Natalie Tereshchenko
Lady In Waiting

A novel by

Elizabeth Audrey Mills

Natalie Tereshchenko - Lady In Waiting

Copyright © 2013, 2016 & 2020 by Elizabeth Audrey Mills
First published November 2013

~ ~ ~~

Paperback (KDP) edition
Published by Elizabeth Audrey Mills
ISBN: 9798611174357

~ ~ ~~

Elizabeth Audrey Mills asserts her right to be identified as author of this work in accordance with the Copyright, Designs and Patents Act 1988. All rights reserved.

~ ~ ~~

No part of this publication may be reproduced, distributed, or transmitted in any form or by any means, including photocopying, recording, or other electronic or mechanical methods, without the prior written permission of the publisher, except in the case of brief quotations embodied in critical reviews and certain other non-commercial uses permitted by copyright law. For permission requests, email the publisher at the address below.

~ ~ ~~

This is a work of fiction. Names, characters, places, brands, media, and incidents are either the product of the author's imagination or are used fictitiously.

Written using LibreOffice by The Document Foundation

Cover by The Cover Collection

Email: elizabeth@itsliz.net
Website: www.itsliz.net

Part One

~

Наталья Терещенко

Natalie Tereshchenko

Diary ~ Thursday 3rd March 1917 ~ 6am

My eyes snapped open, but they revealed nothing. Nothing but darkness. Yet I felt energy building in the air, as might accompany the first distant rumble of thunder, and I sensed a presence. Someone ~ or something ~ was approaching.

Then a hazy shape began to form in the gloom, slowly appearing, like the moon emerging from behind a cloud. When it became clearer, I could see that it was the figure of a woman, walking towards me, glowing as though illuminated by a hidden spotlight.

At first I could still hear the wild wind howling and whistling around the palace walls, lashing the windows with blades of ice and snow, as it had for days and nights beyond counting, but as the vision came closer the noises from outside faded, until there was no sound but the soft swish of her clothes and the echoing 'click ... clock' of her shoes.

She was dressed in a long gown of deepest green, full in the skirt, and high-necked, with a white lace shawl around her shoulders. Her hair was dark, tied up into a bun. I tried to judge how old she was, but could not tell. In fact, it was difficult to concentrate at all, to focus on her for more than a few seconds, because she seemed to shift in and out of sight, like a swan on the lake in the autumn mist. Is that not how it is with dreams ~ someone is there, but you do not recognise them; or they speak, but you cannot hear what they say, and they drift away, leaving only uncertainty?

She stopped beside my bed, within the stretch of an arm if I had felt inclined to reach out.

"Who are you?" I demanded, hearing the words as if someone else had spoken them.

When she answered, the woman's voice was soft, yet clear.

"Hello Natalie," she said. "My name is Myriam."

Part of me was terrified, part fascinated and curious.

"How ... how do you know my name?" I stammered. "Are you a ghost?"

Myriam smiled, and shook her head slowly.

"No, I'm not a ghost; ghosts are a misunderstanding. I am your guardian angel. Everyone has a guardian angel. We are not normally allowed to show ourselves, but I have been permitted to speak to you in this way because you have a part to play in the history of Russia, and I have a warning to deliver."

"What do you want of me, Myriam?" I asked, intending to sound authoritative, but I heard a quiver in my rebellious voice.

She smiled again. "Oh, I want nothing from you, Natalie my love ~ really, you have nothing to fear from me. I have been near to you all your life, watching over you, guiding you. I was with you when you were born and when you were brought to the palace. I was there while you grew from a baby to a little girl, and then into the young woman you are now. I exist only to care for you. That is why I am here now, to guide you through the most difficult part of your life so far. I have come to help you to be prepared for the dramatic events that will soon occur."

She lifted her hands from her side, drawing them together before her, so that her fingers touched as she extended them towards me. Then, as she swept them apart again, images appeared from between her fingers, scenes of people marching and of fighting and death.

"You are aware that Russia is in turmoil," she continued as I watched with amazement the recreation, in miniature, in the space between us, of some of the awful things that have been happening. "You read the newspapers, and listen to the wireless, so you know what I am saying. The Tsar has made too many mistakes and too many enemies; the people are rising up against him. There is revolution in the air. I have come to tell you that, though it seems distant, the conflict is about to come to this palace in a way that is frightening, and will involve you in unexpected and dangerous ways."

She clapped her hands, and the images vanished, then she took a step closer to me. It was then that I noticed that her outline was not quite distinct, as when I sometimes smudge the edges of my drawings to create a softer appearance, yet I could see the intricate gold patterns embroidered on her bodice and the fine, golden lace edges at her cuffs and around her neck. A necklace of silver strands set with pearls glittered at her throat in the flickering light, and tiny jewelled earrings twinkled on her lobes. Her eyes were deep, deep blue, like the summer sky in the east at sunset. I could even smell her perfume! Never in my wildest imaginings would I have expected an angel to wear perfume.

"From today," she continued, "things will begin to change around you. At times you will fear for your life, and you will wonder what to do. I cannot prevent or affect the events that will soon come to pass in Russia and in your life, they are beyond my control, but I want you to know that you are safe for a little while, as long as you are careful.

"I shall visit you twice more. Tomorrow night I will return and tell you some things about yourself that will surprise you, and later I will give you some words of warning and some wisdom to help you, but for now I must leave, and you must consider carefully what I have told you."

I went to speak, but she raised a hand slightly, as though waving goodbye, then her image shimmered, and she faded from view.

Like a black shroud falling, darkness again smothered the room, and in the silence that remained, I lay still and wondered at what had just happened. The strange sound of Myriam's voice still reverberated in my ears, her words swimming wildly around in my head, like fish in a bowl, being pursued by their meaning.

And what of the things she had told me? Was it possible that the security we took for granted was about to be broken? Would my life really be in danger? Despite the recent upheaval, I had so far not felt afraid, but Myriam said that I would fear for my life.

No! It could not happen. Revolution was one thing, but the royal family was at the heart of Russian history and society, surely that could never change?

Then words formed unbidden in my head:

'Ah, but it happened in France, did it not?'

Shocked, I chastised myself:

'Natalie, what are you thinking! That was a hundred years ago. And, anyway, France is France, it is not Russia.'

Slowly I began to hear again the faint hiss of snow ~ driven against my window by the cruel wind ~ and the ticking of the hot water pipes expanding as they ran past my bed on their way to the bathroom. Reason began to return. It was a dream, of course, one of those dreams that seemed profound and real in the middle of the night, but I would laugh at it in the morning. I smiled then at my silliness.

Even so, her words played again and again in my head for what seemed like ages before I finally, imperceptibly, drifted off to sleep.

Chapter 1 ~ Alexander Palace

As I sit on a train, six months later, reading through my old diary entries, this is the event that seems to signal the beginning. All that preceded it, all the sixteen years of my life up to that moment, are like the overture to the opera, a prologue. Choosing this moment gives me a chance to contemplate the background, the scenery behind the events.

I am amused to see how much I, the young Natalie, took for granted. Of course, hindsight is a wonderful way to feel superior, and I have nothing to feel smug about, but I look back at the girl I was then, and smile at her naivety. I remember how I would walk the corridors of Alexander Palace, never noticing the priceless paintings hanging on the walls or the intricate marble mosaics beneath my feet. And if I had looked at them, would it have crossed my mind to wonder if the craftsmen who created those beautiful things also walked upon marble floors, or ate from bone china plates, or looked up at ceilings decorated with flying angels? Probably not. Life changes perspectives ~ I travel back in time, through my diary entries, and it all looks so different.

I lived at Alexander Palace, one of the many residences of the Tsars, hereditary rulers of Russia for over three hundred years. It was the smallest of the palaces, set in acres of beautiful grounds, favoured by the royal family for its relative intimacy, and had been my home since I was eighteen months old.

To picture this modest member of the royal estate, imagine a letter E fallen on its face. The short central stroke represents the main entrance, and the two longer arms are the Left and Right Wings. My master, Tsar Nicholas II, and his family, lived in the Left Wing (also known as The English Wing), while guests and matters of state occupied the Right Wing. As a Lady In Waiting, I had my own room on the first floor of the Left Wing, overlooking the colonnaded Grand Entrance, the sweeping driveway and beautiful gardens.

Had I looked out of my window on the morning of Myriam's first visit, however, the view below my window would have been hidden under a thick white blanket, and seen as though through a moving lace curtain. All winters in Russia are hard ~ it is a source of some pride among patriots ~ but the beginning of 1917 was one of the bleakest on record. Accumulated snow was piled high upon the roofs and windowsills, and spread like a cloak over the gardens. Icicles, three feet long, were hanging menacingly from the gutters, occasionally snapping in the wind and plunging like spears, impaling the mountainous snowdrifts that seemed to be climbing the walls to meet them. The palace resembled a cake, a pretty Battenberg sponge cake, with marzipan windows peering from beneath a thick layer of icing sugar, and all set on a bed of fluffy meringue.

~ ~ ~

Morning arrived like a black cat, invisible in the winter gloom. After only a few hours sleep, and those split by Myriam's unexpected manifestation, I rose and lit a candle. The room, still smothered in deep darkness, was raised to a dim shade of yellow, with shadows that bobbed as the flame caught a draught.

I did not look outside; there would have been little to see. Fresh snow was still being driven against the glass by winds that were born at the north pole, and anyway the sun would not peer gloomily over the horizon for another three hours. But, though dawn in Russia in March arrived late, our days started early ~ our masters and mistresses would soon require our services.

This was the quiet time. Soon enough the sounds of gunfire would begin again, but for a little while a small peace reigned.

I sat at my dressing table, a thick coat around my shoulders for warmth, writing in my diary. I was still pensive and puzzled over the night's unexpected event, and wanted to capture as much as possible while it was fresh on my mind. My thoughts flowed freely, and I scribbled them down quickly before preparing myself for my day's duties.

After a final read-through, to ensure that I had recorded it accurately, I rose from the chair and crossed to my wardrobe, where I selected a maroon satin dress, with long sleeves, and laid it out on the bed. I then pulled on some thick, woollen stockings, before slipping off the coat and shedding my nightie. Shivering, I pulled on a vest, clean knickers and a shift, and was just stepping into the gown when there was a soft knock at the door, almost inaudible, and Polina entered.

Polina and her twin sister, Radochka, were my closest friends. We had shared a room from the time they came to the palace from Azov with their parents in 1912 until I received a room of my own. Now that I was elevated, they insisted on being my unofficial maids. She wore the standard servant's uniform of black skirt and blouse, just as I had worn until recently, with a jacket over it for warmth.

"Good morning, Polya" I said brightly.

"Good morning Nata," she whispered.

Big, dark eyes stared owl-like at me from her pretty oval face, her tiny mouth pursed with anxiety. The tension in the palace was affecting her badly. She was a sensitive, timid girl, unlike her sister, who was brash and confident.

She buttoned my dress down the back for me, smoothing out creases and straightening the bustle. A year younger than me, she was surprisingly tall for her age, and her head was level with mine as she helped with my necklace and earrings. Her eyes, though, were downcast and sad.

I lowered my head so that my face was in her line of vision, and held it there, staring at her, until she looked at me ~ and when she raised her head, I smiled reassuringly. Tentatively, almost reluctantly, her lips curled a little into a nervous reflection of my smile. I kissed her cheek, and we held each other for a moment.

Then, returning to the task in hand, she helped me on with a little pair of French boots, and tied the laces for me, and finally draped a warm shawl over my shoulders. Together, we left my suite and hurried along the corridor. A few doors down, she left me to rejoin her sister, while I continued a little further to Tatiana's rooms.

~ ~ ~

The duchess heard the door as I entered her suite, and called me through to her boudoir, where I found her standing beside the bed, wearing a long, loose nightdress of pale blue flannelette.

She was not the most beautiful of the sisters, but I always thought that she was attractive, in a driven, passionate, sometimes even masculine way. She had beautiful long, golden-red hair, with a stubborn wave to it, and steely blue-grey eyes. Her figure was the best of all the girls, slim-waisted, but shapely.

I looked forward to this part of the day more than I should. In our sterile existence at the palace there were no eligible men, no opportunities to flirt or find romance, and many of us found some pleasure from each other's company, as the twins and I had often in the past. Now I found myself admiring my Lady, and feeling inappropriate desires.

She raised her arms straight above her head, and I stood behind her to lift her nightie over her shoulders, admiring the curve of her back where it narrowed into her waist then widened again at her hips. Her bottom was generous ~ it had a beautiful roundness that was so attractive that I had to fight the urge to run my hands over it.

Closing my eyes for a second to clear my mind, I turned to her closet and brought out some undies. She seemed to be completely unselfconscious as she turned, naked and shivering with the cold, to take the pair of knickers I passed to her.

She thanked me before bending down to step into them. It was the same every day, and stimulated a warm feeling inside me that started in my throat and travelled down to nestle between my legs. I was mesmerised by the sight of her breasts swinging level with the triangle of ginger hair below her belly, until she straightened, and it vanished beneath the silk of her Parisian pants.

She looked up and caught me staring. I lowered my eyes quickly, but it was too late. Her face assumed a challenging expression, and she arched her eyebrows. But instead of covering herself, she reached out her arms and took the remaining clothes I was holding, throwing them onto the bed behind her. Then she stepped back and started to sway her body, like a dancer, twisting her arms like writhing snakes, and all the time staring provocatively into my eyes. She turned, slowly, so that her back was to me, then thrust her arse towards me. I could hear her chuckling.

I smacked the bare bum with the palm of my hand, hard. "Behave, tart!" I said, laughing.

She straightened up, grinning, and I started to sort through the heap of clothes on the bed, passing items one by one as she needed them, helping her into each garment, until she was ready to leave. At the door she stopped, and planted a soft, quick kiss on my lips before opening the door and stepping into the passageway.

~ ~ ~

We turned in opposite directions, Tatiana to take her place with her mother, while I joined Polya and Rada, who were waiting for me in the corridor outside their room. We threaded our way through the maze of narrow passageways on the top floor and took the servant's stairs down to the Palace Chapel below. There we greeted a new girl, Sacha, who I had met for the first time the previous evening.

"Do you go to church, Sacha?" I asked as we took our places in the chapel and waited for the Empress to arrive. Sacha was part of 'The Family', a distant cousin of Tatiana and her sisters. She had some of the Romanov features ~ the bold nose, the red hair, the heavy hips ~ but carried herself differently, less haughtily, as though she couldn't take herself or her life seriously.

"Oh yes, every Sunday," she replied.

"At Alexandra Palace, we go every day, twice a day," I said, noticing Rada smirk. "And four times on Sunday."

Fortunately the doors opened at that moment, and the Empress entered the chapel. It was probably as well I had been prevented from blurting out any more, or I might have said too much, as Rada knew well ~ I had often told her my views. I could, for instance, have added that Alexandra seemed to be obsessed with religion, convinced that she had been chosen by God to rule a nation. I might even have revealed that I found it embarrassing.

Brought up in that atmosphere of reverence, I had at first accepted everything I was taught. But before long I began to wonder why it was that all the prophets were men, why God was male, and why women were so completely subjugated. I quickly became cynical, and formed the view that it had all been invented by men as a way to prop up their petty insecurities and satisfy their need for power. But the Empress was not to be argued with, at least not on matters of religion or state, so the family and staff gathered every morning and evening for a blessing before and after the day's labours.

Alexandra's voice droned on, performing the usual Orthodox rituals. There was nothing for us to do but stand and listen, and it wasn't long before my mind drifted off. Like a gramophone record, I played again Myriam's warning about the dangers to come, and tried to imagine how they might happen. As a consequence, I was oblivious to the progress of the service until I suddenly became aware that Alexandra had stopped speaking, and that everyone else was saying 'amen'. I quickly joined in.

Then Sacha, the twins and I followed the small throng making its way to the exit. As we filed out into the corridor to go about our duties, each received a blessing from the Empress as they passed her at the door. She smiled as we curtsied and she laid her hand on each one's head and said "God be with you, child."

~ ~ ~

Sacha was to accompany me for the morning. Alexandra had called me into her quarters the previous evening to introduce us, and expressed the wish that I should show Sacha some of the routines around the palace. So, when Rada and Polya left us, heading for Aleksey's quarters to begin their day's work, I took her to a hidden door and dark staircase.

As we descended, the icy air trapped in the stairway caught our breath and raised instant goose-bumps on our arms.

"This palace feels even colder than the Winter Palace," she said, shivering, as we began our descent.

Sacha's father, Prince Vassili Dolgorukov, was a general in the army, stationed at the Winter Palace, and that was where Sacha had lived until it became clear that it was going to be overrun by the rampaging citizens of Petrograd. She and her mother were hastily evacuated to Alexander palace, to stay temporarily with her grandfather, Count Beckendorff, one of the Tsar's trusted military advisers and an old friend of the family. The Count and his wife had been living at Alexander palace, in the Right Wing, since the royals moved there in 1905, after the Bloody Sunday massacre.

"It is always cold here," I replied. "There is no heating where we are going." I chuckled. "Most of Russia thinks we live in unadulterated luxury, and I suppose that, compared with them, we do, but it is not as easy as they think."

The stairs spiralled down until we emerged into the vast, echoing expanse that was the palace basement. It resembled a huge cave ~ which, in essence, is what it was, having been constructed in a great hole in the ground before the palace itself was built over it, with rows of pillars supporting the walls above.

People scurried, rat-like, about their duties, carrying blankets, pushing carts piled with boxes, wheeling dinner trolleys with silver-dome-covered plates ~ the whole gloomy edifice resembled a scene from hell. We paused at the bottom, and I watched Sacha's face as she took in the sight, amused as her mouth fell open and her eyes bulged. She turned to me, speechless, unable to express her amazement, and I grinned; it had affected me in the same way, the first time I saw it.

"It's like ..." she struggled to think of a simile, "... like an ant's nest. So busy. I had no idea."

"This is what it takes to keep a place like Alexander Palace functioning," I said. "For each person up there," I pointed at the ceiling, "there are ten people down here, and another ten waiting in the wings."

When she had recovered her composure, I started to lead the way across the great chasm, stepping aside as people hurried past, intent on their errands. The noise of all their activities reverberated from the walls, floors and ceiling, creating a din that made conversation almost impossible.

At odd intervals, seemingly almost at random, more iron staircases, like the one by which we had arrived, spiralled like winter leaves falling from above, their doorways hidden in the darkness.

A troop of soldiers appeared around a corner, marching noisily, and we waited patiently while they passed, receiving more than one appraising, sideways glance from dark eyes beneath peaked caps.

I showed Sacha where furniture was stacked all around the walls, and pointed out several square, wooden structures which rose from floor to ceiling, each containing an elevator. "That's how food gets up to the dining rooms," I shouted.

She nodded to show that she had heard.

Eventually, we reached the far corner, where we entered a tunnel. I located a switch on the wall, and a row of electric lights, mounted at intervals in the domed roof, flickered on, pointing off into the distance, away from palace, under the gardens.

"This is the way to the kitchens," I told her, as we walked along the worn, stone-slabbed passage, the noise of the basement fading behind us, and my voice echoing disconcertingly.

"Do you know how long you will be staying at Alexander Palace, Sacha?"

"No, it is very uncertain. The only thing I am sure of is that we are unlikely to return to the Winter Palace at any time in the near future."

"The last time I saw the Winter Palace was when I was five years old," I told her. "I don't remember much about it, except that it is big."

She laughed. "It's huge," she agreed. "But I hardly saw anything of it. I spent most of my life safely locked away in five rooms on the top floor with my mother."

"What has it been like there, these last weeks?" I asked.

"Chaotic, uncertain. It flared up after Christmas, when thousands of people started demonstrating in the streets outside against the food shortages. The troops who had been stationed around the city were ordered to withdraw into the palace to protect it from being occupied. The revolutionary newspaper, Pravda, is openly urging the overthrow of the monarchy and the election of a people's parliament."

I nodded. "Yes, we sometimes have a copy here in the palace. I don't know who gets it, but it makes frightening reading."

"I wasn't supposed to know anything," she said, "but I saw fighting outside the palace from my window, and my maids relayed quite a bit of information to me. We had hardly anything to eat, supplies weren't getting through, and I was told that often the soldiers had nothing at all for days; many of them just walked out of the palace and joined the revolution."

At the end of the tunnel, we climbed a flight of steps and emerged into the warmth of the palace kitchens, a separate building, about two hundred yards from the palace. This is where I came every morning after prayers.

While Tatiana ate breakfast with her mother and sisters in their private dining room, my primary, self-appointed duty every day had nothing to do with service to the family; it was much more important than that.

Chapter 2 ~ Sacha

The kitchens at Alexander Palace were modest if compared with those at, for instance, the Winter Palace, or St Catherine's Palace, but a wondrous place to me, nonetheless.

As we arrived, staff were scrubbing work surfaces, cleaning and preparing food, cutting up sides of meat, and standing over steaming pots. The clatter of utensils and the buzz of many voices echoed beneath the raftered roof, two floors above us. Doors in the outer walls of the central work area opened and closed as cooks and skivvies came and went from rooms all around it, and there were more doors off the balcony that ran around all four walls at first-floor level. It was hot and steamy, with a strange, exotic blend of smells and noises.

I took Sacha to meet Ivan Kharitonov, the chef ~ tall, plump, pink-faced, with kindly blue eyes and soft-hands. I had grown up with Ivan as a special friend; he was like a much-loved uncle to me.

We chatted briefly, but he was busy, so, clutching a small parcel donated to my mission by him, I led Sacha away, up a short flight of stone steps that climbed beside a ramp leading to the big back door. This was where deliveries of food would arrive each day to provide for the royal family, their staff and the growing numbers of guests.

Sacha, with an amused expression on her face,

listened as I told her my mission, and helped me to pull on a big, old coat that I kept hanging there on a hook. Then she steadied me as I slipped off my pretty French fashion shoes and pushed my feet into a big pair of fur-lined boots, ready for the wild outdoors. With my hood up and tied in place, and a pair of mittens to complete my protection, I unlatched the door.

Even though I knew the storm was severe, I was quite unprepared for the savage force of it that morning. The wind must have turned, from a northerly to a north-westerly, so that it was blowing directly into the sloping gully that normally sheltered the arched access. The heavy door leapt at me as soon as it was released, and the wind burst in with a noise like an explosion, sweeping me aside and hurling me to the ground. Snow that had been piled against the step outside swirled across the floor and down the ramp, like the tentacles of a hungry beast searching for prey, with fresh flakes following, whirling from the skies.

I sat on the cold tiles, shaking my head ~ unhurt but in disarray, and amused at my dramatic downfall. Sacha, seeing that I was laughing at myself, helped me to my feet and vigorously dusted me down, then we grabbed at the swinging door, and, leaning into the raging snowstorm, I struggled outside, pulling it with me. When my feet were on the icy path beyond the step, I turned and braced myself against the wall, heaving on the big cast-iron handle, while Sacha pushed the door with all her strength from the inside; together we managed to close it.

Although it was still dark, and would remain so for another hour, the snow reflected every glow from the palace windows, casting an eerie whiteness over everything.

Head bowed against the stinging, blinding blizzard that was blowing into my face in huge flakes, filling my eyes so that within seconds I could hardly see, I fought my way to an alcove in the kitchen's west wall. There, in the modest protection afforded by the bulk of the building, I paused to look out across the frozen gardens to the estate beyond, where I could see one of the camps of soldiers set in the scant shelter of a small wood. Snow, carried horizontally by gale-force winds, had smothered every detail, until all features had disappeared and the camp resembled rows of dunes in a grey desert.

In this little sheltered corner I had my bird-table. Every day, no matter the weather, I put food out for the wild birds ~ it helped me to keep contact with a reality from which I felt otherwise separated by my insulated life. I quickly scooped off the snow which had been driven under the table's little roof, using a scraper that Ivan had made for me, then piled on the bread and fatty scraps of kitchen waste from the parcel he had given me, and a handful of sunflower seeds that I had saved from the previous summer. That done, I retraced my way along the wall, back to the kitchen. Even in that short time, my coat and hood were thickly covered with snow.

Buffeted by the malignant, driving wind, I turned the iron ring to release the door, and was whipped off my feet again and hurled into the kitchen like a rag doll, in a blast of cold air and snowflakes. Becoming already used to the routine, Sacha briskly pulled me back onto my feet, and we pushed together at the door to close it again, our feet skidding on the wet floor. A kitchen hand came, not to help, but with a broom to sweep up the mess, glaring resentfully at me as I removed the heavy coat and put my own shoes back on. I ignored him, thinking instead about the small creatures out there who were trying to survive in those dreadful conditions.

What I had just done may make no difference in the vastness of history, perhaps it even failed in its aim of saving some of the birds, but at least I had tried to do something. I hoped my little gift of food would help them, although I knew that many would die in that hard weather, just as thousands of the citizens of Russia were also dying.

~ ~ ~

"Have you heard from your father?" I asked Sacha as we started back through the tunnel towards the palace.

"Mother spoke to him on the telephone last night" she replied. "The regiment has left the palace to the Bolsheviks ~ it would have been captured anyway. Daddy is now in the garrison, and hopes to make his way here tomorrow with whatever men he still has. Most of them have deserted."

I nodded, pensively. "It must have been quite frightening, before you were evacuated."

"I suppose so. You don't think about it much while it's happening, only afterwards ~ that's when the reactions set in. I didn't feel personally threatened at first. I believed that we were safe."

Her words echoed from the bare brick walls, and she must have heard the tremor in her voice, because she suddenly became self-conscious and stopped speaking.

We walked in silence for a few moments, and shortly arrived back at the basement. I guided her to another flight of stairs, that would return us to the English Wing. She changed the subject, leaning close to my ear to make herself heard. "Natalie, I'm puzzled ~ how do you fit into things here?"

"Ah," I smiled wryly, as we began to climb the narrow stairs, shouting over my shoulder, "you don't miss much. I am neither one thing nor the other, Sacha. Not family, not staff. My official title is Lady-in-Waiting to the Grand Duchess Tatiana Nicholaievna, but apart from that I have no rank here."

As the stairs entered the cavity beneath the floor above, the outside din faded a little. "Oh," she said, sounding surprised, "that's not the impression I had from Alexandra, yesterday. She was praising you and saying how much they all value you."

I hid my amazement with a cough.

"Anyway," she continued, "what's the agenda for today?"

We reached the little platform at the top of the stairs and I fumbled with the door.

"Well, first we are visiting the sick," I replied,

turning to face her. "There is an epidemic of measles in the palace, you may have heard. For a while last month, we didn't know who was going to flare up in spots next. Anna Vyrubova ~ an old friend of the Empress, and a permanent guest here ~ was the first, then Olga and Anastasia, and finally their young brother, Aleksey, and several members of staff. So far, I've managed to avoid catching it, and so has Tatiana. I think we may have had it when we were younger ~ it was usually she and I who played together."

Silence engulfed us as we stepped through the door into a corridor that led through the Tsar's rooms, and from there I took us to a narrow back stairway that accessed the residential quarters.

"Anna, Olga and Aleksey are still confined to their beds," I whispered as we walked, "and Tatiana has been helping Alexandra and the maids to care for her brother and sister." I paused as we reached the back stairs and began to climb again, then resumed. "She is devoted to her mother, you see, and is determined to help in any way she can. The Empress has been inundated with callers ~ politicians, generals and so on ~ passing on information or needing instructions, and with Nicholas away all the time, she is carrying nearly the whole burden of running the nation; Tatiana wants to take some of the weight from her shoulders."

At the top of these stairs we entered the maze of corridors that linked all the bedrooms of the royal children and their staff. Sacha was pensive. "All this has flared up so quickly. What's gone wrong, Nata?"

I stopped walking and studied the girl's face for a

moment, unsure whether or not I should tell her what I knew, what the real reasons were. My thoughts could get me into trouble, if Sacha should decide to tell anyone.

But there was no-one in earshot, and I felt I could trust her, so I answered truthfully. "The people's frustration is understandable, Sacha ~ it's a cold winter and they have no fuel, food is scarce, the war against Germany is going badly, and their wages are unpaid ~ no wonder they are desperate and angry. The Family seems unaware of the national catastrophe unfolding beyond the boundaries of their little closeted lives. For them, nothing has changed, except for the inconvenient bout of illness that has sprung up among them, and the protests of the citizens outside their gates."

I paused, biting my lip, aware that I had revealed rather too many of my opinions, but I noticed that she was nodding her head, as though I had confirmed what she already thought.

"Sacha," I said, anxiously, "I shouldn't say these things; they are disloyal. Please don't repeat anything, will you?"

She took my hand and gripped it with both of her own. "Thank you for trusting me," she said, giving it a little shake. "I promise I won't breathe a word."

~ ~ ~

Later, as we trailed behind Tatiana on her rounds, I explained more to Sacha about life at Alexander Palace and answered her questions. I also began to feel that I understood her better.

We seemed to have a rapport, to be comfortable in each other's company, able to talk freely and listen easily. She was close to my own age, the same height as me and slim. Her red-blonde hair contrasted with my black, but otherwise we might have been mistaken for sisters.

Tatiana led the way to Aleksey's room, where we found him out of bed and standing pensively on his balcony.

Aleksey was a precocious thirteen; he knew he was heir to the throne, and had already adopted a supercilious attitude to everyone, including his own mother and sisters.

He suffered from haemophilia, a blood disorder ~ any injury could take weeks to heal, and an illness such as measles was a major worry for the family ~ so he was treated like a delicate flower; he exploited it to the full. Just about every doctor in the land had been summoned at some time, then dismissed when they were unable to cure him. I still remember how it was when that self-proclaimed priest, Rasputin, was strutting around the palace ~ though fortunately I only met him once, shortly before he was killed. He frightened me with his intense glare and casual power over the family, but Alexandra was under his spell, and believed that he had the gift of healing. I was not sorry when I heard that he had been murdered.

Tatiana joined Aleksey on the balcony for a while, talking quietly. Of course Sacha and I were not included, so we helped Rada and Polya to make

Aleksey's bed and clean up his room.

Aleksey visited, we moved on to see Olga, and then, finally, Anna, who were both in bed.

They too had suffered badly, Anna because of her age, and Olga as a result of catching influenza at the same time. Alexandra was sitting with her old friend Anna, when we arrived, and she greeted us absently.

I excused us to them, and took Sacha round to the room where, when Tatiana finished visiting her family, we would be dealing with the clerical part of my duties.

Chapter 3 ~ Under Siege

One of several in the palace, the small library that we entered adjoined the Empress's quarters on the ground floor. Tatiana liked to use it as a workroom because it was normally one of the best-lit rooms in the palace, with large windows that faced south-east.

A small coal fire crackled invitingly in the grate, there was a square of Indian carpet covering most of the polished wooden floor, and on it stood a round oak table in Chippendale style, with four matching chairs. Above the table, in the centre of an ornate ceiling, hung a chandelier of crystal and brass, fitted with the new electric light bulbs. On the table, already delivered by one of the staff, was a bundle of letters, neatly tied with a ribbon.

"The electricity is off again," I informed Sacha after testing the light switch. I waved a hand in the general direction of the window and the world beyond: "They keep disconnecting us, just to prove they are in control."

"It was the same at the Winter Palace," she said with a shrug. "All part of the pressure on us to capitulate."

On brighter days, we would not need the lamps - the morning sun often shone through onto the table on which Tatiana and I worked - but it was barely dawn, and anyway for weeks the clouds had been heavy and the windows piled high with snow, so that there was no sunlight, just a pale and watery, grey gloom.

We crossed to the French windows and sat in two of the easy chairs there.

"Tell me about Tatiana," Sacha said.

"Had you met her before this morning?" I began.

Sacha nodded. "A few times, formally. I never had a chance to get to know her, though. Mother says she can be rebellious and headstrong, and often seems to forget her status as a royal princess."

I grinned; it amused me to think of The Royals being talked about outside the palace.

"That's partly true," I said. "She easily convinces herself that she is in love, and has fallen several times for army officers that she has met through her work at the palace hospital. They were not deemed by her parents to be suitable for her, of course, and Alexandra has had to remind her several times of her responsibilities. Tatiana loudly laments her parents' intervention every time, but she is fiercely loyal and would not disobey them."

Sacha smiled, then surprised me by asking: "Have you ever been in love?"

I spluttered. "Me? What chance do I have to meet anyone, let alone fall in love?"

"Ah," she grinned, "love always finds a way."

"Is this the voice of experience?" I asked.

"No. Like you, I don't get to meet eligible young men. But I read a lot of books, and they all say that there is someone for everyone."

"Well, when mine turns up, I hope I'm not too old to enjoy it, whatever it is."

We loaded candles into the heavy brass candlestick in the centre of the table, and were lighting them using the jewel-encrusted box of matches laying at its base when Tatiana arrived.

~ ~ ~

I enjoyed working for Tatiana. I respected her enormously, and felt closest to her of all the royals. It was a comfortable relationship; more than employer-employee, much more relaxed and informal than that ~ and recently even more so. Sometimes it would even begin to seem more like a friendship, and, for a short while, I would have a sense of what it might be like to be part of that family. But, before long, something always happened to remind me that it was an illusion.

As Tatiana and I prepared to plunge into the day's post, Sacha told us that she was needed to care for her mother, who had taken to her bed, suffering from the tensions of the past months at the Winter Palace.

I arranged to meet her again later, then I began looking through the mail with Tatiana, separating the items that needed her personal attention from those that I could take care of on her behalf. We had noticed a dramatic fall-off in the volume of letters in recent days, our conclusion being that the post was being withheld by the revolutionaries, but there was still enough to keep us occupied for a morning.

As we worked, however, everything I dealt with seemed to remind me about the previous night, and set my mind wandering off into questions of whether or not I should take it seriously, wondering what it could mean, trying to guess what might be about to happen. Then I would lose concentration and make mistakes, or find myself standing beside a cupboard but couldn't remember what I had gone there for, or staring at some papers yet not seeing the writing on them.

Tatiana noticed. "You are in another world today," she commented, though she did not seem put out.

I put down my pen. "I'm sorry, I had a weird experience last night; I don't know if it was real or a dream. My guardian angel warned me that our lives are going to be changed. Things are going to become much worse very soon." I recounted the essentials of the encounter.

"It sounds almost like a premonition," she said.

"Mmm, yes, I suppose it does; I don't know whether to believe it or not. I suppose the things going on out there ... " I gestured again towards the window, " ... are bound to be on all our minds, awake or asleep."

After a brief pensive silence, we returned to work, and for a while I managed to concentrate on my letters, interrupted briefly by some tea and cakes brought in at mid-morning by a maid. But, increasingly, the stillness was broken by the sound of gunfire that had started again, as it did every day. Volleys and exchanges echoed around the grounds, some seemingly very close.

At one stage, we heard shouting and singing nearby, and ran to the French windows to see what was going on. Right outside, in a lull in the snowstorm, the gardens were filled with soldiers, many of them drunk, looking up at the palace, waving their fists and shouting obscenities. Their officers were trying to call them into order, but with little success. *Even our own troops are hostile to us*, I thought, watching as they cavorted and staggered and gestured. Tatiana and I stood back from the window, peeping from behind the drapes, hoping the soldiers would not see us.

In the months since Christmas, Alexander palace had progressively acquired the nature of a besieged castle. Straggling remnants of the Royal Guard were camped in the grounds, facing off a small but noisy crowd of demonstrators on the outside, and officers of the general staff were stationed inside the palace building, in some of the rooms of the Right Wing, directing what loyal troops they had left in Tsarskoye and Petrograd.

'Petrograd' ~ still the word sounded strange to me. All my life, it had been Saint Petersburg, but, with the war raging in the west against Germany, the Tsar had decided to replace the Germanic-sounding name with one more Russian. But such small measures were not enough to satisfy the anger of the people. Suddenly the revolution had swelled into frightful reality, and it was happening right outside our home. It was not the first upheaval in recent years, but this time it seemed to be personal.

A shout from outside brought my attention back to the present, and I peeped around the long curtain to see that one of the soldiers was pointing at our window. Tatiana quickly moved back out of sight opposite me, but it was obvious that she had been spotted. All the men transferred their attention to us, shouting obscenities and making gestures with their hands. We ran across the room, close to the wall, so that we were completely hidden from them, then out of the door, desperately afraid that they would storm in and attack us.

From the billiard room, next door, we heard the crack of a single gun shot. I ran to the window and peered cautiously out. The soldiers' attention was still on the French doors of the library. A puff of smoke was just visible above their heads, being whisked away from the muzzle of an officer's skyward-pointing pistol by the wind. It had the effect of quietening the men, and we could hear his shouted commands to them to disperse. Eventually they wandered off, and we returned to the library to finish our work.

~ ~ ~

All morning, while we dealt with the mail, a procession of army officers and government ministers were calling at the palace to report to the Empress, and messages were constantly being relayed to Tatiana, who kept leaving me to consult with her mother. A tense atmosphere was building up, emphasised by the sounds of fighting, both far and near, and exacerbated for me by the family's withholding of knowledge. Tatiana could have kept me informed, passed on what had transpired with her mother, but she didn't, and once again I felt the resentment rising up in my heart.

Early in the afternoon, Count Beckendorff came to the library to talk with her about the current situation. He would normally have been in regular communication with the Tsar by telephone and messenger while Nicholas was away, but I knew that, for the last several days, there had been no news of where he was, or even if he was safe. Tatiana and the Count moved into the next room to talk privately.

I watched them leave, glaring at their backs as they took their little secrets away from my ears.

I rose and stood morosely for a while at the French windows, gazing out at the bleak, white landscape. There was no sign of the soldiers who had been demonstrating earlier, no sign of life at all. A fresh fall of snow had begun ~ tumbling and pirouetting from a leaden sky, floating in the gusting winds, snow falling upon snow, piled in great mounds as far as the eye could see, like a gigantic white sheet thrown over the world, hiding all life underneath.

For something to do, I returned to the table and checked through the letters we had written. It was no distraction, for I found myself frequently staring vacantly at the flickering flames in the fireplace and thinking about my place in the palace. Every day I told myself that I should be used to it, but each time I was excluded from family matters it hurt as much as the last. I felt dreadfully lonely, isolated from almost everyone.

Eventually, Tatiana returned. Her expression was unreadable as she took her seat at the table, her hands clasped as though in prayer, her eyes downcast. I sat opposite her, and as I did so, she raised her head. "It's bad, Nata," she said, softly. "I think your premonition is going to prove to be rather close to the truth."

Diary ~ Friday 4th March 1917 ~ morning

Last night, when Myriam returned for her second visit, she did not arrive slowly, as before, but shimmered into view at my bedside, like milk poured into a glass tumbler, glowing against the darkness of the room. I suppose that, the first time, I had to be introduced slowly to the idea of a nocturnal visitor, whereas now we could dispense with that and get down to the real business. It showed me that Myriam had a high level of control over the situation, and chose the manner of her manifestation and its effect on me.

I was sitting up in bed, propped on two pillows, still wide awake ~ sleep was impossible with my mind in such turmoil. For most of the day, two questions had been racing around in my head, like dogs chasing each other round a flower bed, barking, turning on each other. After her warning on the first night, and the events of yesterday, I hoped to find out more about the news that had upset Tatiana ~ Beckendorff gets messages from the Tsar, so perhaps the war is going even more badly than before, and I wondered if it was possible that Nicholas had been injured, or even killed! I suppose that would make Aleksey Tsar?

But, oddly, that was not my priority. Above all other things, I was desperate to know about my birth, then I may be able to understand why my life is as it is. I knew nothing about my mother or my father, had never heard their names mentioned in all my sixteen years. Oh, I had asked Alexandra a few times, but all she would say was that she took me in when my mother could no longer care for me.

"Ah, you are expecting me," Myriam smiled. "You do not think this is a dream, then?" She knew my every thought.

I shrugged my shoulders. "Myriam, I spent most of the day trying to convince myself of just that. But you said you would come, and I have so many things to ask you."

"I know, dear one," she said, gently. "But remember, there are some answers I will not give, some things you must determine for yourself."

I nodded, quickly, anxious to ask the first question, but when I attempted to speak, my voice caught in my throat, and I coughed. What Myriam might tell me could be painful. I swallowed and tried again:

"My father, Myriam, who was he, what was his name? And my mother? Tell me about them, please."

"Ah, your parents, yes, that is understandable, I expected it. But you must accept that I cannot tell you all you wish to know ~ some things would torture your mind, and I will not do anything to harm you."

I nodded again, vigorously, impatiently.

"As for your father," she continued, "I can tell you this ~ he is no longer alive, but he was a nobleman, a

member of the royal family."

This was a shock. "I have royal blood in me!" I thought, excitedly. "I am related to the Tsar of Russia and Queen Victoria of England."

But was this good news or bad? Suddenly, I was afire, my curiosity aroused, my imagination running wild.

Myriam read my mind and, before I could speak again, she said:

"It is just a fact, my dear, neither good nor bad. Nothing in life is ever really all good or all bad, as you will learn with time. Even the most awful things bring strengths, and when you think you are lucky to find sweet fruits, look for the sting from the hidden insect. For every gift there is always a burden, it is the way the universe is balanced. The challenge is to see which is the gift and which the burden, because they are never quite what you think, and may even be both at the same time."

At this, she paused, and raised her eyebrows, with a quizzical expression on her face, amused at the confusion I was feeling and showing.

"But, in any event, your royal blood is not something you should seek to use. For one thing, you cannot prove it; and, when you think about it some more, you will not wish to. The life that awaits you will be the one you create for yourself from the circumstances that assail you, not something handed down like a hereditary disease. I have to warn you, though, that

you will meet people who will try to manipulate you because of your father; you must resist them." She leaned closer. "Natalie, can you see now why you received the same education as the duchesses and enjoy special privileges which none of the other servants have, but yet you don't feel quite part of the Family?"

She was right. I remembered my childhood: days in the care of my nanny, Katerina Nikolevna, and happy times playing with the duchesses in the nursery; then lessons in the study with various tutors ~ arithmetic, history, English, Russian, French. None of the other servants received these things, and I often wondered why I was singled out. Yet, as those very privileges set me apart from the rest of the staff, they did not make me the same as Tatiana or her sisters. I always felt isolated from the Family, unloved, like a dog that is fed scraps at the table, but must sleep outside. The Empress and the Duchesses treated me well and with kindness and respect, but always with a reserve that showed that I was not one of them.

Myriam waited patiently as I sat silently for a few moments, reliving times when I had cried after being shut out yet again from the intimate moments between the mother and her daughters, wondering why I was different. But I had taught myself to fight those tears, to take hold of my emotions and suppress them, to turn them to anger and hide them behind a cloak of self-sufficiency.

"And my mother," I asked, eventually, "was she also of noble birth?"

Myriam shook her head. "Your mother worked here in the palace. That's how it began; the Duke saw her and was immediately taken by her beauty. He began to pay attention to her, and she was flattered. Before she knew it, she was pregnant."

'Oh, great,' I thought, all hopes of royalty snatched from me, 'I'm a bastard!'

She smiled kindly, but did not comment on the fleeting thought; instead, she resumed her narrative.

"To his credit, your father accepted his responsibilities ~ he was not a philanderer like many in the Family. He provided a house and income for your mother, so that you would be well cared for, and it went well for the first year after you were born. He visited whenever he could; he really did love your mother. Unfortunately, his career in the navy brought everything to a tragic end. He was killed in a battle at sea against the Japanese fleet, and, of course, all the payments to support you and your mother ceased. In desperation, she came to the Empress and told her everything; she knew that Alexandra would have to take you in, and she did. But there was a sacrifice: Alexandra took you from her to avoid any scandal, but your mother had to promise that she would leave the palace and not return, and she must never try to contact you. Alexandra gave her some money to help her restart her life elsewhere."

"Where is she now? Can I meet her?" I asked.

"No, that is beyond my powers. Events will unfold in their own course, and you will know more."

She stepped back a pace. "Natalie, I must go. Think about what I have told you ~ how you use it will decide your future. Tomorrow, when I return for the last time, I will give you some final important words of advice." She raised her hand again in that little wave, and as she faded from view, I heard her say: "Goodnight, dear."

Chapter 4 ~ Petr

Sacha joined me in the chapel, and remained with me all morning. It was the day Tatiana had set aside for her hospital visit. She had trained as a nurse and, while she dressed wounds, we girls helped her, or sat on beds and chatted with the patients.

The hospital was a large brick structure, located a short distance from the palace and accessed in the winter by a temporary tunnel of steel poles and canvas running from a corner of the right wing, providing passage sheltered from the raging storms. It was set up to care for officers of the armed forces sent home for repair. There were no common soldiers or sailors there ~ they would be treated on the battlefield, if they were lucky enough to receive any attention at all; it seemed likely to me that few would survive in the dirt and mayhem.

After about an hour, the Duchess was called into the operating room to assist the doctors, so Sacha and I separated and wandered between the rows of beds, looking for anyone who needed company or comfort.

Seated in a chair beside a window I found a young officer smoking a cigarette. The left leg of his brown uniform trousers had been cut off above the knee, and the limb below it was encased in a large plaster cast. Propped against the wall under the window was a walking stick.

I sat in the vacant chair opposite him, aware of his

immediate interest. "You're not a nurse," he said tartly, scrutinising me as though interviewing me for a job.

"I'm glad to see that they haven't reduced the standard of the intelligence test for officers," I retorted, returning his gaze.

He looked about twenty, a bush of wild brown hair sat above a face that was handsome and full of confidence. He grinned and relaxed, attempted to nonchalantly cross his legs but remembered that was not possible, and instead leaned toward me, taking a packet of cigarettes from his breast pocket. He offered the packet to me, but I declined by holding up a hand.

"Don't blame you," he grunted, returning the pack to his pocket, and pinching out the remains of the one he was smoking, dropping it into a bin beside his chair. "Filthy habit. Do you have any vices?"

"None that I admit to. What happened to your leg?"

He looked down at the limb. "Copped a bullet. Instead of passing through, it smashed the bone, then stopped. My gunner was not so lucky, he died."

"I'm sorry. How did it happen?"

"We were on a reconnaissance flight over the German lines. Someone with a machine gun managed to rake us from front to back ~ I still don't know if it was one of ours or theirs. Lucky the bastard didn't hit the engine, or I would be dead too."

"You're an aviator!" I gasped. I had read a little about the young men who flew these amazing new machines. It seemed such an impossibly dangerous yet romantic thing to do.

"Yes, ma'am," he grinned and stretched out a hand.

"Lieutenant Petr Nikolaiev Novichkov, by Royal Command."

I accepted the handshake. "Natalie Tereshchenko, Lady in Waiting to the Duchess Tatiana."

He didn't release my hand, and I thought for a surreal moment that he was going to kiss it, but instead he held it firmly and looked intently into my eyes. I felt drawn into his gaze, as though he was reading my innermost thoughts.

Feeling my face becoming red, I looked away, and after a moment, he let my hand go. When I turned my head back to face him again he was smiling.

"You are very beautiful, Natalie Tereshchenko. Do you have a boyfriend?"

My equanimity destroyed, I blushed again. "What a question to ask," I spluttered.

He laughed. "Why? I need to know what competition I'm up against."

My head was in a state of confusion, this was not something I was used to dealing with. I felt flattered and flustered and, yes, attracted.

By way of changing the subject to allow myself to recover some composure, I asked: "What is it like to fly above the ground?"

'Above the ground'? I thought. *Of course it's above the ground, that's what flying means, you silly woman. What is the matter with you?*

Still grinning, perfectly aware of the effect he was having on me and the reason for my question, he sat back in his chair and thought for a moment.

"An aeroplane is like a lover," he said, pensively.

"She wraps herself around you and carries you into heaven. But you depend on her completely; she is your salvation and your angel of death. It is frightening at first ~ the roar of the engine as you hurtle along the ground, gaining enough speed so that the wings can lift you free of the earth. But when that moment happens, when the horizon suddenly drops beneath you, when you and your aircraft become one, a bird in the sky, it is like no other feeling."

As he spoke, I saw Sacha coming towards us. I made a movement with my head and eyes to tell her to go away, but she continued relentlessly. Lieutenant Novichkov saw my gesture and turned to see who I was addressing. He smiled and made to rise, but was reminded at once by his leg that it was not something he could easily do, and flopped down into his chair again, an expression of angry frustration on his face.

"Sorry," Sacha flapped, "I have to give Natalie a message."

"Then give it you must," he grunted.

She turned apologetically to me. "Natalie, we have to return to the palace. Tatiana has been called to see her mother. Something has happened."

Damn!

I stood at once. "I must go," I said, reluctantly.

He grabbed my hand. "Come back and see me again, pretty young Natalie, will you please?"

"Yes," I said, rather breathlessly. "Yes, I will try to."

~ ~ ~

Emerging from the tunnel into the right wing of the

palace, Sacha and I decided to go to the library and wait there for the duchess to return. There was nowhere else to go, really; outside the weather was wild, while inside was at least relatively warm and comfortable. We picked up a book each and sat beside the fire, but though Sacha soon became immersed, I could not concentrate on mine.

I was angry at the peremptory summons by the duchess, leaving us without any kind of explanation, and now there was nothing to do but wait until someone deigned to inform us. As we sat in silence in the library, I started to sink into a dark mood. After learning so much about myself from Myriam, I had thought I would become immune to such slights, but it seemed to be worse this time than before. I knew I should have been included in things, at a level comparable to the duchesses, and their rejection of me as a Romanov burned like acid in my heart. But there was no-one I could talk to about the hurt and anger I felt, not even Sacha, as much as I had grown to like her. This was something that would always be held inside me, secretly growing hard and cold, like a stone.

And Petr ~ I was just beginning to enjoy his company ~ now, here I was, kicking my heels back in the palace, waiting for their Royal Majesties to command us, with only Sacha for company. As soon as that uncharitable thought rose to the surface of my mind I felt immediate remorse ~ what a horrid thing to think about my new friend!

"Sorry, Sacha," I mumbled.

"What?" She raised her head from the book and

looked at me, puzzled.

"I'm not good company," I said lamely.

She shrugged. "Is something getting to you? Was it that handsome young officer?"

At the mention of him, I relaxed a little and smiled. "Do you think he's handsome?"

"Are you kidding me?" she screeched. "He's gorgeous. What were you talking about?"

I told her what he had said about his aeroplane being like a lover, and she laughed. "That beats most chat-up lines. Are you seeing him again?"

It was my turn to shrug my shoulders. "I would like to. He's very nice."

As we talked, I felt my bad temper ebbing away.

"Then what you must do is make him wait," she said firmly. "He mustn't think you are keen. Men like to have to chase their prey."

I looked at her quizzically.

"I read it in a book," she said by way of explanation, and grinned.

~ ~ ~

Eventually Luba came to tell us that we were required by Alexandra to attend with all the staff in the central hall at once. A summons from on high, and now so urgent!

We followed her through corridors and abandoned rooms in silence. I was sure Sacha must have noticed that, apart from delivering her message, Luba was not inclined to talk to me. She would find out in time that it was this way with most of the staff; they resented my relative closeness to the family, not realising that it was a superficial thing, a source more of pain than comfort.

When we arrived at the hall, a huge, high-domed, semi-circular room in the centre of the palace, with tall windows, hanging drapes, and a chandelier on long chains, the rest of the staff were already assembled, clustered near the fireplace. We joined Polya and Rada, standing quietly at the back of the group, wondering what it could be about. Hushed whispers were being exchanged by some of the girls, but the twins simply greeted us with hugs, and we waited patiently to find out why we had been called together; no doubt all would be revealed in the Romanovs' own good time.

Chapter 5 ~ Rodzianko

Shortly, a sombre Alexandra entered the room, accompanied by the Princesses ~ all looking very pale and worried. Even Olga and Maria had risen from their sick-beds to be with their mother. This was clearly a significant moment.

The Empress's shoulders were down, her face was grey and drawn; she looked frail and old. In recent months, she had found it increasingly difficult to walk any great distance, and appeared always to be in some pain as she moved. She was only in her forties, slim and normally pretty, with beautiful golden hair, but the years as Empress of Russia had weighed heavily on her. In some ways she had been prepared for this life ~ she came from the German royal family, and was accustomed to wealth and authority ~ but, particularly in matters of running the nation, both she and Nicholas were woefully inexperienced and naive.

The small group stopped before the assembled staff, and Alexandra looked slowly around the room; she seemed at a loss. Then she turned to the man who had entered the hall with her. Without speaking, but with a sweep of her open hand, she indicated that he was free to address the small crowd. Then she sat down with her daughters, her expression unreadable.

When the man stepped forward from the group to speak, I was shocked at his appearance. Revealed fully at last, he was huge ~ not just tall and broad, but fat in the extreme. The excesses of some in our royal family, and others around Europe, had led many of them to rotundity, and this man was as obese as any I had seen. In order to balance the weight of his great belly, he had to lean backwards, meaning that he looked down his fat nose at everyone. Yet he spoke in a rich, musical baritone, though with each enunciation, the accumulated fat around his neck and jowls quivered.

"My name is Mikhail Vladimirovich Rodzianko" he announced. "I have the sad duty to tell you about the current sorry state of our country's affairs."

I recognised the name: he was the President of the Duma, the token elected government set up by the Tsar to placate the people after the 1905 uprising.

Despite the cold weather outside, the hall had become quite warm, with the small fire and the collective heat of all the bodies clustered there, and he paused to remove a handkerchief from his waistcoat pocket to wipe the sweat from his forehead. He kept it in his hand, and frequently dabbed at his perspiring face. I found myself becoming distracted by watching as, with every movement, his belly rippled beneath his waistcoat, and seemed to be trying to escape from its confinement.

"You are aware, I assume, that there is violence on our streets," he continued in that oddly beautiful voice. "The citizens are starving, their wages have been unpaid because the economy has collapsed, and they are freezing to death because there is no fuel to burn. When they riot, the troops sent to control them desert their duties and join the rebels.

"Furthermore, our soldiers at the front in the war with Germany have no ammunition, and they too are starving. All the wars of recent years have ruined our country, and the people are revolting against the leaders who they see as responsible; in other words, the royal family. I do not believe that any of you realise the extent of the poverty of the nation, or how angry the people are, and how much they hate the monarchy at this time."

Looking around at the other members of staff, I wondered if he was right. How many people in the room actually did know what a mess the Tsar had made of the country? They surely could not all be ignorant of the fact. After all, it was impossible to read a newspaper or listen to the wireless without being aware of the catastrophe that was unravelling. But, as I studied the expressions on their faces, I realised that they did not comprehend; I wondered if I was the only one who thought about such things. Worse, perhaps they knew but didn't care. If even the royals had closed their minds to the consequences of their actions, what hope was there for those who just followed blindly.

"For these reasons," boomed Rodzianko, "yesterday, the generals of the army and navy, and members of the government, including myself, advised His Imperial Highness that the only way to regain order in Russia is for him to abdicate, to give up his position of supreme authority and hand power to the Duma until such time that a proper government can be chosen. I am sorry to bring you this news, but it is the end for the monarchy in Russia."

Sudden chatter and questions erupted in the hall at his words, echoing around its marble walls, until Alexandra stood and spoke, in a voice that was hoarse and strained.

"Children, please, act with decorum; listen to Mr Rodzianko." She scanned the room, glaring at wherever she still heard muttered voices, and the din quickly subsided. Then she sat down again, her face set.

Rodzianko stepped forward once more, dabbing at his face. With each movement, his shirt was pulling out of his trousers; a flap of it was hanging below his waistcoat.

"The Tsar has accepted our advice, and has announced to the country on the wireless that he is stepping down immediately. There is to be no successor. For his own safety, the young prince will not be elevated, and the Tsar's brother has wisely declined to accept the role. I have advised Her Majesty to evacuate the palace and go somewhere safer, as I cannot guarantee the family's safety here."

She would most likely ignore that advice. Over the past few days, as fears of an uprising had grown, the Empress had been pressed by many people to take the family elsewhere, but she refused to go until her husband returned.

He was still away at the front, directing his generals in the war against Germany. It was his favourite place to be, and he often spent weeks at a time away from the palace, sometimes only returning for some state occasion or other before disappearing off to war again.

But while he was playing his boy-games, a new, different kind of battle had sprung up on his doorstep.

Rodzianko had finished delivering his message. He turned to the Empress, bowed stiffly, and walked out of the room. I could hear his footsteps echoing as he crossed the parquet floor of the entrance hall beyond, then a door closed and silence fell upon the hall.

So that's that, I mused. *The Romanovs no longer preside over Russia. Despite their belief in their divine right to rule, they have been unable isolate themselves from the woes they have brought upon the country, and have been rejected by their subjects. I wonder what it will mean to our lives.*

~ ~ ~

For a long time, no-one moved. But then Alexandra slowly rose to her feet. She looked exhausted. Every day she woke with the responsibility for a whole nation weighing constantly on her mind ~ but she had failed, failed as none of her predecessors had ever done, and she was ashamed at letting them all down.

"Today," she began, but her voice caught, and she hesitated, her head lowered. She swallowed, took a long breath, then raised her head and resumed. "Today the world has been turned on its head. Those horrible little people have conspired to overthrow the monarchy! A family that has served the people of Russia for hundreds of years is to be discarded because of a few greedy and power-mad intellectuals."

Alexandra was a traditionalist; she had no time for the aspirations of the 'ordinary people' to run their own lives; she truly believed that the leadership of the nation was given to the royal family by God.

However, she knew that she was personally disliked in Russia because of her German beginnings ~ both by the people, who mistrusted her, and by the gentry of the Petrograd court, who resented her presence in their society. That those things upset her was a sign that she was human after all, not the demi-god she wanted to believe she was.

"The next few months are going to be difficult enough for all of us," she continued. "You need to know that I am strong enough take care of you, and I will do my best for you and all the people."

I could not believe it! Even with everything in tatters around her, she was unable to accept that 'the people', as she thought of them, were rejecting her; in her mind, they were simply being misled and corrupted by the Bolsheviks.

"Nicholas has announced his abdication in a broadcast on the wireless, and we no longer have a role in running the country. But we have to carry on here as best we can until things are sorted out, continue as though nothing has changed. I do not know what will happen to us, but for now, in this house, we must remain the same as we always have been. Today and tomorrow, and each day to come, we will all continue to do what we do so well; we will smile at each other, and work and help each other as we always have."

She paused again to look slowly around the room, as though she expected someone to speak, or perhaps applaud. Then, with a fleeting, rather forced, unnatural smile, she brought the meeting to a close.

"Now, I need to spend some time with my children and my husband."

She beckoned her daughters to follow her and, after they had left, everyone else shuffled out of the room, most lost in their own thoughts of what had just happened, some muttering quietly together.

Diary ~ Friday 4th March ~ evening

So, it is abdication. Probably the bravest and best decision Nicholas has ever made, though what it will mean for all of us I can't imagine. I was stupid to over-react yesterday, thinking Nicholas might be dead; of course he's not! The clues were there for me to see: Tatiana would have been in a much worse state, and would not have returned to work. Sometimes I get so angry with myself for not thinking straight.

And the declaration: I had to fight the temptation to laugh at Rodzianko. It struck me that, in his tight, white suit and with his bulging waistline and invisible neck, he looked just like a ball of ice cream on a glass.

I have quickly grown to like Sacha. We get on very well. She is smart and willing to listen; and though she is the daughter of a prince, she does not seem to think she is above me. And I have met a man, a wonderful, sexy man. His name is Petr Valeriev, and he is an airman; how romantic is that? He is handsome and tall, with disturbing eyes that make my legs go weak. Sacha says I must not encourage him; I must wait for him to chase me. I hope he doesn't take too long.

Diary ~ Saturday 5th March ~ morning

I think I have been told off! Myriam was her usual, gentle self, but after she left I had the strangest feeling that she had been wagging her spiritual finger at me.

"Natalie," she began after greeting me, "tonight, for my last visit, I am going to tell you about yourself. You may not like everything I say, but you need to hear it. The first thing I want to tell you is this: I know your heart, and how lonely you feel, here in this palace. Although you have the twins and one or two friends, you are not accepted by most of the members of the household staff, yet neither do you feel part of the family; you yearn for the comfort of belonging. You feel that what you have now is a substitute, not a real family, not a true home. That is true, isn't it?"

She raised an eyebrow, and I nodded.

"Well first you must stop blaming others for your feelings. Whatever they may do to you or for you, the people around you are all following their own dreams, confronting their own fears; I want you to learn to do the same with your life. So, you feel unloved and want to know if that will ever change? Look around you, Natalie, you are loved more than you realise. Don't look so surprised, you know it is true. Your friends Rada and Polina love you, and you love them; they are like sisters to you, and sisterly love is just one of the

many faces of love. Alexandra loves you, too."

I opened my mouth to speak, but she held up a hand.

"No, dear, listen. I know it is not the same as the love of a mother for her own offspring, but it is closer to that than you think. The only love you truly lack right now is the kind that binds you to one person, one man, and I promise you, that will happen. You are still young, just be patient."

I thought at once about Petr. "When, Myriam, and how will I know?" Could it be him?

"Oh, it is coming, and you will know beyond doubt. When you least expect it a man will enter your life, and from the first moment you meet you will know he is the one, and you will remember my words."

Yes, I was sure she meant Petr!

She did not elaborate, but smiled again. A smile filled with warmth, radiating understanding and confidence.

"Now, I am going to repeat something I told you before. It is important, more important than anything else, so make sure you grasp it. If you apply what I am about to tell you to every part of your life, you will have all the strength you need to pass through the trials that will soon assail you."

She paused and leaned towards me, gazing intently, hypnotically into my eyes. Close to, I noticed that her image was shimmering slightly, like a reflection on ripples in water. I could not shake the feeling that I knew her, or recognised her from somewhere.

"Natalie, listen carefully. Everything that happens in life is a lesson to be learnt, a gift from the future, sent to strengthen and guide you. No matter how bad it may seem to you, or how good, all things are part of life and part of you. What you have to do is to try to understand what you see, then accept it if you want to, or fight it if you need to ~ the choice is always yours.

"But I need you to learn to be more confident in yourself, less subservient. You are an intelligent girl, so take control over your life; you can do it. Over the next few weeks and months, when the world seems to be tumbling in disarray all around you, remember what I am telling you. Keep a clear head, because you have a purpose, and every day you live will lead you forward to your future, if you let it. Do not be passive. Absorb every experience, question it, remember it, look for ways to change it if that seems the right thing to do. Always be aware that what you learn from each experience prepares you for the next, and what you do with what you learn will become the measure of you. Trust me, you will become greater for it.

But listen, my dear Natalie: my visits here have been for one purpose, to warn you. There will be people who you have yet to meet who will help you, and some who will seek to use you for their own gain. You must learn to question their motives. A day will come when you will hold the balance of history in your hands; I will not tell you what to do, the decision is yours, and you are free to choose the path that is right for you ~ but you must choose."

She tilted her head to one side in that odd way she had, studying me again.

"That is my gift for you, the reason I have been allowed to visit you. Do you understand it, Natalie?"

I nodded, slowly, uncertainly, then changed my mind and shook my head.

"I don't know, Myriam. I understand your words, but not what they mean to me, or how I am to apply them to my life."

She smiled, gently. "I know, it seems too much to grasp right now, but you will understand, sooner than you think. Yesterday you were a child. Tomorrow (yes, it is that close) you will see the start of changes in your life that will make you a woman or, perhaps, even an angel.

"Goodnight, Natalie, remember my words, be confident of your future, and know that I am always here for you; ask me in the quietness of your mind, and listen ~ I will answer."

She lifted her right hand again in that little wave, then shimmered and faded from sight.

Chapter 6 ~ Romance

When I reached Tatiana's suite that morning, to dress her, I found the door locked. I knocked, but there was no answer.

Puzzled, but assuming she was with her mother, I went back to join the twins, and we took the stairs down to the chapel for the morning service. When we arrived, several members of staff were gathered around the door, deep in conversation. They immediately fell into silence at the sight of me and wandered off in small groups. I shrugged as I watched them go, accustomed to their cold attitude, then turned to see what they had been looking at.

There was a note pinned to the door: '***There will be no prayers this morning. Please go about your duties as normal, and help each other whenever possible***', it read.

This was a shock. Never, in all my years at the palace, had she cancelled a service before.

"What does it signify?" Rada said, thinking aloud. "That the Empress has withdrawn from palace life?"

I doubted that. "It is more likely that she and her daughters were deciding what they should do next."

With nothing to detain us, they set off to begin their routines, and I headed for the kitchens to attend to my birds.

Once outside, I found that it had at last stopped snowing, so I took my time, carefully cleaning all corners of the little feeding table. When it was done, though the wind was filled with the menace of more snow, I paused to look around.

The sun was still below the horizon, but his first rays were painting swathes of pink across the bellies of the clouds that hung in garlands over the glittering skyline to the east. A fluttering in the branches nearby told me that my little friends were queuing for their breakfasts, so I departed to allow them to feed.

Back indoors, I took a little breakfast to the small library to eat while I waited in case Tatiana wanted me, though I doubted I would see any of them ~ the note hinted at that. They would be discussing the events of the previous day and considering the outcomes and implications.

I sorted through the post, sparse as it was, and replied to any that I could. Those that needed Tatiana's attention I tied in a bundle and locked in the safe, then I carried my letters down to the entrance hall, where there was a box for outgoing post. Normally, the letters would be collected by a messenger, but every day something was changing, so there was no way of being sure that the mail would go out, or that it would be delivered.

My letters disposed of, I stood at the centre of the palace, in the great, empty, echoing expanse of the entrance complex, and looked around pensively at the architecture. It was a magnificent welcome for any arrivals at the palace. A polished parquet floor flowed from where I stood before the front doors, through marble columns into the semi-circular hall. There, tall and wide windows, decorated with more marble, rose to a domed ceiling high above, creating a light and airy chamber. A huge chandelier, suspended from the centre of the dome, matched one above my head in the entrance hall. On each side of me, arched openings led to a pair of staircases leading to the upper rooms. The one to my left, by which I had arrived, waited for me to return; the other to my right gave access to the state rooms and guest quarters. At the far corner of that wing, along a short corridor, was the entrance to the tunnel leading out to the hospital.

A thought had been tickling at the edge of my mind, a desire manifesting itself. As I allowed it to form, to become real, an unexpected feeling gripped my stomach, and my heart began pounding. I hesitated briefly, excitement building as I tried to decide if I should do what I suddenly wanted to do. The decision, apparently, was not mine. As though controlled by someone else, my legs began to walk, footsteps ringing on the polished floor, carrying me through the arch, along a short corridor and through deserted rooms, into the canvas tunnel. My eyes watched the walls passing on each side, and took in the sight of the rows of beds as the owner of those eyes emerged into the hospital and stopped, panting nervously, scanning the chamber for a familiar face.

I began to feel foolish. What would I say if anyone asked why I was there? What was I going to say to him, for goodness sake? All my confidence deserted me; I turned to scuttle back to the safety of the palace, but collided with a tall body blocking my way.

"Sorry," I mumbled, eyes downcast, trying to sidestep whoever it was and make my escape, but I became aware that I was looking at a plaster cast and a walking stick.

Simultaneously, a friendly voice said: "Would it be terrible vanity if I were to assume that you're here to see me?" and I looked up to see those brown eyes twinkling at me.

"Yes, it would," I stammered, lowering my head again hastily. "I'm just here on a .... for an .... umm ... a routine visit."

Why did he affect me like this? My heart was fluttering, I knew my (inadequate) bosom was heaving in a most provocative way, and I couldn't stop it.

"Are you ok?" he asked, anxiously, stooping down to look into my eyes. "You seem out of breath. Have you been running?"

"Yes, running, that's what it is. My chest ..." (*argh! don't draw attention to your chest!*) "... I'm panting because ... umm ... I ran down the corridor. You see. Because it was cold. In the corridor. From the weather."

"You had better come and sit down," he said, grinning, and led me to a rumpled, vacant bed.

"This is my bed. Sit here until you get your breath back."

I nodded and sat obediently.

His bed! I'm sitting on his bed, where he sleeps!

"Stay there," he ordered, and hobbled off, returning moments later carefully carrying a chipped enamel mug of steaming tea.

"It's from the urn," he explained, with a twist of his head towards a great copper cylinder on a trolley by the wall. "Horribly stewed, I'm afraid, but it will help to settle you."

I accepted the mug and sipped, clutching it with both hands. "Thank you."

He settled onto the bed beside me, studying my face with those soft, dog-like eyes. "Better now?"

I nodded, and took another sip.

"I have come to see you, really," I admitted. "Sacha said I should ignore you, make you chase after me, but I seem to have rather shown my hand."

He gave a little laugh. "I'm glad. Right now I'm in no position to run after you, though I would."

He reached out a hand to touch mine gently. I looked at it ~ a smooth hand, but a wisp of brown hair peeped from the cuff of his sleeve, hinting at a rugged arm beneath. I could not help myself, I looked up to the open neck of his army shirt to see if his chest was also covered. I could see enough to satisfy my curiosity, but I also saw that he had noticed me looking. Immediately, I was flustered again, my cheeks burning.

He smiled, tenderly. "I think you are feeling what I am feeling, Natalie," he said softly. There was no denying the emotions that were running through me; was this the love that Myriam had told me to expect?

Unable to speak for the thunder in my chest, I nodded, looking up into those hypnotic eyes. As he leaned closer and gently gripped my shoulders with his hands, my lips parted to receive his kiss, and when his mouth touched mine a surge ran through me like fire. I lifted my hands to his face and clasped it as I responded with my whole body.

A sudden clattering roar shattered the silence, and we pulled apart. In my confused state, I had forgotten that we were in a room full of men, soldiers, who were now loudly cheering and clapping their hands.

Acutely embarrassed, I jumped to my feet, feeling my face burning with humiliation. Petr also stood and wrapped his arms around me protectively. I buried my face in his shoulder, tears flowing, chest heaving. He thrust a handkerchief into my hand, which I gratefully used to cover my face as he led me gently off to the tunnel, to the sound of continued applause, which only stopped when we were out of their sight.

Once away from the prying eyes I removed the handkerchief and turned my tear-soaked face up to look longingly into his eyes. He kissed me gently.

"I'm sorry that happened," he said sincerely. "They are separated from their loved ones, surrounded by nothing but violence and death. A little bit of romance is a treat. Are you all right now?"

I nodded. "Thank you. I should get back, anyway, in case I'm needed."

I felt his arms tighten around me, and his breath hot on my face as he held me close and kissed me again, long and with increasing passion. His nose pressed into my cheek, his mouth bore harder and harder against mine, his tongue forcing its way between my teeth. I did not resist. I felt his arousal against my belly, and longed to know it better.

Reluctantly we parted, and with a sigh I began to walk, backwards, waving my hand foolishly, away from him and back to my duties.

Chapter 7 ~ Nicholas

But no duties awaited me. At a loose end and feeling rather dreamy, I went to my room, put on several layers of warm clothes and my heavy boots, pulled a good hat down over my ears, and wrapped a scarf about my face. Then I clumped down the stairs and out through a back door for a walk along the path that ran around the rear walls of the palace, ultimately ending in the family's vegetable garden. The path, bordered by little box hedges, was just passable for part of its length, where it was sheltered from the prevailing northerly wind by the bulk of the building. An almost continuous rattle of distant gunfire formed part of the background noise, along with the nearer hiss of windblown snow and the chirping of sparrows. Gun shots were occasionally exchanged much closer, like dogs barking in response to each other. Each time a ragged volley happened I jumped, but could see nothing, not even the soldiers on guard.

I reached the limit of my walk, where the path ahead was blocked by a drift of snow, and pulled the hood up over my hat, holding it around my face with my mittened fingers against the icy wind, while I gazed out across the palace grounds. The low sun struggled to illuminate the ethereal, monochrome landscape, casting long grey shadows across a bright white canvas. It seemed to fit the mood of the day, and I felt as though I was standing in a dream, somehow apart from the real world, with events of huge import swirling around me, buffeting me like the cold northerly wind.

Myriam's predictions were already coming true; things were certainly changing in so many ways, both for me and for Russia. As I gazed beyond the trees to the snow-topped dome of the church, glowing golden and white against the leaden sky, I remembered her instruction to absorb and learn from every experience. Obediently, I set my mind to flick through the events of the past days, assembling them like pages in a scrapbook. But what was to be learned from them? That we were powerless? That our lives were in the hands of others? No, she had told me that I could influence things, though I had no idea how. Confused, I resolved to be more attentive to the lessons as they happened.

Eventually, the cold wind biting at my nose and ears began to penetrate my skin, despite all the layers of clothes, and became too much to bear. I turned to follow the trail of my own footprints back between the snowdrifts. My breath was rising in clouds, and, looking down, I noticed that my skirt had picked up a crusty hem of ice, but it had been pleasant to be out of the house for a while.

I re-entered the palace and climbed the back stairs. On the way to my room, I passed the bathroom, and decided to treat my cold body to a soak in lovely hot water infused with lavender bath salts. It seemed likely that there would be no work that day, and anyway, Tatiana could always find me if she needed to.

After my bath, I wrapped a towel around myself and ran, steaming like a racehorse, along the cold corridor to my room to dress.

~ ~ ~

Later, as I was adding some random thoughts to my diary, Rada burst in through my bedroom door.

"There you are," she said, breathlessly. "I've been looking all over for you. Nicholas is on his way!"

"When? Where is he now?" I asked, glad of some activity.

"Sacha heard from her grandfather that he is at Mohilev, riding across country to avoid the rebel patrols. She asked if I knew where to find you. She's waiting in the big library, downstairs."

I hugged her, gratefully, then hurried off to see Sacha, trying not to run, as running was strictly forbidden in any part of the palace.

Sacha greeted me enthusiastically, and we sat down together on one of the sofas.

"Grandfather had a telephone call last night from Nicholas," she began at once. "He was in the garrison at Mohilev, resting before resuming his journey this morning. He must already be well on his way, now. He thinks he could be home sometime tomorrow afternoon. He has given orders that the troops in Petrograd are to use whatever force is necessary to regain control. Grandfather has been in touch with Daddy, and he is briefing the officers of all units, coordinating a breakout." She smiled nervously. "Perhaps this is the start of our lives getting back to normal."

"I hope so," I answered, dubiously. "How is your mother?"

She shrugged. "Not awfully good. She had seemed to be a little better, before this news came in. Of course, if Daddy is going to be involved in fighting, she is bound to be worried about him."

Suddenly, she jumped up. "Would you like to meet her? Some company might help to cheer her up."

I grinned and nodded, and together we made our way through empty rooms until we reached the stairs leading up to the guest accommodation. I had never been to Count Beckendorff's apartments before ~ in fact, I could not recall that he had ever spoken more than two words in succession to me ~ so I was surprised when he greeted me warmly when I entered. He was dressed casually, looking elegant in a neat tunic and baggy woolen pants. Sacha explained that she had invited me to see her mother, and he cheerfully led us through to her bedroom.

We found her sitting up in bed, reading a book. "Sacha, my wonderful child," she exclaimed when we entered. "And who is this you have brought? I think I recognise you." She stared at me appraisingly. Her eyes were sharp and alert, in a face not unlike Alexandra's. Her hair was steel-grey, tied back severely.

"This is Natalie Tereshchenko, mother," Sacha said.

"Tereshchenko, yes, of course. That's why your face seemed familiar. I know your mother, young lady," the Countess chuckled. "You look just like her."

"Good afternoon, Countess," I said formally, trying to cover my confusion and surprise. *My mother!*

She noticed that I was flustered. "Ah, I detect something," she said. "Alex hasn't told you about your parents, has she?"

I looked at the floor and shook my head.

"But you know, anyway!" She laughed. "I know you know, I can see it in your eyes and the way you carry yourself. Who told you?"

It was clear to me that there was no point in denying it. "Myriam," I said, simply.

"Myriam?" she screeched. "You can't have met Myriam, she died before you were born."

"You know Myriam?" I heard my voice rising in amazement. This was becoming surreal.

"Oh yes indeed, I knew her well. She was your grandmother. But how do you know her? That's what I want to know."

"She came to me in a dream, recently."

I paused, collecting my thoughts, and she waited for me to continue; but I had a question.

"Countess, is my mother still alive?"

A sly smile crossed her face. "You want to meet her, don't you?" she stated.

I nodded.

"She was well enough, last time I saw her; but I don't think it will be possible to arrange a rendezvous for some time, with you being here in the palace and her in Moscow, and a revolution going on in between. Perhaps, when things settle down, you may be able to meet. But you know she was forbidden from seeing you, don't you?"

"Yes, but that was when I was a child, and when Alexandra thought I would never find out."

She nodded, slowly, thoughtfully. "I will try to arrange it for you."

I was about to thank her when the door opened, and her father-in-law entered.

"The doctor is here to see you," he told the Countess.

I stood and took her hand. "It has been wonderful to meet you," I said, sincerely. "May I come again, please?"

"I hope you will visit me many times," she smiled.

~ ~ ~

As I left Sacha and her mother, I felt happier and more at peace than I could recall feeling for a long time. My mother was well, and within reach. '*Thank you, Myriam*' I whispered.

On my way back to my little suite, I called in to see Polina and Rada, in the room that I had once shared with them. They were my oldest friends; the three of us had shared the room as junior maids, before Tatiana gave me one of my own, in keeping with my new role. We had always slept together in one bed, snuggling together for warmth, and often spent our spare time together, chatting and giggling, sharing all our secrets. They smiled as I entered, and jumped up to hug me.

"How were things in Aleksey's rooms?" I asked.

"Oh, he was his usual, talkative self," replied Rada, grinning.

Although they were the same age, Rada had always seemed older than her sister. She was more confident, somehow tougher, yet more outgoing, with a lively mind and piercing green eyes. She had long fingers, and could play the piano well. She could also dance very competently, and she seemed to be ready to break into a little twirl at any time, with an unexpected smile on her lips. Her black hair was cut short, like a boy's, and she rarely wore jewellery, or any kind of decoration.

"The rumour is that Nicholas is on his way back," she continued, "What's going to happen now?"

"Yes, it seems sure he will be here tomorrow," I nodded.

"That's not good, is it?" she said. "When he gets here, all the family will be together, then the trouble will really start."

"I think you are right. It fits in with the worsening of our situation that Myriam predicted."

"Yes, but what next?" said Rada. "If Myriam is right, what will happen to us all?"

"I have a feeling we will find out when Nicholas arrives," I answered.

We sat silently for a while, our imaginations running wild.

The room had become quite dark, and Polina stood to turn on the electric light.

"I have something to tell you," I began, as she sat again, then paused, uncertainly. "Perhaps I shouldn't; it could break the spell."

"Oh come on!" Rada chided. "You can't start

something like that and then not tell us!"

"Well," I said shyly, "I have met someone, a man. "

Suddenly they were excited. "Who?" said Rada. "Where?" asked Polya. "How?" Rada added.

I laughed and told them about Petr.

"I can't explain how he affects me. It's like, when I'm with him, or even if I just think about him ~ which is quite a lot, actually ~ my body takes over from my mind. I just want him to make love to me."

They laughed at me, but hugged me gleefully.

By then it was late, so we kissed each other goodnight, and I took a candle to walk slowly along the dark corridor to my own, empty suite. I sat for a few minutes at my dressing table, adding the latest events of the day to my diary, then, with a sigh, undressed for bed. I really did not like having my own room. Oh, it was a sign of my elevated status in the hierarchy, and it was warm and comfortable enough, and nicely furnished, but I felt even lonelier than ever, separated from my two special friends, my only real family.

When I slipped between my sheets, however, I found other thoughts occupying my mind. The memory of Petr's kisses filled me with a warm glow, and thoughts of other delights.

Chapter 8 ~ Frederick

The next morning, our routines were re-established, and Tatiana was in her room when I arrived to dress her. She was understandably subdued, and few words passed between us. I felt that it would be wrong for me to try to improve her mood, so we spent our short time together in respectful silence.

Later, after prayers, and a quick visit to my bird-table, I joined her in the library, where she was already sorting through the post. She handed me a small envelope: "This one is for you, Nata."

"Oh, yes, of course, it will be from the Queen of Africa asking me for money again," I smiled, throwing it back on the little pile without even looking at it. "Tell her to ask the King of America."

Tatiana's mouth turned up a little; a brave attempt, but her eyes did not smile. "No, really, it has your name on it, look. And a foreign stamp."

I took it back and it was, indeed, addressed to me. It had, of course, already been opened by the censor, so, with a puzzled look at Tatiana, I pulled out the letter and read it.

10th February 1917

My Dear Natalie

I so much enjoyed our dance together, and wished we could have talked for longer. The evening, drab and boring until that moment, became alive when I met you, and became mundane again when we parted. You have brightened my life and filled it with beauty.

My journey home was not too difficult, except the drive to the port. In many parts of Saint Petersburg, we passed scenes of fighting between soldiers and civilians, which I have never seen before and found disturbing.

And when we joined our ship and set sail, we were still not sure of safety from attack by the German navy. Of course we fly our Swedish flag of neutrality, so they should leave us alone, but we could never be certain. However, the crossing was not so bad, and we arrived home on Sunday morning.

After a few days with my family, I must now rejoin my ship on patrol along our coast.

Although I have only met you on that one occasion, I already miss you very much and think of you all the time. Do you have a photograph of yourself that I could have to keep near me, please?

Your devoted friend,

Frederick

Tatiana was regarding me with a quizzical expression, so, with a grin, I passed the letter over for her to read. When she had finished it, she looked at me with an unexpected smile and raised eyebrows.

"Don't look at me like that," I laughed.

"I'm intrigued, I want to know every detail."

The letter seemed to have raised her spirits a little.

"Very well. Do you remember the state ball in January, at Catherine Palace? You lent me that gorgeous blue satin dress."

She nodded, enthusiastically. "You looked amazing in it, with your beautiful pale skin and your long black hair gathered up. The belle of the ball."

"Hmmmph, belle of the ball with a big nose and uneven teeth!"

She slapped my hand. "Don't be hard on yourself, you are a lovely young woman. Your nose is not big." Then, when I pursed my lips at her, she conceded, "Well, perhaps it is, just a bit. But no-one notices it except you, honestly. What they notice are your lovely big green eyes and your slim figure. Not many people could wear that dress, especially that neckline, but it perfectly suited your shape."

I smiled, and grabbed her hand. "Thank you," I said, giving it a squeeze. Then, looking into her eyes, and with a mischievous grin, I added: "I wish I believed you."

She shook her head as she handed the letter back to me.

"Come on, tell me. What happened at the ball?"

"Well, I was standing in the corner over by the big doors through to the dining hall, watching the couples dancing, swaying to the music, totally absorbed in the occasion. You know how much I love the colour, the beautiful gowns, the smart uniforms of the men, and the glitter of the chandeliers, picked up and scattered by the mirrors. I had been so engrossed in watching the dancers sweeping past me just a few feet away, that I did not see him at first. Then I became aware that someone was standing still in my line of vision, and I looked up to see who it was. He was standing quite close, looking directly at me, with a faint smile on his lips. I saw that he was about my height, a bit older than me, and very good looking, with neat blonde hair and a shadow of a moustache under his nose. He wore a dark blue military dress uniform, which suited him very well. He bowed, and asked me to dance. I was surprised, and looked quickly around me in case he was really addressing someone else, but there was no-one nearby. I stammered that I was not royalty, just a Maid, and he smiled and said that it didn't matter to him, I was the most beautiful girl there, and he wanted to dance with me."

~ ~ ~

As I recalled that evening for Tatiana, my mind filled again with the sights and sounds and the flow of events. I remembered feeling embarrassed, and telling him that I was a bad dancer, because I never had the opportunity to practice.

"Do not worry," he replied gently, "I will not tax you."

He held out his hand to me, and when I took it, I felt a tingle in my fingers and a flutter in my heart; it was the first time my hand had touched a man's, and it was a nice feeling.

He walked me to the dance floor, smiling, looking straight into my eyes in a disturbingly frank way.

"Just relax and follow my lead," he said, and we danced.

It was a magical moment, like a dream come true. He gently guided me around the floor. I scarcely noticed that I was dancing; it was like floating in a warm bath, my movements seemed to happen without my control.

~ ~ ~

"And we talked," I continued to Tatiana. "He was attentive; he asked my name, and said it was lovely. He asked me about myself. What is more, he listened to my answers and responded with sensitive comments.

In turn, I asked him his name. He told me that it is Frederick Froeda, and added that he is from Sweden, the son of a duke who is close to the Swedish royal family; and he is a cadet in their Navy."

"I know the family," she commented, "I think I met Frederick once."

"Ah, good; I knew nothing about him until he told me. His voice was soft and cultured, with a fascinating accent that was both lyrical and sexy. I found his company delightful and felt completely comfortable with him. It was as though we had known each other for years, but needed to catch up with what had happened in each other's lives.

We talked about so many things that the time passed quickly, and I was surprised when the dance ended. He walked me back to where he had found me, and we sat for a little while talking some more. He asked if he may write to me, and of course I said yes.

But then his mother suddenly arrived and, with a glare at me, told him to return to his family. I found that he had been holding my hand the whole time. He gently released it and, with a last, tender smile at me, stood and followed his mother.

Then he was gone, and I returned, alone again, to my little reverie, floating on a cloud."

Just remembering the evening was making me feel dreamy.

"You clearly stole his heart," Tatiana said, indicating the letter.

"I suppose so," I replied, hesitantly.

"What's wrong?"

"I'm confused, Tati. If this letter had arrived a week ago I would have been thrilled. I am thrilled, it's like a fairytale. But since then I've met someone else, another man, and my feelings are all mixed up."

"Another one!" she exclaimed. "Nata, do you have some kind of secret life? Who is this 'other man'?"

"He is Lieutenant Valeriev, an airman. I met him in the hospital on Friday, and I went to see him again yesterday. You must know him; he is probably the only flier we have had here."

"Yes," she said quickly, "yes, I have met him. So, what makes him special?"

"I don't know, that's the puzzle. I mean, he's handsome and exciting and all, but I can't pick out anything that would help me to understand why I feel like this. We have only talked a couple of times, for goodness sake! Why does he set my heart thumping like this? Tati, all I can think about is wanting him."

She shrugged, seemingly in her own thoughts. And why not? Her life was in turmoil, and here I was going on about a man I had hardly met.

I remembered Frederick's request for a photograph, and decided it was time for action.

"Tati, would you take my photograph please? I have no pictures of myself to send him."

"Yes!" she said, galvanised into action.

She jumped up and ran to a cupboard, emerging a few seconds later with one of those new, small Kodak cameras and a roll of film, which she deftly loaded into the little black box.

"Come on, out onto the balcony," she ordered.

Although it had stopped snowing, it was still freezing outside, and neither of us was dressed appropriately. We stood shivering in the crunchy snow that was piled up on the balcony as Tatiana took six pictures, peering down into her hand cupped around the window of the little black box and instructing me to stand "so," or "so."

Then we returned to the warmth of the library, where she carefully removed the film and put it back into its little tube.

"There, Aleksey will develop that for you later, and you shall have your pictures tomorrow."

~ ~ ~

We returned to the table to resume work, but after a

while I noticed that her head was down and she was staring thoughtfully at her hands.

"Are you alright?" I asked.

Without raising her head, Tatiana said quietly: "I want to tell you something I've never told anyone. But Nata ..." she leaned across the table and gazed intently into my eyes: "... you must never breathe a word of this. Promise?"

"Yes, of course. What's wrong?"

"Oh, nothing's wrong. This is just something I have kept hidden inside me for a year, but your letter from Frederick has started me thinking, and I want you to know about it." She paused, resuming her examination of her hands, her mind clearly in turmoil.

"Look," I said, "you don't have to tell me if it makes you feel uncomfortable."

Tatiana was silent for so long that I thought she had decided to keep it to herself after all.

Then, suddenly, she said: "I made love with a man once."

She stopped again, her mouth pinched tightly closed, as though she was afraid she had said too much. This time she did not meet my eye.

After a stunned silence, I asked, hoarsely: "Who?"

"Lieutenant Kuznetsov. You remember, he came to the hospital last year with a head wound? I fell in love with him as soon as I saw him. He was in the cavalry, and we talked about horses and riding; we spent hours together. When he was sufficiently recovered, the doctor discharged him from the hospital, but told him to spend a month at the barracks before returning to duty. We saw each other every day for that month, and on his last day before going back to his unit we made love in the woods. Mother must never find out; she will be very angry with me, and will surely tell my father."

At last she looked at me, a tear running down her cheek. "Nata, my body is filled with yearnings that I am forbidden from easing. Sometimes I feel like screaming with frustration."

I understood that feeling very well. "I know what you mean, Tati," I said, "it is the same for me, except that in my case I have never had the opportunity. Until Petr, I never met a man who showed any interest in me."

At the thought of him I felt again that rising inside me, like a thrill of excitement.

"And Frederick," she added.

"Pardon?"

"Don't forget Frederick, your Swedish prince."

"Oh yes," I said, embarrassed. "And Frederick, of course. Anyway, I promise I will never tell anyone what you just confided."

For a while, we sat quietly, but my curiosity eventually became unbearable. "What was it like?" I asked, keen to have some insight into what, at that moment, I could only imagine.

Tatiana laughed; it was lovely to see her face shed, for a moment at least, the tension that she was suffering.

"You evil girl," she chided, pushing me away. "You don't care about me, you just want the sordid details!"

~ ~ ~

Throughout the morning, and the early part of the afternoon, I could think of nothing and no-one except Petr. The memory of his kiss was on my lips, and I felt again the insistent pressure of his body against mine. As soon as my work with Tatiana was done and she departed to spend time with her mother, I hurried through empty rooms to the hospital, resolved to see him again.

But when I reached the hospital, he was not to be seen. As I stood beside his bed, looking around, perplexed, the man in the neighbouring bed spoke:

"A messenger brought a note for him, about an hour ago, and he left at once," he informed me.

Disappointed, I thanked him. "Do you know what was in the note? Or who it was from?" I asked.

"No miss. He put it straight in his pocket after reading it and hurried out. They removed his plaster cast this morning, did you know?"

I shook my head, partly in answer to his question, but also in puzzlement. Where could he go? Perhaps one of the generals wanted to talk to him, there were enough of them around the palace.

I thanked him again and began to sadly make my way back to the left wing.

Diary ~ Sunday 6th March 1917 ~ evening

From a life of nun-like celibacy, I suddenly find myself with two men in my thoughts: young, refined Frederick, and rugged, sexy Petr. I am thinking about them all the time, but my mind switches from one to the other unexpectedly, as though weighing them up ~ and it is always Petr who rises to the top. I long to see him again, but have no idea where he is; I am worried that he may have been called back to duty.

I could not tell Sacha or Tatiana, but his presence, or even just a thought of him, makes something happen to my body, a warm feeling in my thighs that takes control of me. I know that, if he were to kiss me again, I would be his, I could not hold back. Even as I think about him to write, now, I am tingling. When I put my hand down to where the tingle is, I am wet, and my touch sends waves of feelings through me.

Oh Natalie, stop it. Forget these erotic fantasies. Write, write, write ... What else has happened?

The palace has been busy all day, with diplomats and army officers calling constantly to talk with Alexandra. She sees them in her private quarters, away from any ears, so I have no idea what is going on, but all this activity must mean something significant is happening. Rumours abound that the Tsar is on his way home, but no-one seems to know where he actually is, and I can't believe that all these visitors are calling about that. In the event, he didn't show up today, as had been expected.

People are saying that Petrograd and Tsarskoye are now in the hands of the rebels. It seems likely, as I have seen a change in the attitude of the soldiers in the palace and the grounds, an air of defiance. They are more scared of the communists, now, than of the royals, and it shows in the way they speak and behave when any of us are near.

Chapter 9 ~ Betrayed

All was quiet and dark in the palace as, unable to sleep, and early for once, I sauntered along the passageways, through eerie fluorescent amber pools thrown down onto the carpets by the electric lamps hanging at intervals from the ceiling. My thoughts, from the moment I had wakened, were on Petr. I resolved that, as soon as possible, I would go again to the hospital to find out what had happened to him.

I met no-one on my short journey until, as I turned the final corner before Tatiana's suite, I was stunned to see someone, a man, emerging into the hallway from her door. I stopped, and stepped back quickly out of sight as he turned to look nervously around. He did not see me, but I recognised him immediately ~ it was the man who had been occupying my thoughts for every waking moment, and my dreams when asleep ~ Petr!

The strange twist made my head reel. Tatiana and Petr?

I waited a few seconds, hearing their whispered voices, then his fading, irregular footsteps and the clump of his stick, followed by the sound of her door softly closing. Furious, I marched up to it and flung it open again with a crash. Surprised, on her way back to her bedchamber, she turned quickly at the sound.

"Natalie," she said, guiltily, "you're here already."

"Yes," I snarled, "I'm here, and I saw who was here before me."

Her face coloured up, and she turned away from me.

"How could you, Tatiana? You knew how I felt about him, yet you have had him in your bed!"

"Keep your voice down," she hissed, "someone will hear."

"Why should that be a problem to me," I responded, sharply. "Hmm? I've not been caught in the act! Though I can see why you would not want your mother to find out!"

She turned angrily to face me. "Don't you use that tone of voice with me! Just remember who you are talking to!"

"Oh, how could I forget that?" I answered, stepping forward and standing intimidatingly close, glaring into her eyes, my hands on my hips. "After all, who am I?"

She flinched, and turned her head away from the blast of my breath.

"Well, I don't care, Tatiana. What are you going to do, sack me? Send me away? How will you explain that to Alexandra?" I tilted my head, arrogantly, provocatively.

She moved away and sat in a chair.

"No-one was supposed to find out," she whispered. "I've been seeing him for a week. Last night was the first time ... the only ..."

Her voice trailed off.

My righteous rage was quenched as though cold water had been thrown over me. I was struck speechless. When Petr had been leading me on, sweet-talking me, he was already having an affair with

Tatiana!

I, too, flopped down in a chair, my head reeling; this was all too much to take in. Then I noticed that the door was still open, and automatically got up to close it before sitting again.

As my anger shifted from Tatiana to Petr, I felt tears running down my face, and when I looked at her, she too was crying. I could not feel sorry for her.

~ ~ ~

Later, as I sat alone in the small library with my hurt pride and my angry thoughts, Tatiana sent Luba with an envelope containing the six photographs she had taken of me the day before, and which her brother had developed in his darkroom for me. She could not face me herself.

I morosely selected one to send to Frederick, and began to write a letter to accompany it, feeling guilty that my thoughts constantly wandered back to Petr.

After several spoilt sheets of paper, I finally had a version I could send:

Monday 7th March 1917

Dearest Frederick

Thank you for your lovely letter. I am so relieved that you arrived home safely, though it was clearly a challenging journey. I have read about some of the dreadful sea battles that have happened in this war, so I am happy you are unharmed.

As you may have heard, the situation here is

becoming quite serious. The fighting in the streets is continuing, worse than ever; the Tsar has abdicated and everyone in the family has lost their title. We are now under constant guard, and are very uncertain what the future may hold for us.

Thankfully, the snow here has finally stopped, and we are hoping for warmer weather soon, though spring is still some distance away, and there is every chance that we could have more snow. Do you have similar weather in Sweden? I have looked on a map, and can see that you are at about the same latitude as we are in this part of Russia, so I expect you also have had it.

I, too, fondly remember our dance together, Frederick my dear, it will stay with me forever. But I am sure you will have many dances with many beautiful princesses, and will soon forget this little servant girl.

As you so sweetly requested a picture of me, Tatiana has taken some photographs, and I enclose one for you to keep. We stood in the snow to take it, so my nose is shining with the cold! It is the first time I have been photographed, and it feels strange to see myself as others see me; I hope you like it. Will you please also send me one of you?

With fond thoughts

Natalie

I checked the letter before placing it in the

envelope, and heard again in my head the sound of his soft voice with its haunting accent. The memory of his arms around me as we danced brought a comforting feeling inside me that was quite different from the rush of passion that I had felt for Petr.

Petr! Again jealousy surged through me. I stood angrily and marched down to the entrance hall to despatch my letter.

~ ~ ~

Turning from the post box by the main doors, my little pastel pink envelope addressed to Frederick deposited in the "Mail Out" box, I paused and looked through the arch leading to the Right Wing ~ the route that, two days earlier, I had walked as though intoxicated, to meet the man who had so raised my temperature and my hopes. Now I felt empty and broken, like a jug that had been filled to the brim, then smashed on the ground.

A movement on the stairs from the guest wing caught my eye, and I looked up to see Sacha descending. Her head, too, was down, and she took each step slowly, as though in deep contemplation, only half concentrating on walking. I wandered over to wait for her at the bottom step, and she smiled when she saw me.

"Something is troubling you," I stated.

She nodded. "I can't tell you here," she said, looking around, though we were alone. "Can we go to your room?"

"Of course." I looped my arm in hers, and we

crossed the hall towards the other stairway.

"You look sad, too," she said, studying my face.

As we began to climb the stairs, I told her about Petr and Tatiana.

"The rat!" she exclaimed as we reached the top, then gave my arm a squeeze. "You don't blame Tatiana, do you?"

"I did, and I am still angry that she didn't tell me. But she is as hurt as I am. No, it was that despicable man who misled me, made me think I meant something to him."

"Some men are like that," she said. "Always after conquests."

"Well I'm avoiding them from now on," I stated firmly.

We reached my room, and I closed the door behind us.

"Now," I said, as we sat in my two easy chairs, anxious to move my mind away from my aching heart and damaged pride, "what's your secret?"

Her face became grim, her lips pressed tightly together, as though she was fighting to keep her emotions from escaping.

"I have to leave," she whispered. "Daddy's not coming here. He's travelling south to meet up with officers from the old army, to organise some kind of resistance to the Bolsheviks. He says that it is too dangerous for Mother and me to stay here, so we have to go into hiding."

"Oh my goodness!" I said, shocked at the implications. "When? Where?"

"Perhaps later today, or early tomorrow morning. I don't know where; perhaps out of the country. He is arranging an escort for us to get us through the cordon and take us southwards, away from Petrograd. Nata, I'm scared. I was just settling in here; just met you. Now it's all mystery and danger."

I moved from my chair to sit beside her, and put my arm around her. She leaned closer to me and rested her head on my shoulder. She wasn't crying; I suspected she was holding the tears in, afraid that if she started she would not stop; I felt the same.

Diary ~ Wednesday 9th March 1917 ~ Evening

Now I am really afraid. Nicholas returned to the palace this afternoon, and was promptly placed under house arrest, along with Alexandra, the duchesses and Aleksey. The palace is now filled with soldiers, guarding every corridor and following everyone around. These men have hate in their eyes and murder in their hearts.

My friend Sacha has gone, I know not where, nor if I shall ever see her again. I hope she will be safe. I shall miss her; in our short friendship I have discovered a kindred spirit.

The snow, which has been a constant in our lives since December, has finally given up and headed back north. A weak sun, still low against the horizon, managed to slant through the palace windows as I sat in the library today, lifting my spirits slightly. But there is no joy in my heart, and so little for any of us to do ~ Tatiana is not allowed to work, and Alexandra cannot instruct any member of staff except in the presence of a guard. All the royals are confined to their quarters, with armed men on their doors, and the rest of us are unable to move about the building without an escort.

Diary ~ Sunday 15th April 1917 ~ Morning

Many things have changed in our everyday lives since the abdication; some subtle and insidious, some more dramatic, and some increasingly frightening.

Firstly, because Nicholas is no longer Tsar, we cannot call any of the family 'Your Highness', or anything of the sort, or refer to them as 'His or Her Imperial this or that', or use the titles 'Empress' or 'Tsar' at any time ~ each has to be addressed by their given name. At first, this felt very strange and disrespectful, but most of us have quickly adapted. Actually, I rather enjoy the fact that one of the walls surrounding them has been removed ~ it puts me a little more on equal terms with them all.

The family is also now forbidden from entertaining or communicating with the royal families of other countries, presumably because the communists fear they will hatch a rescue plot (which, of course, is just what they would do if they could). And Alexandra, Tatiana and Olga have been told that they are no longer permitted to work in the hospital. One by one, all our freedoms are being removed.

We are short of fuel for the fires and the boilers, so the gardeners have begun to cut down trees from the wooded parts of the grounds under the scrutiny of a troop of guards.

There is still a complete military cordon around the palace, sealing it from all contact with the outside world; the subtle shift from the previous state is that now they are holding us in, not keeping the protesters out. No-one, family or personal staff, is allowed to leave the palace for any reason; all trips outside, for food or other supplies, must be made only by diplomatic staff. A blessing from this is that almost all the shooting has stopped; the constant background of gunfire has been replaced with birdsong.

Chapter 10 ~ Isolated

Nicholas received a visit from Count Beckendorff, who gave him a newspaper, and after the Count had left, Nicholas sat in an armchair reading it. For once, inexplicably, there had been no guards watching over us that day, and we had gathered in the Purple Room for companionship.

It was unusual to see him dressed casually; most often he preferred to be in uniform, as it gave him added stature. But, confined to the walls of the palace for weeks on end, he had slowly settled into a more relaxed style. As he sat reading the paper, his brown hair grown rather longer than he would previously have worn it, and slightly dishevelled, he looked less like a ruler, more approachable. His familiar square beard and bushy moustache made him look more like a friendly old grandfather.

He began to chuckle.

"There, you see? I told you so, did I not?" he suddenly exclaimed, waving a letter. "I knew George would not let me down. He has offered to give us a safe place to stay in England."

Alexandra looked around, anxiously. Although we seemed to have been left alone for a while, she was acutely afraid that he could be overheard.

"Where did you get that?" she whispered.

"Beckendorff hid it in the paper," he grinned.

A secret chain of loyal supporters had sprung up,

who smuggled messages into the palace, aware that they risked losing their lives if they were caught. The provisional government provided couriers for non-contentious mail, but we all knew that the letter from King George that Nicholas held in his hands would not have been delivered if it had fallen into their hands, and the messenger would have been found dead. Everything was censored ~ what little post we did receive through open channels was frequently so obscured by black marks as to be unreadable.

"George says that negotiations are being opened with the Duma to arrange for us to be transported by sea. Is that not wonderful news? At last, something to smile about."

Alexandra was cautious, anxious to avoid raising false hopes. "We must be careful not to let on that we know about it," she warned.

"Yes, indeed," he responded, trying to assume a serious expression. But he was not to be subdued, and he sat in his armchair, flapping open the newspaper again, noisily, a big smile on his face.

I stood at the window, gazing across undulating green lawns and neat flower beds, where the first shoots of spring bulbs were beginning to appear, to the lakes beyond, framed by trees fuzzy with new leaves. Winter had not yet fully relinquished his mastery over Tsarskoye Selo ~ there were still mounds of snow in hollows and shady corners, and it would take a little while yet for the warmer air and sunshine to remove all traces of the months of relentless blizzards ~ but the seasons were moving as they should, and I felt a momentary sense of rightness in the world.

But a commotion in the room behind me made me look around, and I saw a dozen or so soldiers pouring through the door and taking up positions around the room. Nicholas rose to his feet and moved to stand protectively beside Alexandra. In the doorway stood an officer with his hands clasped behind his back, surveying the room.

He was tall, blonde haired, proud of his new uniform, with its sword and buckles and shiny boots. His piercing pale blue eyes glared at each person in turn. No-one dared to move ~ it was as though a spell had been cast, freezing everyone except the newcomer, who moved between them with an arrogant swagger, like an attentive visitor to a waxworks exhibition. He was very tall, and when he reached Nicholas and Alexandra, he stopped, looking disdainfully down at them. Alexandra was still sitting, with Nicholas beside her, the newspaper gripped tightly in one hand.

"Romanoff," the officer declared in Russian, "you and your wife are henceforth forbidden from meeting with each other like this, except under supervision, and only with my personal permission." His voice, deep and resonant, was heavy with disdain. "You will each be escorted to your quarters and will remain there."

He fixed Nicholas with a fierce look, towering over the diminutive former Tsar to such an extent that he was able to look down on the top of his head, and Nicholas was forced to either crane his neck to look up, or stare impotently at the buttons on the front of the man's uniform.

Spinning suddenly on his heels, the officer swept the room with his gaze. "Every one of you is confined within the walls of this building," he barked. "My men have orders to shoot any member of the family or staff who steps outside. Have I explained myself adequately?" To the grim silence that ensued, he said, smirking, "I will take that as a tacit affirmation."

~ ~ ~

As the door closed behind the departing officer, Nicholas returned to his armchair and sat down with a sigh. "Does anyone want to tell me who that was?" he asked.

"That was Captain Zakharov, the new commandant of the garrison," ventured one of the guards.

"Thank you," Nicholas muttered, thoughtfully, standing again as soldiers took up position beside him and Alexandra. When they were ready, they were marched out of the door, and I heard their footsteps resounding on the marble floor beyond, until the closing of doors brought a heavy silence. The air was awash with tension.

I stood still for a few minutes, but could not stay there, so I walked slowly, carefully, from the window towards the exit, and asked the guard standing there if I could be allowed to go to my room. He opened the door and stood silently aside for me to pass, then followed me, closing it behind him.

No further words were spoken as we passed through a library and an office, and into the corridor leading towards the back stairs. I could hear the clump of his boots a couple of paces behind me, and I saw his reflection in a mirror hanging on the wall as we turned a corner. He was holding a pistol across his chest, a finger on the trigger in readiness. Did he think I would attack him or try to run away?

Another soldier entered the corridor from the opposite end. He glared at me as he came closer, and stopped, obstructing my path. I took a step to my right, to pass him, but he stepped left to block me again. I looked up at his face; it was filled with hate. I felt every muscle in my body suddenly tense with fear.

"You're the lackey for that Romanov whore," he spat, raising the barrel of his rifle and pushing it against my chest.

My heart pounding, I looked down at the round black hole that was pointing up at my face, then raised my eyes to stare defiantly at him, believing that these were my last moments.

"I'm not a lackey and she is not a whore," I retorted angrily, my indignation overcoming my fear, though I felt my voice quiver. His whole countenance exuded violence, and I turned to the guard behind me for support; but he just shrugged, grimly, as though to say that it was my problem, not his.

"Why do you stay here working for them?" the other man shouted, poking me with the muzzle of his gun with each word. "They are finished. The people have taken control. Soon the Romanov dog and his pups will be dead. What will you do then? Huh? Maybe you will die with them"

He laughed at his own crude joke, then continued

on his way, making sure to barge against me with his shoulder.

My whole body was shaking, and I felt tears pressing at the corners of my eyes. Stubbornly, I took a deep breath and pulled myself up straight. With an angry look at the guard still with me, I marched ahead toward the stairs.

Diary ~ Sunday 6th May 1917 ~ Evening

Today, all the garden was bright with colour; the forsythia bushes and daffodils are opening and birds are declaring their territories in song. Summer is just around the corner, though I fear we may never see it. I really think these are our last days. Things surely cannot continue like this, something dramatic must happen soon.

I have been trying to compose another letter to Frederick, but it has been hard to find the right words for what I want to ask him. My idea has been to find out if he has any access to the Swedish Royal Family, to see if they could act as intermediaries in the arrangements to get Alexandra and the family to England. At any rate, events have overtaken me: only a few weeks after Nicholas proudly waved that letter from his cousin, King George, he has received another, rescinding the offer. It was a huge blow, both to our hopes for the future and to Nicholas's confidence.

The days are dragging, we have so little to do, nothing to distract us from our predicament, and that makes our treatment by the guards even harder to swallow ~ there is time to dwell on every incident. Still, I am taking advantage of the inactivity to start reading again. I raided Nicholas's library and found a copy of 'Pride and Prejudice', which I devoured in two days ~ wonderful! I love Jane Austen's style ~ her characters are so rounded, and she writes in a way that makes me feel that I am living with them. Currently, I am reading Mark Twain's 'Adventures of Huckleberry Finn'; how very different life is in America.

Diary ~ Friday 15th May 1917 ~ evening

It is reassuring to find that not all the guards are ignorant louts ~ well, one of them isn't, anyway. While I was sitting in the small library downstairs today, reading Dostoevsky's 'Brothers Karamazov', the soldier on guard came over and started talking to me.

His name is Andrei Petrovich Sokolov. He is educated and well-spoken. He told me that he loves books, and has read Leo Tolstoy's 'War and Peace' and books by Chekhov and Garsin as well. I invited him to sit with me, which he did, though he was rather nervous in case any other soldiers saw him consorting with 'the enemy'. He does not speak any English, so we talked all afternoon in Russian, about books and about the state of affairs in Russia.

As the afternoon progressed, I found myself watching his face as he spoke, enjoying the expressions he made while talking. He is a little taller than me, dark-haired, with an olive complexion, and eyes the colour of emeralds. He grew up in Moscow, and had known only that city all his life until his conscription into the army, where he is a musician, and plays in the regimental band.

I have never had a male friend before. It is a nice feeling. But when I told Tatiana about him, she urged me to be careful. "You don't really know anything about him, Natalie. These soldiers are rough, he could get the idea you are ... well ... 'interested' in him."

"What do you mean, 'interested'?" I grinned.

"You know damn well what I mean," she retorted, returning my smile. "I don't want my friend getting a reputation, it might rub off on me!"

"Reputation?" I snorted. "We are hardly objects of veneration as it is; there's not much I can do to make them despise us any more!"

Diary ~ Monday 11th June 1917 ~ evening

With the warmer weather, the garden has sprung back into life, and the girls have started to spend time in the vegetable patch. This is not so much to supplement food supplies, because the gardeners have always maintained a large area of fruit and vegetables in the walled gardens, but more to keep themselves occupied. Sometimes all four of the sisters are at work in their garden together (Aleksey rarely leaves his quarters, except to sometimes watch from his balcony), although all of them are losing weight and suffering increasingly from various illnesses ~ one or more of them might be confined to their bed at any time.

Andrei tries to be assigned to guarding me whenever possible. I am sure his superiors must know what his motives are, but they seem to be willing to turn a blind eye. He is a very sweet man, and I have grown to enjoy his company very much. Today he told me about his two sisters, who are both older than him, and married, with babies of their own. I asked him why he has not married; he seemed embarrassed and muttered that he hasn't met the right person yet.

Time hangs heavily over us all, with the family no longer able to perform the duties with which they used to fill their days. I have used some of mine to watching and drawing the small birds that came to my feeding table. In order to learn about each one as they feed, I searched through Nicholas's books until I found one with pictures and the names of the various kinds of birds, plants and animals, and have quickly become familiar with the most common ones.

Paradoxically, although we have more free time, we are progressively less free. What we have in the palace now is nothing less than imprisonment ~ watched over by soldiers of the new government, with strict rules about what we are allowed to do, where we can go and who we can talk to.

The police are also under the control of the provisional government, which is now making little pretence to be loyal to the royal family. This morning, a troop of uniformed policemen marched into the palace and arrested Anna Vyrubova, claiming that she is a German spy. She is still weak from the measles, but they took her, without compassion, from her sickbed and drove her away to prison. Alexandra tried remonstrating with the police officers, but without success, and received only verbal abuse for her trouble.

Diary ~ Sunday 8th July 1917 ~ evening

Spring turns to summer, and our captivity continues. We are never allowed to be alone, a guard always accompanies each one of us, no matter what we are doing. Nicholas and Alexandra are kept apart, except at mealtimes, and we are now forbidden to speak English; it has been decreed by our masters that only Russian is allowed (so we cannot conspire together, presumably).

I have not seen Andrei for some time. Perhaps he has been stationed elsewhere, but I think he would have told me if he could. I miss him.

As the winter was cold, so the summer is proving to be hot. The air is heavy and oppressive, with regular thunderstorms rolling in from the plains. The grounds are patrolled by new army regiments which are loyal, not to the Tsar, but to the government, which is now controlled by the Bolsheviks. The duty of the soldiers is, nominally, to protect those inside the palace from the mob beyond the gates ~ it is clearly a task they do not enjoy. I suspect that many of them sympathise with the revolutionaries, and thousands have already deserted; those who remain to watch over the royals are, for the most part, sullen and resentful.

Today, the duchesses were gathered in the Purple room under heavy guard. Anastasia had her sketch pad on her lap and was drawing a portrait of her mother from a photograph. Olga and Tatiana had opened a window, and were sitting on the sill, looking out across the garden and enjoying the cooling breeze. I was standing beside the other window, gazing out at the lakes in the distance. Suddenly, there was a shout from the lawn nearby. I looked over, and saw one of the guards, glaring at the girls from the lawn below.

"Get your ugly faces inside, and close that window!" I heard him shout.

"But we are sweltering in here," said Olga.

At that the guard raised his rifle to his shoulder, and pointed it straight at the sisters, as though to shoot. "Shut the fucking window. Now!" he ordered. Shocked and scared, the two sisters jumped back into the room and closed the window. As they did so, a shot rang out and a bullet ricocheted off the wall outside. We realised that he had fired deliberately to scare the girls, and I glanced at the other guards who were in the room. I saw that some of them were smirking and laughing. 'Why?' I wondered. 'How can one person hate another so much without even knowing them?'

Diary ~ Friday 9th August 1917 ~ evening

Like a small ray of sunshine through storm clouds, another letter has arrived, via the secret courier network, from Frederick. That I, lowly Natalie Tereshchenko, am receiving mail through the palace grapevine is rather exciting.

Alone in my room I eagerly opened it, and as I did so, a photograph fell out. I picked it up and smiled to see Frederick, dressed in an open-neck shirt and the baggy trousers that are all the fashion in Europe this year. My eyes lingered over the picture; he really is a very handsome young man, with his wild hair and his relaxed smile. But I was dying to read what he had written, so I put the photo on the table and unfolded the letter.

Dear, dear Natalie

I cannot tell you how happy it made me to receive your letter, and to see your beautiful face again in that photograph. Surely, no princess in the whole of Europe could be as lovely as you.

With this letter, as you requested, I have included a photograph of myself. I have many official pictures, but they are all dreadfully starchy and pompous, so instead I have plundered my mother's photo album and found a nice casual one, taken recently in our garden.

It is with great concern that I hear of the state of affairs in your country, and I fear very much for your safety. Please be careful, as far as it is possible my darling, to keep away from danger. I will speak with my parents, and try to find out if it would be possible to bring you Sweden, for your safety. Word has reached me that your mail is now being censored, so I am sending this by courier. I urge you not to write again using the normal postal service.

The summer weather here is very pleasant, and I often walk in the beautiful parks and gardens here, remembering the feeling of holding you close as we danced, hearing the sound of your voice in the songs of the birds and the humming of the bees. And I smell your sweet perfume in the flowers, but though they are very beautiful, they cannot match your beauty, my love.

I miss you, dear Natalie, and truly think of you every moment. I hope we may meet again soon.

With deepest affection,

Your loving Frederick

I was shocked to read that Frederick would try to arrange for my rescue; it seems to be a sign that he cares far more than I had realised. Although his notion to rescue me is far-fetched, the romantic prose of his letter raised my spirits and put a smile back on my face for the whole of the day. Tomorrow I will tell Tatiana, if I have a chance to speak to her.

Chapter 11 ~ Summer

With Frederick's letter hidden in my bodice, I waited until twelve o'clock. Tatiana and I were allowed to socialise, under supervision, and we had taken to sitting in one of the drawing rooms, passing the time in sketching, sewing or reading. At noon each day we looked forward to watching, with some satisfaction, the slovenly process of changing the guard in the palace. The men who had been slouching in doorways and corners would scurry off quickly as soon as the clocks started to chime, and often we would be left unsupervised for a while before new soldiers arrived.

Alone with Tatiana, I quickly told her that I had received a letter from Frederick, and asked if she would like to see it. I handed it to her, conscious that his mention of rescue was for me alone, and also nervous in case anyone came in ~ the letter must not fall into the hands of the guards.

Tatiana sat silently reading the letter. When she was finished, she lifted her eyes from the page and gazed at me intently. There was an odd expression on her face as she passed the letter back to me, and I slipped it inside my dress. She leaned forward and took hold of both my hands.

"Nata," she said, gravely, "I want to tell you that if you have a chance to escape from here you must do it."

I tried to protest, but she stopped me by gently

shaking my hands, still held tightly in hers.

"No, listen," she said. "I no longer have a title, there is nothing to protect me now from the hatred felt by these people towards my family." She looked meaningfully at door. "But they do not resent you as they do us. They have already allowed many of the staff to go, and they don't know that you are related. If Frederick can get you safely away, I beg you, please go."

I noticed at once her reference to me being 'related' to the family. She knew! Her mother had told her about my parents. And what was more, she assumed that I knew, that Alexandra had told me. But the sly witch had been deliberately keeping it from me while, it seemed, telling everyone else. Fresh anger boiled up inside me; how dare she!

Tatiana was still speaking. "I know we had that falling out, but we can be friends again, can't we?"

She smiled nervously, and I knew she meant every word, but I was still reeling from her revelation, and my instinctive reaction was to withdraw into my protective shell.

I couldn't blame her for her mother's actions, she was not responsible for those, but neither did I feel particularly charitable. The passing months had helped me to subdue the anger I had felt at her betrayal over Petr, and a kind of forgiveness had replaced it. But though I felt compassion for all the family, for what they had lost, it was, after all, no more than the same thing that they had always denied me.

Still, I tried to reassure her. "Tatiana, do not worry

that anything will happen to you," I said, carefully. "Everything will work out fine, you will see."

"No, Natalie, please, you must understand. It is the Bolsheviks' resentment of the royal family that is causing all this unrest; they will not be happy until we have been removed. But as far as they know, you are not part of it ~ if you are careful you could save yourself."

"No," I said defiantly, "nothing will happen."

In my heart, though, I was much less confident about the future than I was trying to appear to Tatiana. A combination of the facts of our situation and the mystery of Myriam's visits had made me fear the worst.

A few moments later, the door in the far corner of the library opened and an officer of the guard looked into the room. He turned to speak to someone behind him in the corridor, and admitted two soldiers.

My heart leapt, and I had to suppress a smile when I saw that one of them was Andrei.

Tatiana noticed the expression on my face and guessed the reason. After a decent interval, she stood and, with a little smirk in my direction, gathered up her book and walked to the door. She did not acknowledge either of the guards, just opened the door and walked out; her only concession was that she did not close it behind her. The other man followed her, and Andrei shut the door behind them.

He came to sit beside me, smiling, and I leant over to plant a gentle kiss on his cheek. "I have missed you," I said softly.

"I have missed you too," he answered sincerely. "We have new officers, angry, difficult men, and it is becoming hard to get myself assigned to you without arousing suspicion."

"You must be careful. Avoid anything that might cause trouble."

He nodded. "In any case, I fear that I may soon be sent elsewhere. The band has been rehearsing new music and new marching routines, all very stirring stuff for the revolution. Something is being planned, but of course we will be told nothing until the last minute."

I bit my lip, sad that he may be taken away from me. "So much change," I whispered. "No chance to settle."

He placed his hand reassuringly on mine, and we fell into contemplative silence.

Chapter 12 ~ Kerensky

A week later, and I was with Tatiana again when Luba, accompanied by a very young and nervous-looking soldier, arrived with a summons for her to join her mother and father at once, to be addressed in the Purple Room by the new leader of the provisional government, Alexander Kerensky. Instead of waiting behind and feeling resentful, as I normally would, I decided to accompany her; I didn't say anything, just stood up when she did and walked with her behind Luba to Alexandra's Formal Reception Room, where the meeting was to take place. She didn't comment, nor did she seem to mind.

I had never heard of Kerensky before, but Tatiana whispered to me as we made our way through empty rooms, that the family considered him to be an arrogant and untrustworthy man, who pretended to act for the general good and security of the country, when really he was in league with the Bolsheviks, and obeyed them in everything he did.

He proved to be a slender man, quite elegant in appearance, not very old, possibly about thirty, with sharp features and a birdlike manner, quick and twitchy. His thick, dark hair was slicked back with grease. His new position of power seemed to suit him well, and he had a swagger about him that I found immediately offensive. He wore a traditional style of long tunic, but apparently made of silk, in deep brick red, with a colourful embroidered panel, and pulled in at the waist with a silk belt. It was ostentatious, and contrasted conspicuously with Nicholas's smart, but casual, plain woolen jerkin and loose trousers.

When we arrived, Kerensky was telling the royal couple that they were to be moved away from the palace "for their safety."

"Very well," Nicholas replied, "we will go to our summer palace in Crimea."

"No," Kerensky stated peremptorily, in a condescending tone, "Ukraine is also overrun with revolutionaries, we cannot guarantee your safety there. You will go to the Urals. The Governor's mansion at Tobolsk is a safe distance from Petrograd and is being prepared for you now. We must move quickly. You have one week to pack; it will only be possible to take essential possessions and a minimal number of staff. You will travel on the train."

"The Royal Train?" asked Nicholas, innocently, unthinking. He was fond of the train, which he had created for those times when the family had long distances to travel. It was luxurious, a miniature palace on wheels.

"There is no royal train," snapped Kerensky. "It is now the property of the people, who paid for it and built it, as is this building and all the other palaces and houses and lands. You must remember that you no longer enjoy the privileges you used to take for granted."

With that, and a piercing glare at Nicholas, he turned on his heels and marched off, with his armed bodyguard strutting behind him. I heard them clattering down the corridor in their polished boots and clinking swords. I was amazed at his dismissive, rude attitude toward the royal family. We were well enough aware that things had changed, but it was as though he was enjoying his position of power over them and intended to exploit it.

~ ~ ~

Nicholas glared at the door through which Kerensky had just left, and I saw that he was clenching and unclenching his fists at his side. Alexandra moved closer to him and looped her arm in his. She leaned close to his ear and whispered something, and he patted her hand and gently kissed her forehead. It was a simple and tender moment between two people who were clearly still very much in love.

Anastasia was standing, quietly sobbing, in a corner, and Maria crossed the room to comfort her, putting her arm around her shoulders and stroking her hair, talking softly. The other two sisters moved to their parents' side and began a quiet exchange.

It was, by then, early afternoon, so in an attempt to lighten the mood, I asked if they would like some lunch. Alexandra, after a glance to her husband and daughters, smiled and nodded.

I was glad to be busy. Taking my lesson from Tatiana, I did not ask the guards for an escort, but simply walked out of the room, leaving it up to them to decide what to do about it; I heard one of them fall into step behind me.

The door to the stairs leading from the ground floor to the basement was now locked and guarded by two bored soldiers. At my request, one of them unlocked it and allowed me through, followed by my escort, who spoke to them, briefly. As we went down the stairs, I heard the door slam behind us and keys turning in the lock.

I was nervous at being alone with the guard, but nothing untoward happened and no word was spoken as we descended the stairs and passed across the great chasm, now quiet and almost deserted. Another door, a new one, with another pair of guards awaited us at the tunnel entrance, and after a similar routine, we entered the dingy passage.

When we reached the door at the far end, the soldier with me rang a bell, and it was opened from the other side. I was then allowed through into the kitchens, while the man who had accompanied me stayed chatting with his companion.

As I walked between the rows of preparation benches, I could see about five or six kitchen staff hard at work, standing over large steaming pots or cutting away at various meats, fruit and vegetables. Soldiers watched warily at intervals around the huge room, and from the balconies above our heads. Kitchens, of course, have many knives, and could be a good place to start an uprising.

Ivan himself was preparing the evening dinner, and I told him what the family wanted. He smiled at me and immediately began to assemble the requested meal.

I watched him cutting and arranging. I had a serious crush on him, and had done so since I first met him three years earlier. He was such a lovely person: kind, cheerful, friendly and outgoing. I supposed him to be about forty or forty-five years old, with pale, wispy brown hair, already thinning and receding, and a small moustache. He was tall, much taller than me, and I liked to stand close to him, so that I could look up at him. I loved to watch him at work, he was so quick and yet precise. He always chatted away to me as he worked, and I used to fantasise that we were secret lovers, and that later we would meet at our usual place and hold hands and talk about our dreams and hopes.

His voice was gentle and, although he managed to speak a little English, as most of us were expected to, he did so with a strong Russian accent, which I found electrifying; mostly, we conversed in Russian. Of course, he knew nothing of my fantasy; or, at least, I hoped he did. I would have been mortified if I thought he knew the images flying around in my head, some of them not so pure and innocent. And, of course, it was never more than my imagination, a young girl's hormones running amok.

"How is my favourite girl?" he enquired. It was a term he always used for me, although I was also under no illusion that it meant anything special; he probably said the same to every one of us. Somehow, though, he managed to make it sound affectionate ~ personal, yet not flirtatious.

"I am well enough, thank you," I answered, "but cannot be happy while the Family is under such a cloud."

"Dear Natalie," he chided, grinning, "you always carry everyone else's problems on your shoulders. Are you still writing your diary?" I nodded. "Good," he said, "perhaps one day the world will know what happened in this place."

Plates were soon covered with slices of different cold meats, accompanied by little jars of various pickled vegetables and a bowl of mixed salad. A loaf of bread, still warm from the oven, had been sliced and laid on a plate. Beautiful silver pots were filled with butter and jam. He laid out some cheeses, and little biscuits, and a bowl of caviare, poured a jug of fruit juice and one of white wine, and chopped some fruit into a bowl.

I watched, enraptured at his skill and the beauty of his movements. His hands moved so fast, and the knives were so sharp, that it seemed a miracle he never cut himself.

Chapter 13 ~ Yuri

Soon enough, the meal was ready, and Ivan called for two assistants to protect the food with domed silver covers and load it onto trolleys. We walked together back through the tunnel with the gloomy, silent guard keeping a safe distance behind us, his gun at the ready. Emerging through the doors at the far end, we crossed the basement to a lift entrance, the assistants pushing the trolleys and Ivan walking beside me.

Ivan took one of the trolleys and wheeled it into the lift, then he and I travelled with it on its first trip up to the ground floor, I savoured the moments pressed close to him, feeling the warmth of his body and breathing the smell of cooking that lingered on his clothes. The elevator emerged beside the Purple Room, where the family was gathered, and there we waited while the car returned for his assistants. I noticed that our guard declined to travel in the lift with any of us ~ perhaps he was afraid we would overpower him.

When we arrived in the Purple Room, we cleared a sideboard and set out the plates of food there, and on the table. Alexandra thanked Ivan and his team as they left, then the family quickly set to, serving each other and talking with their mouths full, for all the world almost like ordinary folks. Everyone's spirits seemed to be lifted by the meal, and we relaxed in a way that I had not seen for some time.

There must have been a change of guard while I

was on my trip to the kitchen, because there was a single soldier on duty. He watched us for a while, then shrugged and moved himself out into the anteroom, leaving the family unguarded. I noticed his resigned expression, and felt sorry for him, so I put some of the food on a plate and took it out to him. He was clearly taken aback at the kindness, when I shyly handed it to him, and thanked me with a look of surprise on his face.

I could not help grinning as I returned to the party; it felt good to break down one of the barriers between us, even if only in a small way.

Later, when we were clearing away, he came in and gave me the empty plate with a smile and a small bow.

~ ~ ~

An hour later, and we were in the Oval Hall. I had resumed my place among the servants, Olga and Maria had returned to their quarters, and Alexandra was explaining the situation to a meeting of all the palace staff.

Pairs of armed soldiers stood at each of the three doors that accessed the hall. We were a depleted group, about forty in all, huddled in a corner of the huge, echoing, formal room ~ many servants had been laid off, as there was so little to do, and some had chosen to leave the palace to be with their families.

Alexandra paced back and forth as she told those present that they would all be needed to help with the packing and preparations for the long trip the family must take to Tobolsk.

"Also, we will need some of you to come with us, though we will be restricted in how many we can take," she said. "But I fear we are entering a period of great danger, and I cannot force anyone to make this journey into the unknown. So it is open to each of you to volunteer, or not, for this fearful step. Come to me in my quarters after this meeting, and I will select those we can take."

As we filed out of the hall, Polina and Rada told me that they intended to go to Alexandra to offer their services.

"Please don't," I begged. "The situation can only become worse."

I could not bear the thought of my young friends putting themselves in danger.

I looked from one to the other. "Polya, Rada, this is not wise, we don't know what terrible things might be about to happen."

But they were quite resolved to do it, and I could not let them go alone, so the three of us marched through the public halls to Alexandra's rooms together and joined the short line that had already formed outside her door. One by one, as each volunteer came out, another was invited in, and more joined the back of the queue; when it was our turn, we three shuffled in together.

~ ~ ~

Afterwards, the twins went off to finish whatever duties they had, but with Tatiana engrossed in other matters, I was left with time on my hands again, so I put on a wide-brimmed hat, took my sketch pad and pencils and walked down to the lake to watch the swans. I noticed that the soldier who elected to accompany me was the same one who had been on duty in the Purple Room, earlier. I smiled, as he seemed to be a good man, and I felt safe in his company,

I needed to relax, to absorb myself in nature for a while. It seemed to me that events were carrying me along, that there was nothing I could do to prevent them. I wanted time to think, and the peace of the lake beckoned me.

It was a fine, bright afternoon. A light breeze had moderated the smothering heat of the day, but it was still pleasantly warm. It had been weeks since we had any rain, and in different circumstances it would have been an idyllic summer. Of course, there were still the odd flurries of distant gunfire, but compared with the fierce battles that had raged in recent times, the bursts were few and separated by long silences. And in any case, I did not want to dwell on our predicament.

I unfolded my little canvas stool and sat quietly by the lake, conjuring up romantic thoughts about my foreign Prince; well, not exactly a Prince, I realised, but he might as well be from my perspective. Was it really possible that Frederick could take the girl he only knew as a Lady In Waiting and turn her into a Princess? A thrill passed through me as I thought about it, and I shuddered involuntarily. It happened in some of the books I read, why should it not happen to me?

My guard had settled down to lay casually on the

bank a short way off; I turned to him, and saw that he was quite relaxed, so I risked a smile and a wave; he raised a hand and pinched the peak of his cap with his fingers.

One of the black swans obligingly stopped to observe me studying him, and I managed several good sketches as he circled, majestically. I could not forget that these were my last days at Alexander Palace, that soon we would begin our exodus. Aware as I was that The Family did not confide in me, I wondered if they could have some kind of escape planned at some stage of the journey.

Slowly, the afternoon drifted easily past and the sun became a red disc settling onto the leafy horizon. As I pensively gazed across the glittering waters, I saw, in the long shadows on the far side of the lake, a herd of the deer that ran free in the woods and fields of the grounds. In past times, the Tsar would gather his retinue for a day's sport each autumn. I had watched them with disgust as they rode out with their rifles slung over their backs, bent on killing for the fun of killing, and I felt physically sick when they returned with the carcasses of these beautiful animals draped like trophies over their saddles. I took some comfort that it only happened once a year, and that the meat was used in the kitchens to feed the household and retinue.

I called quietly to my guard, to attract his attention, and when he looked at me, I pointed across the lake. He turned to see what I was indicating, and I saw his eyes widen as he spotted the deer and watched them pick their way to the water's edge to drink. After a little while, they scampered off, and he turned back to face me with a smile and a nod of his head.

The sun settled like a Chinese lantern behind the trees, and the light began to fade into that beautiful shade of peach that makes the world look like a dream.

It was time to return to reality, to forget my silly fancies.

Chapter 14 ~ Packing

The palace became a scene of intense activity as we pitched in to sort through the duchesses' clothes and personal possessions, selecting the ones to be taken. We started in Maria's rooms, carefully wrapping any fragile items in tissue, inserting them between layers of clothing, and packing them into trunks. As each box was filled, two or three of us together carried it out into the corridor, adding to the others, lining them up along the walls. At the same time, male staff were helping Nicholas to sort through his and Aleksey's possessions and pack them ready for travel. Surprisingly, as the day progressed, it took on a kind of quiet party atmosphere, with everyone helping and some gentle banter taking place. We tried to ignore the guards who stood with their guns ready beside the doors and windows, although of course we could not forget them completely, and their presence cast a shadow over everything. Still, we made good progress, working our way through the rooms, with Alexandra supervising and making decisions when she considered any items to be less than essential.

After Maria's, we moved on to Tatiana's rooms, and, over the following days, Olga's and finally Anastasia's. When we were done each afternoon, there was a stack of boxes and trunks in the passageways and corridors, which the men then carried, huffing and puffing, down to the main Formal Receiving Room, off the entrance hall. Gathered together like that, there looked to be a huge amount of stuff, but actually, for each piece taken, fifty had been reluctantly left behind. Finally, on day four, we started on Alexandra's own possessions.

~ ~ ~

On the afternoon of the fifth day, we were all called into the garden, where tables had been laid out with food and drink for us by the kitchen staff. We tucked in, with gratitude, watched over by the guards, who also helped themselves to anything they fancied, without waiting to be invited, sometimes pushing us aside to reach something that caught their eye. It was a warm and pleasant evening, which reminded me of happier days, but there were dark clouds gathering.

After a while, Nicholas and Alexandra appeared together on the balcony, flanked by armed guards on each side. They were pale shadows of their former selves, but they thanked everyone for the hard work done. We all gave them a cheer, much to the evident disgust of the guards, and then they were taken inside again. When they were gone, our collective mood turned sombre; the sight of them between armed soldiers was disturbing, and we had little appetite after that.

Our guards, however, had no such reservations, and quickly polished off everything that remained, although I noticed that some of them did not eat much, but instead wrapped food in serviettes and pushed the little packages into their pockets and the flaps of their tunics.

One of them was the man who had accompanied me a few days earlier to the lake. I helped him wrap a few pieces, and he thanked me. As I stood beside him, he told me that his wife and two children were starving ~ his soldiers wages had not been paid for weeks, and they had no money for food. I learned that his name was Yuri, that he was 19 years old, and that he had been a soldier since the age of 16. He was wounded at the front in the war against Germany, and had returned to his family in Petrograd, but was now posted to protect the Romanovs. I said that, if he needed anything, I would try to help if I could, and he thanked me again.

As though to match the collective mood, it began to rain, at first just light, but soon becoming heavy. We quickly cleared the tables, in almost total silence, and helped the kitchen staff to carry everything back inside.

When everyone had dispersed, I sat in the great central hall until nightfall, watching through the French doors as the rain swirled around the garden in gusts of wind and beat hard against the glass, running down in a cascade like one of the fountains in the park. I was aware of being watched in turn by a bored, sullen guard, who had seated himself beside the fireplace. Presumably someone thought I was a danger. I considered trying to talk to him, but realised it was not wise; he was not like Yuri.

My mind went back over the few years I had been in the palace before the uprising. Although I was too young to remember the move there from the Winter Palace in 1905, I had some happy memories of better times as I grew older ~ of trips to the theatre with the family (a special treat) and of grand balls at St Catherine's Palace. Usually, I was not able to take part in the balls, until that magical evening ~ the night I met Frederick. Now, as I sat in the huge hall, alone but for the guard, I heard again in my head the music, the chatter and the shuffling of feet, like echoes repeating forever, taunting me with their gaiety.

Eventually, as the beating of the rain on the roof stopped and the sun began to set, I got up and went to my room. I hesitated at my door, wondering whether to call in on Rada and Polina, but decided that I was not good company, and besides, it was getting late.

Despite being very tired, I sat at my desk and wrote out the day's events in my diary, before undressing and climbing between the cool sheets. But sleep would not release me, my mind kept repeating over and over the scenes and the words of the day and worrying about the future. I found myself crying. I felt so helpless, so vulnerable. I hoped for another visit from Myriam, I desperately wanted some words of comfort or advice, but she did not appear. Eventually I drifted off into a restless sleep filled with wild dreams of soldiers and shouting.

Diary ~ Monday 20th August 1917 ~ evening

There are reports in the newspaper of an attempted coup. Apparently, General Kornilov of the Imperial army managed to put together a force to march on Petrograd a few days ago. The paper doesn't make it clear what he hoped to achieve, but I suppose he was hoping to snatch control from Kerensky's government. At any rate, he was dissuaded by representatives of the various communist groups, and his army dispersed. Kornilov's body was found last night ~ they say he committed suicide. How very convenient for Kerensky.

I have spent much of the day pondering over the way our captors feel about us. I know that there has been a growing tide of discontent among the people for a long time, and thought I sympathised with them. Certainly it is easy to see why they are so resentful of the royal family ~ while they have lived in poverty, and watched their families and friends die of cold and hunger, we have enjoyed a surplus of comforts. But the way some of them are behaving towards us is beyond hostility, more even than hate; it is inhuman, sadistic. With a few exceptions, such as Yuri and some others who are at least more civilised in their behaviour, most seem to enjoy treating us badly. The trouble is, I have no way of really understanding them. I am only now beginning to imagine the lives that have led them to despise, not only Nicholas, but the rest of the family, and even those of us who work for them.

Chapter 15 ~ Frustration

The next morning, as Tatiana was still not available, I spent a few pleasant hours with the twins, changing beds, cleaning rooms, dusting; you know, all the fun stuff. At two o'clock in the afternoon we were called into the Oval Hall, where we found the rest of the staff gathering. Soon after we arrived, Alexandra entered regally, with her daughters following behind, like a mother duck with her brood of chicks in a line ~ the royal image rather marred by the presence of four fierce-looking guards. Anastasia closed the doors behind them, then the girls sat down on a settee near the fireplace, and waited patiently while Alexandra called us all closer, and greeted each of us by name. She chatted easily for a few minutes, relaxing in the company of familiar faces. After a while, though, she stepped back and addressed us all.

"Thank you everyone for your hard work over the last few days. We have done all we can for now."

She began pacing thoughtfully in front of us, looking down at her feet, suddenly the matriarch again, feeling the burden of her position. Then she seemed to become aware of what she was doing and, with a determined effort, stopped and turned to face us again. The strain of it all was showing on her face, already lined with worry.

"Soon, most of us will be parted forever, and it seems likely that I and my family will never return to this place. I'm afraid I do not know what will become of those of you left behind, but I hope you will be safe, and will take with you fond memories of our times together here; I certainly do. We have lived through some tempestuous and troublesome times together, have we not?"

She paused and smiled, wryly. "As I look back over these last twenty or so years, I have accumulated some unhappy memories along the way, it is true, but I want you all to know that my times with you will remain in my heart always. And I wish to thank all who came forward and volunteered to accompany us to Tobolsk. It was a lovely surprise that so many of you wanted to do so; I know you are aware that this is a perilous time, and it was courageous of you to offer. However, I have no wish to put any of your lives in unnecessary danger, so we have deliberated carefully as to who we need to take, and who should stay, and this is what we have decided."

She turned to Olga, who handed her a sheet of paper.

"Our loyal physician, Yevegny Botkin will be much needed for the foreseeable future, as Aleksey's health remains fragile; the good doctor will be accompanied by his son and daughter, who will act as his assistants.

"My own Lady's Maid, Anna Demidova, will also come with us, and Natalie Tereshchenko as maid to our four daughters. The twins, Radochka and Polina Petrov will be our junior maids."

I looked at Rada and Polya, just as they turned to me, and we smiled nervously to each other. I knew that we had been chosen to stay together, Alexandra would not split us up.

"We will take our dear chef, Ivan Kharitonov," she continued, "and two assistants of his choosing, plus Alexei Trupp, who will act as valet to Nicholas, and we will take two housemaids, Svetlana Alekseeva and Luba Kuzmina."

She smiled at us all again, "That's it. Thank you once more to those who offered to come with us, but to those who we could not take, I would like ... "

She was interrupted by a commotion outside the hall, followed by the doors flying open and Kerensky and his bodyguard marching into the room. Without any polite preliminary greeting, he confronted Alexandra and barked: "I cannot find your husband." He was much taller than her, and towered over her, glaring at her down his sharp nose as though it was her fault.

"He is in the billiard room," Alexandra responded coldly.

"Well, I do not have time to find him now, you can tell him yourself. You are to be ready to travel at six o'clock tomorrow morning. A local train will take you to Petrograd, and there you will join the Trans-Russia Railway to take you to Tobolsk."

"But we were to have a week to prepare," she protested, "we are not ready."

"That is your problem," he snapped. "The situation here is very dangerous, we must move quickly; be sure you are ready."

And, with a disdainful glance across the room at the

assembled staff, he was gone again, leaving us all stunned. Another strange twist had inserted itself into our fate, another unwelcome intrusion from the world outside.

"Well, it seems that is it," said Alexandra, sadly, "We are, as always, in God's hands; He gives, and He takes away. Let us pray together."

I suppressed a groan as we stood with our heads bowed in respectful silence, and she prayed for our safekeeping. I started to plan in my head what of my own things to pack, for I was completely unprepared. When she finished, and we had all mumbled our "Amen", she looked sadly around the room once more, then walked slowly out with her procession of ducklings winding along behind her, preceded and followed by the armed soldiers.

~ ~ ~

While the men set about moving all the trunks and boxes and bags from the Formal Receiving Room, and stacking them up near the mounting doors of the left wing, ready for the morning, I headed straight up to my own room to start packing. But I had scarcely begun to pile my things on my bed to be sorted into what was needed and what was not, when I was called to Alexandra's private rooms. Luba smirked when she delivered the message ~ she could see that I was put out. It was irritating and frustrating to be interrupted, when I suddenly had so little time to myself, but of course I had to obey the summons.

Alexandra was in her bedroom, the only place

where the guards were not allowed to follow her, along with her daughters and Anna Demidova, who were all seated around, sewing. She explained quietly to me that there was a secret job she needed me to help with. She wanted to be prepared in case those of us travelling eastwards were left without means to support ourselves, so she had decided to hide as much of her jewellery as possible and take it into exile. It could then be sold to obtain some money, if the need and the opportunity should arise. So we sat, the two ladies in waiting and the four daughters, carefully sewing precious heirlooms between the layers of their skirts and into the stuffing of some cushions.

~ ~ ~

It was late by the time I was able to get away, and already dark. I returned to my room and quickly sorted through my own clothes and possessions, packing whatever essentials I could fit into my two carpet bags. They did not hold much, but then I didn't have much to take; many of my older clothes could be left behind, as they were too small for me ~ I seemed to have grown in all directions very quickly. I did not know what it would be like in Tobolsk, but assumed I would be most glad to have winter garments, so I packed long, warm dresses and thick skirts, woollen jackets, pantaloons, some blouses, petticoats, stockings, vests, a scarf and gloves, boots and a coat. Any remaining space I filled with lighter, summer things.

Inserted between the clothes, to protect them from damage, I inserted my hand mirror, the silver one that was my 17th birthday present from Alexandra and the girls, and my little bottle of real French perfume. I put my own small collection of jewellery into a soft cotton bag with tie strings; it was my intention to wear the bag under my travelling clothes, for safety.

My diary, precious and secret, was in the form of several exercise books, and I had a number of empty books so that I could continue to record everything; I carefully laid these all in the bottom of a portmanteau that I would carry onto the train, with some soap and a towel, my hairbrush, sanitary pads and a change of underwear on top of them. I also put in the book I had recently started reading, 'Anna Karenina', by Leo Tolstoy. I had been told that it was not a suitable book for refined young ladies to read so, of course, I had to find out why; the long journey would give me an opportunity to really get into it.

After some uncertainty, I pressed all my drawings between two pieces of stiff cardboard, tied around with string, to create a kind of portfolio. It was the only safe way I could think of transporting them.

When the bags were full, I took a final look around my room to see if there was anything else I might need, but actually there was very little left that I could practically take, and nothing much that I would miss. I started to drag the carpet bag out of my room. It was hard work, and I was glad when Rada and Polina come out to see what was causing so much noise in the corridor so late. They helped me to carry it to the lift and from there to the entrance hall, where we left it with all the other items. It was well past midnight when we parted and retired to bed.

Part Two

~

неумолимый

Inexorable

Chapter 16 ~ Departure

Six o'clock, the hour of pre-dawn. The sky to the east was streaked with orange, charcoal and light teal as the sun poked tentative fingers at the thickening cloud from below the horizon. The air was clean, blackbirds were vocally contesting territory, and flowers were beginning to open ready for the sunrise. I stood with Polya and Rada and the rest of the staff in the entrance hall, nervously clutching my portmanteau and my makeshift portfolio. There was no conversation in the small crowd, all were silent, deep in their own thoughts and fears. Our lives were suspended by threads under the hands of hidden puppeteers.

Through the open doors we saw two large, canvas-covered, army horse-drawn carts arrive with a clatter at the front of the palace, accompanied by a motor cycle rider. They circled clockwise round the island of grass and flowers, mutely observed by the statues of athletes and mythical beasts. The tension in the air rose as we watched them ~ it was happening, another link in the chain of events that was carrying us inexorably to some unknown fate.

One of the carts drove up and around the curved ramp that served the door at the end of the Left Wing, then stopped, ready to be loaded. At the same time, the motor cycle skidded to a halt outside the main doors, in a spray of gravel.

The rider jumped from it and marched into the entrance hall, unbuttoning his heavy, brown leather coat. Under it, he wore the grey uniform of an army officer, while on his head was a rather amusing leather helmet, with side flaps that dangled unfastened, topped with a huge pair of goggles. He surveyed the pile of boxes and trunks, then pointed to the male palace staff who were standing nearby, a total of about twenty men and boys. "Here, you men, help load these things!"

Soldiers from the palace guard who were loitering nearby were also directed to assist the palace staff, an order they accepted with bad grace. Trunks and boxes and bags were carried out and thrown onto the tail of the cart, from where two men transferred them to the swiftly growing pile at the front. The younger boys and the more elderly of the palace men tried gamely, but clearly were not strong enough for such work, and the more robust ones had to help them. I noticed that none of the soldiers would assist, and not one friendly word passed between the guards and palace staff. There was a friction in the air, a deep-seated animosity that seethed just below the surface.

Eventually, everything was loaded and the cart was full. The sweating men sat down on the steps to rest, and the officer gave orders for the family to be brought through from their quarters. Four of the palace guard departed, reappearing some minutes later with the royals. They approached us from the end of the corridor in solemn convoy. The women looked dreadfully vulnerable, Nicholas was defiant. This was a significant day, a huge step away from all the security they had known for their entire lives. They knew the true meaning of their exile, and the dangers they faced. Things could only get worse from this moment.

Tatiana had her little dog in her arms, and all of them were carrying their own hand baggage, as well as some blankets and cushions. With them were doctor Botkin, Anna Demidova, and Nagorny the sailor, who carried Aleksey. The boy was very pale, and looked as though he may have been developing another fever.

Nicholas recognised the officer, and became noticeably more relaxed.

"Lieutenant Izakov, how good to see you again," he beamed. They shook hands and spoke briefly, and Nicholas introduced the Lieutenant to Alexandra. "We were together at the military academy in 1887," he explained.

Izakov bowed to Alexandra, and apologised for the primitive transport that had been arranged for this part of their long journey; he told them that he would do all he could to help, but added gravely that he expected it to be an arduous trip.

~ ~ ~

Along with the rest of the staff, I picked up my hand-baggage and followed them as they were escorted to the central hall at the back of the palace, then taken out onto the balcony. From there, they descended the steps into the garden, where they climbed into two of the large automobiles waiting for them. These were Nicholas's own cars, from his personal collection, of which he had always been rather proud. The first, with Stephan Stephanovich, the family's chauffeur, at the controls, was occupied by Nicholas, Aleksey, Nagorny, the doctor, and Alexei Trupp, Nicholas's valet. All the women took the second car; I saw Tatiana tearfully hand her little dog to one of the servants ~ her mother must have decreed that the creature could not travel with us.

Aware that this was probably the last I would ever see of the palace, I paused at the doorway and looked back around the hall, seeing ghosts of my younger self and all the other people who had walked its marbled floor in my time there, hearing their voices echoing across the years. I came there as a small child, and it was the only home I remembered. Now, leaving it, I realised how familiar it had become, and how that familiarity had hidden from my eyes the ostentatious wealth in its gold decorations and polished marble. I was aware that it had been a privilege to live within its walls, pampered, educated, warm and, until now, safe, but suddenly realised that it was all false. How had my mother lived since handing me over? Not in luxury like this, I was sure. For us to enjoy such opulence, how many others had paid for it in suffering and hardship?

And, now that I was alerted to the substance of my home, I sensed the smell, too ~ a familiar mixture of furniture polish and old wood, of fresh flowers and stale tobacco smoke, but now mixed with the sweat of the people bustling about and the dust rising from the soldiers' boots.

Everyone seemed to be ignoring the rest of us who were to travel with the family, so eventually we just walked outside into the sunshine and waited for instructions. Somehow, Yuri appeared among the men assigned to escort us and, when the important people were seated, he politely directed us to climb into the remaining vehicles. The kitchen staff took one car, leaving the last one for the twins and I, along with the two maids.

Once seated, I looked back at the palace, with its white and mustard coloured walls, its balconies and railings, and the beautiful gardens in which I had so much enjoyed walking. My eyes wandered over to the corner of the kitchen block, half hidden by shrubs, where my bird-table stood, and I felt a pang of guilt because I had not put out any food; the poor birds would have to survive without me now.

~ ~ ~

Soon we moved off with a roar of engines and a cloud of smoke, and circled anti-clockwise around the walls of the palace to arrive at the front. As we passed the colonnaded main entrance, I saw that all the remaining staff had collected at the steps, and were waving us goodbye. Among them was Katerina Nikolevna, my childhood nanny, who was waving a white handkerchief; I waved back, tears suddenly in my eyes.

The motor cars spluttered to a stop beside the two carts, and waited while the soldiers boarded the empty cart. When they were ready, we moved off again, preceded by Lieutenant Izakov on his motor cycle, the carts following our cars.

For as long as the palace remained in view, I looked longingly back at it, but it was soon obscured by trees as we followed the road that wound through the rolling gardens. The throaty roar of the motor cars was the only sound I could hear. In any case, we were all silent, disinclined to talk, absorbed in our own memories, some quietly crying at what they are losing, and the friends left behind. At least I did not have that problem; apart from Katerina, there was no-one back there who cared about me, or who I would miss. My only friends were with me.

We bumped through the woods, and between the huge iron gates that marked the end of the stately grounds. There, a sparse crowd was waiting, and they began to shout abuse at us and to throw rotting vegetables at the cars. Some of them ran alongside our vehicle for a while, shouting and making obscene gestures. The soldiers at the gates, who should have been restraining them, seem to be unwilling to try, either through fear or sympathy. I stared at my feet, and breathed a sigh of relief as we gathered speed and they were finally left behind.

The sky had by then become overcast, with dense black clouds building over to the west, but the weather so far was not unpleasant. It was the first time for six months that any of us had been outside the palace, and I felt a surge of relief to be away from that place at last. We emerged onto the short road through Tsarskoye Selo, the pretty little town that served the palace, with its bakers and butchers and its fairyland houses, towards the little railway station.

~ ~ ~

The heavy black clouds had arrived overhead, blocking the sun, and a drizzle had begun to fall, as we stopped beside the entrance of the station. We climbed anxiously from our cars, and the soldiers spilled out of their cart, running to create a protective barrier around us, separating us from a small crowd of curious onlookers which had gathered, and forming a corridor through which we passed to enter the station building. Whether it was to protect us, or stop us trying to escape, I was not sure, though I suspected it was the latter. We emerged onto the wooden platform beside a small train, consisting of just two carriages and a neat little engine, painted bright red, which sat patiently, hissing steam and occasionally releasing a cough and a puff of smoke.

Izakov rejoined us. Having shed his leather coat and the funny helmet, he looked smart in his grey uniform, peaked cap and polished boots. He led Nicholas and Alex to the front carriage, and opened the door for them.

"Please take your seats, we shall depart as soon as your luggage is loaded," he said, before turning away to direct the soldiers.

These little coaches were very different from the luxury to which the royals had previously been accustomed on the royal train. I had never travelled in it, but had seen photographs, and it looked palatial.

The train we were boarding certainly did not resemble those pictures, consisting as it did of just one passenger coach and one closed goods wagon, but as we followed the family aboard, the coach itself appeared to be reasonably clean and comfortable. There were four private compartments, accessed by a corridor, and each compartment could contain up to six people.

While the family found its seats in the first compartment, Polya, Rada and I moved along the corridor to the opposite end of the carriage and sat in the last compartment. We heard all the others finding places, and were joined shortly by the two upstairs maids, who steadfastly avoided meeting my eyes when I looked in their direction. If there had been another compartment free, I am sure they would have taken it. Well, let them ignore me, they were nothing to me, what did I care?

We sat in silence, waiting for the train to move off. My feeling was one of impatience; the constant uncertainties of recent months, and the fear of what might happen next, were worse than having something tangible to deal with. I hated to be a victim, passive and powerless. At last a new phase was beginning, things were happening, and I had some sense of self-determination.

I watched through the window as the soldiers loaded our luggage into the goods wagon, and when they were done, they climbed in with it. Then, at last, with a sharp whistle and ear-pounding, drum-like beats of smoke and steam, the engine jerked forwards and our journey finally started.

Slowly at first, Tsarskoye Selo slipped behind, and the train began gathering speed across the open countryside, a trail of smoke gradually dissipating above the track in the steady rain which was now falling.

Chapter 17 ~ Petrograd

An hour passed, and the fields and forests began to give way to buildings that appeared, sporadically, on either side. Soon they became denser as we entered the outskirts of Petrograd, and it was not long before the train stopped at the station.

With shouted orders, the soldiers jumped out and took position at the doors, alert, with their weapons in readiness. Everyone seemed to be very tense. We could hear the sounds of an angry crowd close by, a clatter of gunshots not far away, and an explosion in the distance.

There was a strange 'ping-ping' sound, and small holes appeared simultaneously on both sides of our carriage as a shot passed right through the thin wooden panels. We threw ourselves onto the floor, but no more bullets followed, and mercifully no-one was hurt.

More soldiers arrived and helped the men to unload the other carriage, while we remained seated, then Lieutenant Izakov came aboard and told us we were to leave the train and follow the soldiers. I was puzzled, and asked Tatiana, as our little group clustered on the wooden boards of the platform, why we were disembarking.

"The line ends here, Natalie. We have to cross Petrograd to the other station, from which the Trans-Russia train departs."

For some reason, I had thought that our train would

simply switch to another line and proceed.

We waited there for a few minutes, hearing a cacophony of shouts and banging from beyond the station walls and an incessant beating of rain on the roof. A man appeared, handing out an armful of umbrellas; I grabbed two, handing one to Rada.

Eventually, we were escorted out of the building, surrounded by our constant phalanx of soldiers, into the street beyond.

Outside the station, the rain was now falling steadily, bouncing on our umbrellas with a noise like the crunching of a thousand feet on gravel. The city looked bedraggled; limp flags drooped from their poles, large puddles of water lay everywhere, and drips splattered at our feet from awnings and roofs as we stood by the station entrance.

A crowd of people had gathered nearby, held back by a line of police, and when they saw us emerge they began to shout abuse at the former Tsar and his family. Our guards, with grim expressions and alert eyes, gathered around us, forming a tight cordon, and we walked quickly past the crowd with our heads down as they shouted at us and threw stones. The stones mostly fell short, though I saw one or two bouncing off the uniforms of the soldiers, and one or two struck our umbrellas.

An assortment of vehicles was waiting for us. I recognised some of them as the huge state coaches from the Winter Palace. The last time I saw them was about ten years earlier, when there was a royal procession through Saint Petersburg, as it then was. I couldn't remember the reason for that celebration, but there had been sunshine and marching bands and cheering crowds ~ so very different from this bleak day. The grand golden coach was understandably absent, but there were several others, with their hoods raised to protect the occupants, and there were also a few taxi cabs, looking small and drab beside the grand ceremonial carriages. All the horses were nervously stamping their feet and tossing their heads, upset by the noise, and their drivers stood reassuringly beside them, steadying them, talking to them.

Nicholas and Alexandra were taken to the first two large coaches, along with their children; the doctor, his son and daughter, and Alexandra's friends occupied the next. The rest of us climbed in wherever we could find a space. The twins and I hopped up into one of the small taxi cabs, and were joined again by the two upstairs maids; five of us squeezed into the tiny compartment. We kept our heads down and avoided looking at the jeering crowd, not far away, who were still shouting obscenities and throwing stones at us.

With as little delay as possible, we set off, the skittish horses clopping through the grey, wet streets, away from the booing mob. There were mounted soldiers riding along beside us, forming a protective wall on both sides, and I noticed that there were police and armed soldiers in force at every junction we passed, blocking access to the wide avenue along which we were passing. It soon became clear why: beyond the human barrier formed by the police and soldiers there were enormous crowds of demonstrating citizens. Stones were constantly bouncing off our cab, the noise mixing with the drumming of rain on the roof to create a frightening din, and our driver struggled to control his scared horse.

Off to our right I saw that some people had managed to break through the cordon and run towards the procession, throwing stones and shouting obscenities. The soldiers ran after them, grabbing them and pulling them to the ground, but one man was more determined ~ he struggled free and staggered towards us. Not more than thirty feet away I saw him raise his hands, as though pointing at us, and I saw that he was holding a pistol. Even above the shouting and the beating of stones and rain, I heard a sudden rapid burst of gunshots and saw puffs of smoke whisked away from the gun barrel by the wind.

All this noise was finally more than our horse could stand, and we were thrown about inside the cab as the poor creature reared and bolted. It seemed that the driver was unable to restrain it, and we careered out of control across the avenue, gathering speed, swaying and occasionally leaving the ground momentarily as we bounced off curbs. We were all thrown to the floor in a tangled mass of limbs and bodies, struggling to separate ourselves, groping for something to hold onto.

As I pulled myself up by the door handle and my eyes reached the height of the window, we swerved back towards the other coaches and struck a glancing blow against the side of one of them, smashing one of our wheels. I watched the spokes splinter and fly off, one by one, as the wheel turned, then the rim distorted for a moment, before collapsing. I saw the horrified faces of Tatiana and her sisters flash past, then the road rose towards me as the cab began to tilt. Still we hurtled along for a few more yards on the axle, rocking wildly, being thrown around inside like dice in a pot, until suddenly the cab rolled right over with a crashing, scraping noise and one side and the roof were ripped away.

I found myself flying like a bird. I looked down on the scene of destruction as though merely an observer. Then I was falling, the ground looming, hitting me. I bounced, once, twice, all my breath knocked from me as I rolled over and over on the rough, wet road. Pain! My left side scraping and my head hitting something hard ...

In a kind of dream I saw my mother; I knew it was her, even though I had not seen her since I was six months old. She was talking to me, smiling, I watched her lips move. She looked into my eyes and stroked my hair with her fingers. Gently she rocked me in her arms, then laid me in my cot and kissed my forehead ...

Katerina, feeding me, helping me to walk. Tatiana chasing me around the garden, then stopping to pick strawberries. Classrooms, lessons, deportment, English, French, Russian ...

Birds at my table, butterflies in the buddleia, bees humming in the lavender, warm sun ...

Dancing with Frederick, his smile, his voice with its lilting accent, fading, fading ...

My eyes re-opened upon a world turned on its side. Water was dripping on my face and I could hear the sound of many voices all around. Someone was holding an umbrella over me, but my clothes were already wet, and sticking to me. I shivered. A man was leaning over me, but not Frederick. It was Doctor Botkin.

"What's happening?" I croaked.

"There's been an accident, Natalie," he said, "you have been injured. I need to check to see if any bones are broken. Tell me if anything hurts as I do this."

I felt his expert hands on my arms and then my legs, as he pressed and pulled at them. I winced a few times, but it was from scrapes, not the grinding of bones.

He smiled reassuringly, then turned and spoke to someone nearby: "Nothing appears to be broken, she can be moved."

Then to me, "Natalie, a Hansom cab is here to take you to the station."

Someone came running over and addressed him, and immediately he turned and walked quickly away towards the remains of the cab, which I could then see were close by.

Two soldiers, one on each side of me, gently slipped their arms under my body, legs and neck, then lifted and carried me away between them, still horizontal, as though on a stretcher.

As we passed the wreckage, I could see that the doctor was kneeling beside another casualty, who was lying still on the ground, surrounded by the debris of the crash, and I noticed that a young woman was beside the doctor, leaning over the body, crying out in anguish.

I was seized with fear. I could not see clearly, was it Rada?

Oh no! My friends were hurt!

I tried to struggle free, but the men restrained me, speaking quietly, telling me that I must keep still.

We stopped, and they carefully passed me up to someone, another man, through the door of a small carriage. Effortlessly, he took me from them, then turned and lowered me onto a seat. He covered me with a blanket, and called up to his driver through a flap in the roof; immediately we began to move.

The constant baying and stoning of the crowd appeared to have stopped, leaving an eerie lightness in the air. The only sounds were the metallic slapping of the horse's iron-shod hooves on the paved road and the steady pattering of the rain on the roof, creating a soothing background noise that hypnotically filled the ears and eased the senses.

I looked around and found that I was lying in a small vehicle, like one of the private carriages I had sometimes seen nipping about the city with their wealthy passengers. On the same seat, at my feet, was a man I did not recognise ~ middle aged, very smartly dressed, sporting a large black moustache.

He saw that I was studying him, nervously.

"Do not be alarmed, madam, my name is Pavel Sergeyevich Lukashenko, I am a businessman from Belarus. I am taking you to rejoin the rest of your party."

"What happened to my friends?" I asked, anxiously.

"I'm afraid I don't know much," he replied, shaking his head. "I witnessed the accident as I was leaving my hotel, and when your vehicle overturned, I saw you lying on the ground. So I spoke to the doctor to offer my carriage, if it could be of use."

"Do you know who is hurt?"

"All I know for sure is that the driver of your cab was shot, I think he is dead. I saw him fall from his seat as the horse bolted, and he did not get up. Now please rest, we will soon be at the station."

And before long we came to a halt, the cab doors were opened from outside, and I was carefully passed down into the strong, upward-reaching arms of a huge, ugly soldier, with a shaved head and pock-marked face.

My initial fear at his appearance, however, disappeared instantly when he blessed me with a warm, broken-toothed smile and said, albeit it in a gruff voice: "Just relax, young lady, you will soon be with your friends."

As he held me, I could see that we were outside the Petrograd Moscow station, a large, ornately decorated, cathedral-like building with arched doors and windows. Another man was holding an umbrella over me. The crowd was subdued ~ I wondered if they had seen the royal family pass and vented their anger on them, and were now just waiting to see what would happen next.

My saintly ogre carried me effortlessly through the grand entrance and across the echoing gallery of the station, sheltered at last from the rain. Now the sounds I heard were the hissing of steam and occasional cough from a railway engine, like the breathing of a great, sleeping animal.

Chapter 18 ~ Reunited

There was only one train in the station, a great long chain of assorted carriages stretching far into the distance. The man carried me to a compartment near the back of the train, deftly side-stepped through the narrow doors, and laid me gently on a bench, accepting a pillow from someone and placing it carefully beneath my head.

As he was about to go, I caught his hand and looked up at his big, kind, ugly face ~ but after struggling to say more, all I could manage was: "Thank you."

His mouth cracked open with one of his captivating toothless smiles and he touched my cheek with his fingertips, then turned and left.

Immediately, Tatiana appeared at my side.

"What happened to you?" she enquired as she removed the blanket and surveyed my scraped skin and bedraggled clothes. "We saw your cab careering around without a driver, and thought you would all be killed when it crashed into the side of our carriage then rolled over in pieces."

What could I tell her? I knew so little myself. "The man who brought me in his Hansom cab told me that our driver was shot," I began. "I think the gunman intended to hit one of us ... or you. It seems that the driver is probably dead, and I fear for one of our group, who was still lying in the road, being attended by the doctor, when they carried me away. Tatiana, I'm afraid it may be one of the twins."

I had reached a point close to hysteria. The shock of what had happened was finally impinging on my mind and body, images of the crash flashed past again and again, like one of those moving picture shows, and I was desperately afraid that I had lost one of my dear friends.

"Natalie, stop talking and listen to me. I will try to find out more for you, but, in the meantime, I want to check you over for injuries and get you cleaned up. So I have to get those wet clothes off you, do you mind? I will arrange a screen for privacy."

I nodded, and she stepped away from me and spoke to her three sisters, who returned with her, carrying some sheets. They stood beside my bench and held up the sheets to hide me from view while Tatiana started to remove my clothes.

"I will need to cut some of these to get them off, is that alright? They are already quite badly torn, and I will be as careful as possible."

She expertly cut away until she could see my damaged skin underneath, then carefully cleaned the grit and blood from my wounds, taking each of my scraped and muddy hands and gently bathing them with a small bowl of water, patting them dry with a piece of cloth. As each cut and graze was revealed and cleaned, starting with my legs and working methodically up my body until finishing with my head, she bandaged it using strips cut from a sheet. And all the time she worked, she was asking questions ~ Where did it hurt? Did I see the gunman? Who rescued me after the crash?

There was sudden noise and activity at the door of the carriage, and she looked over her shoulder. Then she turned back to me and leaned closer.

"The twins have just walked in, and they both look fine," she announced.

"Oh thank God!" I cried, realising as I did so what a hypocritical thing it was to say. "How are they?"

She turned away again, and spoke to someone.

"It appears they were trapped inside the overturned cab," she relayed to me. "It protected them from any serious injury."

More words came from behind her, then she continued.

"It seems that Svetlana and Luba have the worst injuries, but they have not yet returned, and no-one here knows how they are. They were still at the scene of the crash with the doctor, when Polina and Rada were brought away."

She stood up. "There, all done."

Olga brought me a skirt and blouse from somewhere and Tatiana helped me to dress. The reversal of our roles was not lost on me, and when I caught her eye and grinned, she too realised it and winked at me. Then her sisters lowered the screen and they all helped me to move into a sitting position.

Having attended to me, they crossed the carriage to care for Rada and Polya, and I was able to look around for the first time. What I saw was not edifying.

Our compartment was nothing like the comfortable one in which we had travelled to Petrograd from

Tsarskoye Selo earlier in the day. This one was primitive and basic. The seats were bare wooden benches, running along each side for nearly its entire length, with two further rows set back-to-back down the centre. There were no comforts, apart from a lavatory cubicle at one end, with a wash stand alongside. The floors were plain wood, scratched, dented and stained with unknown substances, and the air had a smell of urine and worse about it.

There were twenty or so armed guards outside on the platform, forming a barrier all along the coach. I saw people walking past our windows, some of them staring in at us, probably not believing their eyes at who they could see sitting in here, but they were brusquely moved on by the soldiers.

I recognised Yuri amongst the guards who passed through our compartment, and realised with a shock that these men, too, were being uprooted from their homes to make this journey. He came over and gently asked how I was feeling. I smiled and thanked him, and assured him that my injuries, though they looked bad, were superficial. I did not admit that, actually, they hurt like hell.

~ ~ ~

Doctor Botkin arrived in a flurry of activity, followed by two soldiers carrying a stretcher, the diminutive form on it covered by a blanket.

Yuri went to help. He returned to tell me that it was Luba Kuzmina on the stretcher. Her friend Svetlana Alekseeva died in the crash, and Luba herself was seriously wounded. They had been on the side of the cab that came to rest on the road, and Svetlana was thrown partly through the opening and crushed by the impact. I shuddered as my imagination painted a terribly vivid mental picture of that happening.

He also handed me a bedraggled bundle of papers.

"These are your drawings, but they are rather spoiled by the rain. I recognise them because of that day by the lake, and I have often seen you in the garden, sketching the birds. The men at the scene of the crash picked up everything they could."

He pointed to a corner, where his colleagues had put the dripping collection of personal items they had gathered from the wreckage. "All the bags are over there, but I do not know which is yours."

I held his hand. "Thank you, my friend, I am very grateful. And please will you also thank your colleagues for me?"

He smiled and touched the peak of his cap with his fingers, then departed to rejoin his troop.

My home-made portfolio had burst and the drawings were all soaked. Where I had used paints, the colours had run quite badly, but I was happy to have them back. I looked around for somewhere to dry them, and spotted a curtain rail above my head, running the length of the carriage windows. There were no curtains, so I draped my pictures over it to dry; they were a sorry sight, and on reflection I doubted that they could be saved.

Chapter 19 ~ Lenin

With the arrival of Luba and the doctor, there was nothing more to detain us; everything was ready for our departure. I watched through the window opposite as Lieutenant Izakov and the soldiers who had been on guard duty outside our carriage climbed into the coach ahead of ours.

Then a man in dark blue uniform waved a red-and-yellow flag, and blew a whistle. With a hoot and the now familiar gasps from the engine, the clanking and squealing of wheels and couplings, and the lurching of carriages, we were on our way again.

As the train emerged slowly from the station, I saw the city slide past like a diorama, sometimes obscured by a cloud of sooty smoke from the engine.

Inside, the doctor and Alexandra were treating Luba, and Tatiana was talking with Rada and Polina, while dressing their cuts and scrapes. Others sat in small, quiet groups, or stared out of the windows.

When Tatiana was done with the twins, they came over to see me, bruised, dishevelled and limping a little, but smiling as we were reunited. They sat beside me, and we held hands, relieved that we had survived, though our eyes were fixed on the small huddle around poor Luba.

"I am so glad to see you, I thought one of you had been killed," I told them.

"It could have been any of us," Rada said. "As the

cab rolled, I saw one side fly right off, and you were catapulted out. When we came to rest, we were all in a heap, with Luba and Svetlana underneath Polya and me, and there were cushions and bags and all kinds of stuff on top of us."

"Svetlana was screaming," added Polya, shuddering. "We struggled to try to free ourselves, but were pinned down until some soldiers arrived and pulled us out one by one."

Rada was nodding her head. "The royals had continued on their way," she continued, "and the crowd seemed to be subdued after they had passed. No more stones were being thrown at us, and the chanting had stopped.

I saw the doctor a short way off, he must have jumped from his carriage as soon as the accident happened, and was kneeling beside someone who was laying on the ground; I was sure it was you. When Polya was freed, we came over to see how you were, but before we got there the men had carried you off to a carriage that was waiting."

"Svetlana is dead," I added.

"Yes. One of the soldiers spoke to the doctor, and together they ran back to the wreckage. I could see that the men had freed Luba, and they were pulling the cab apart with their bare hands, ripping panels off and throwing them aside to reach Svetlana. But when the doctor examined her there was nothing he could do, she was already dead."

I looked across at the huddle on the other side of the carriage. "What do they say about Luba?" I asked.

Polya shook her head, and Rada said quietly: "It's not good."

~ ~ ~

Over in the far corner of the carriage was the pile of hand baggage that had been with us in our cab, now bedraggled, wet and dirty. We sorted through it and I found my portmanteau, which I carried back to my seat, placing it on the floor to finish dripping. Opening it, I found that the contents were dry and undamaged. I removed my diary and Anna Karenina; Anna, I placed on the bench next to me, while I found my last diary entry and re-read it.

Wednesday 22nd August 1917 ~ morning

Today we will leave the protection of the palace and set off into the unknown. Is this the end? Are we being taken to our deaths? Who knows what they have planned. All I know is that they are capable of anything; there is no cruelty that is beneath them. My heart is tight, as though my chest is bound in a corset. Myriam, please protect me.

Suddenly we were alerted by Alexei Trupp, who exclaimed "Look!"

We clustered around him, peering through the windows.

The train was still close to the city centre, slowly passing a large open market place, just a short distance away. Despite the rain, which was still falling steadily, the square was filled with a huge crowd of people.

They were facing a platform that had been erected at the far end, upon which someone was speaking, gesticulating wildly with both his arms outstretched. The crowd seemed to like what they heard, and were cheering so loudly that we could even hear them in our carriage, despite the rumbling of the wheels and the pulsing beat of the engine dragging us up the incline.

"Is that Lenin speaking?" Olga asked her father.

"I believe it could be," he replied, "it is hard to be sure at this distance."

Then, unbelievably, columns of soldiers appeared from the side streets, knelt, and opened fire with their rifles indiscriminately upon the crowd.

People scattered, running from the carnage towards whatever shelter they could find, but they were gunned down as they ran. Within seconds there were twenty or thirty bodies on the ground, with desperate people jumping over them as they fled.

The train seemed to be almost stationary, and we could clearly see the events unfolding so close that I saw the blood flowing in the puddles and the terror in people's eyes. Lenin had disappeared from the platform; I did not know if he had been shot or had fled.

We were all shocked at what was happening before us, and Alexandra crossed herself and began to pray. Nicholas was more forceful. "Who ordered these soldiers to attack the crowd?" he shouted at our guards, who merely shrugged. "This is absurd, you are making enemies of the people. Can't you do something?"

Before any more could be said, we saw more troops, about fifty men mounted on horseback, riding into the square and charging at the fleeing crowd, scattering bodies as the citizens tried to escape, hacking with their sabres at everyone in their sight.

All this happened in, perhaps, one or two minutes at the most, while the train was creeping along, until the scene mercifully passed from our view as we accelerated away.

Nicholas sat down heavily and put his head in his hands; Alexandra ended her prayer and placed a hand on his arm. He lowered his hands and gazed at her for a moment, then took both of her hands in his.

"What can I do, Sunny?" he said, hoarsely. 'Sunny' was his affectionate nickname for Alexandra. "They are making things so much worse, and the people will blame me. I feel so powerless!"

The carriage became heavy with silence as we returned to our seats. Everyone was looking glumly and morosely out of the windows as the buildings became more sparse and the train eventually gained speed as it fled through the suburbs and into open country. So deep in my thoughts did I become I that I saw nothing of the beautiful landscape passing by.

Tatiana broke into my reverie. "Luba is in a bad way," she said quietly, sitting on the bench beside me. "Both of her arms are broken, and she has internal injuries. The poor girl is distraught, because she was laying on top of Svetlana until she was released, and her friend was screaming in pain and begging Luba to free her, which of course she was powerless to do. She is nearly hysterical and the doctor has had to give her morphine to ease her pain and calm her down."

I looked across the packed compartment to where little Luba lay, peaceful for a little while, sleeping. She had always avoided me in the past, as did most of the staff, wary of my relationship with the family. Relationship! If only they had known how tenuous was my connection with the royals, and how lonely I really felt. But the past was irrelevant. Things were different, we had shared a dreadful experience, and I felt a surge of tenderness for that tiny girl and the loss she had suffered.

~ ~ ~

Two hours passed, and as the train slowed again for Moscow, we briefly observed a running battle between a small group of soldiers, dreadfully outnumbered, and a large mob. The crowd seemed to be mostly throwing rocks and anything they could pick up as they pursued the soldiers, but some had come prepared ~ they were throwing bottles which, when they smashed near the soldiers, burst into a cloud of fire. I was thankful not to see anyone engulfed in the flames. The soldiers seemed to be unwilling ~ or, perhaps, were unable ~ to use their weapons, and they suddenly stopped running and turned to face the crowd, throwing their guns down onto the ground before them and raising their hands in surrender. Buildings obscured my view and I did not see what happened next; I hoped the men would be safe.

Witnessing all these events on this journey, our

familiar world distorted into a kind of hell, with killings and hatred sweeping through our society, was deeply disturbing and upset me greatly.

~ ~ ~

Soon we pulled into Moscow station with a screeching of wheels and brakes, and sat, with the hiss of the engine, and the strangely sweet smell of the smoke that drifted all around, looking out onto a crowded platform. People were pushing to get on the train, and our guards had difficulty keeping them from entering our carriage. As I looked upon the desperate, contorted faces, I realised that this revolution was affecting citizens of every class. There were women in fine clothes and men in rags, children, old women, families. All ... what? Fleeing the city? Joining loved ones?

After a brief stop, the train pulled away again. At every intersection I was shocked to see how many people were begging at the side of the road. In our comfortable, protected environment at the palace, we had never seen the hardships being suffered by the ordinary people; perhaps things would have been different if we had been more aware of them.

And when we rode high over part of the city, as the railway passed along an embankment, I could see long queues of people outside shops in the streets below, shuffling forwards a few steps at a time, empty shopping baskets in their hands. When I saw someone emerging from the building, after queuing for what I guessed could have been an hour or two, they were carrying no more than a cabbage, or a small loaf of bread.

Not everyone was as restrained as those patient shoppers. In other places I saw gangs looting shops, running off with whatever they could steal, and there seemed to be no-one to stop them.

I tried to imagine the homes these poor people would return to, but realised that I knew too little. Did they even have houses? Perhaps they lived in flats or rooms rented from more fortunate people? Or, dreadful to consider, did they sleep on the streets? I was seized by an urge, which I only just resisted, to grab Nicholas and Alexandra and point to all these things I was seeing and shout, "Now do you understand?"

Diary ~ Wednesday 22nd August 1917 ~ Late Morning

The rain has eased, and the sun has appeared through cracks in the clouds, casting shafts of light onto the Earth, like spotlights on a stage. A semblance of normality is resumed in our little, enclosed, false world. At last the train has escaped the city and its violence and hardship, and is running beside the beautiful river Volga ~ I have never before seen such a wonderful sight. As the train rounds a bend, and the whole spectacular panorama sweeps past, Rada, Poya and I crowd at the window to watch. Another bend, and I can see the engine and the first the coaches start to clatter across a huge iron bridge with ten arches. Then it is our turn, and below us we see ships and barges of all sizes, swarming like water-beetles, all with a purpose, a destination. I wonder if they look up at the train, passing caterpillar-like above them. Then it is behind us as the engine pulls us relentlessly onward, through woods and fields, cities, towns and villages towards our fate.

Most of the fields are bare, the harvest having been already gathered in. But peasants are sometimes to be seen walking behind a horse-drawn plough, or gathering hay, using pitchforks to throw it up onto carts. Where there is grass, I have seen cattle, goats and sheep grazing. We have passed through forests, and I have glimpsed a brown bear and, later, a pack of wolves ~ exciting moments for me. When we crossed the great prairies, seeing little human life for hours, just miles of flat, featureless scrub-land, I saw herds of bison, roaming as they have since the birth of the world.

I have noticed a change in the attitude of the soldiers towards the twins and me. It is as though they have accepted that, despite the privilege of our lifestyle, we are really more like them, just minor pieces in a game bigger than all of us, not part of the ruling elite. Perhaps the crash has affected them, and surely Luba's sad state must touch their hearts. And so a strange duality has developed: where the royal family are concerned, the men are cold and unhelpful, but if I should as much as groan from my injuries, one of them will be there in a flash, asking if I need anything.

Chapter 20 ~ Luba

Swaying, clattering, the train plunged on. Minutes ticked away into hours, each much the same as the one before. We were not cold, and all of us dozed occasionally throughout the day; perhaps it was the motion, or the rhythmic sound of the wheels.

I spent much of my time watching through the windows as the land slid past in an endless tapestry. For a while, the railway ran alongside a canal; it was beautiful, glittering in the afternoon sun like a priceless jewel. There were barges, weighed down with coal or grain, being hauled slowly by huge horses which plodded steadily along the tow-path. Ducks, geese and swans glided on the sparkling water, or waddled on the banks, flying off angrily when a barge crudely thrust itself through their world, returning as soon as it had passed.

Luba regained consciousness, and I crossed to kneel on the floor beside where she lay on the hard bench. The train had just left a rural station, where we received some water, so I brought her some in a cup. I carefully raised her head and shoulders and helped her to slowly sip the cool liquid. When she was done, I lowered her head gently back onto the pillow.

"Thank you, Natalie," she whispered, smiling gratefully.

I held her hand and returned the smile. "It's no trouble. Is there anything else you need?"

"No thank you. You know what happened to Svetlana?"

I nodded. "I'm so sorry, Luba, it must have been a terrible ordeal for you."

"It was. She was screaming with pain, begging me to get her free, but I was laying on her, unable to move myself because the others were on top of me." Tears slowly trickled down her face as she recounted the awful experience. "She died as they were trying to release her."

There was nothing I could say, so I just gently squeezed her hand, and we sat in silence, each reliving our own memories.

"What caused it all?" she asked, suddenly.

"As I understand it, a gunman fired a few wild shots at the carriages and hit our driver."

"I couldn't see you," she said. "What happened to you?"

"I was thrown out," I began, but stopped talking when she suddenly gasped with pain and gripped my hand tightly. Doctor Botkin, sitting close by, came immediately. He placed a drop of syrup on her tongue and, after a little while, her grip on my hand relaxed, and she drifted off into sleep again.

The doctor indicated with an inclination of his head that I should follow him. When we were out of her hearing, he said: "Her external injuries do not worry me very much, but I'm afraid some of her internal organs are ruptured. She needs a hospital, but there is no hope of getting her to one. I have very little morphine left, perhaps enough for one day, then there will be nothing I can do to help her." He stopped, and looked at me. "It will become very distressing as the pain builds. You are her friend, are you able to be with her, to comfort her?"

I chose not to disillusion him about the extent of my relationship with Luba. I supposed that, at that moment, I could be considered her only friend.

"Certainly, I will do anything I can. Is it not possible to get more morphine from one of the towns when we stop?"

"I have asked the lieutenant about that, and he has told me he will telephone ahead from the next station for a doctor to meet the train and provide me with some."

We returned to our seats, and I picked up my diary. But every thought carried images of the crash. Those pictures are imprinted forever in my mind like photographs ~ bodies thrown around inside the swaying cab, the sight of the royal carriage looming closer and Tatiana's shocked face, the rolling, splintering, flying, and finally the sight of Luba's hunched little body leaning over her dead friend.

Diary ~ Thursday 23rd August 1917 ~ morning

We receive very little food from the guards; mostly it is just rough bread and coarse sausage, once or twice each day. Yesterday evening, we had a pot of warm soup, of uncertain content, which we scooped up with cups and devoured with our bread. I have observed that all the family pass some from their portions to supplement what Aleksey has.

The soldiers in our carriage eat the same as us, and it is clear to me that there is not much food available. What little there is has to be shared between everyone ~ the twenty-two of us and the twenty or so guards.

Chapter 21 ~ Nights

The first day ended, and the train rattled on through the night, occasionally stopping at stations and outposts. The temperature dropped considerably, and there was no heating in the carriage, so we covered ourselves with blankets and coats and slept fitfully, shivering in our seats, often awakened by sudden shaking of the carriage, or at station stops.

I had weird, fitful dreams. In one, I was driving the train, but from a position on the roof of one of the coaches, and did not know how to steer it or stop it. It careered across fields littered with dead bodies before overturning in the kitchen garden at Alexander Palace.

In the depth of the night I heard whispered voices across the carriage; a strange conversation taking place between Tatiana and her father. Curious, I lay still, so as not to alert them that I was eavesdropping.

Nicholas was saying something about King George of England, and Tatiana asked in reply "Can he do that?"

"He could if he wanted to," hissed Nicholas. "He is my cousin, after all."

"But surely, father, the time is past when he could arrange it?"

"Admittedly it will be harder now; he should have kept to his agreement when I first asked him, on the day I signed the abdication document. It was that damned Prime Minister of his, Lloyd George, who persuaded him to change his mind, I know it was. But perhaps something could still be negotiated with Kerensky, possibly to have a ship waiting for us on the Black Sea coast, from where we could sail across to Constantinople."

"But if the British Government has advised the King against getting involved, where can we go?"

"Yes, they have, blast them! But blood is thicker than water; surely George must act for his family. And if not England, then perhaps Greece, or even America."

"I don't see how we can communicate with anyone, now that we are in exile. We have lost all our contacts." Her voice wavered; I could hear that she was close to tears.

"Don't despair, Tata," her father said, tenderly. "All is not lost. Good people are still trying on our behalf."

As their voices faded, and I floated away in that uncertain state that is neither asleep nor awake, I saw Nicholas and Tatiana standing at the gates of a cemetery, he in full military uniform, she dressed as a small child, holding his hand. A man arrived, wearing a voluminous black robe, with his head and face lost in a vast hood. He led them through the gates to a graveyard, where rows of white stones radiated to the horizon, like a child's drawing of sunbeams. Alexandra spoke, and when I looked, she had appeared as an angel, with wings of white feathers.

"The greatest shall become the least," she said, "and the least shall be the greatest."

Bright flashes suddenly flickered like lightening

through my closed eyelids, and when I opened them, the door linking our coach with the one used by the soldiers had opened, and a figure stood there, carrying a torch. Without moving, I watched as Lieutenant Izakov passed me on his way to where Doctor Botkin was asleep. He shook him gently awake and, after a quiet word, they walked to the end of the carriage and waited by the door.

Soon the train slowed for a station, and when it came to rest, the two men stepped out onto the platform. I tiptoed across the carriage and peered through the grime on the window as they walked together towards the shadows of the station building.

A man, wrapped in a large overcoat, emerged into the pale yellow glow of a lamp and spoke briefly to the lieutenant and the doctor. Botkin reached into his coat pocket and handed over something, presumably money, and a package was passed to him in return. The man disappeared, and Botkin and the Lieutenant turned back to the carriage. As he passed my window, the doctor saw me watching, and held up the little package with a tight smile; he had his morphine, Izakov had been true to his word.

I returned to my seat beside the twins and, once again, closed my eyes and tried to sleep, but it eluded me. So many things had happened, and were still happening, that my mind was racing around like our runaway cab, crashing into memories, sparking new images of possible futures, that themselves careered out of control, becoming terrible nightmares. However, after a little while, a new sensation intruded into my reveries and brought me back to reality; I felt a dampness between my thighs, as though I had wet myself. "Oh, bother!" I muttered to myself, realising that my period had started early.

I grabbed my handbag and hastened to the toilet compartment, where I cleaned up as best I could in the darkness, and applied a pad. As I worked, I remembered how terrified I had been when the first one happened; I thought I was bleeding to death. Thankfully, Tatiana explained everything to me, and showed me how to make the pads. I had prepared several before the journey, using a layer of cotton wadding stitched into a skin of muslin, and they were in my bag in readiness for my unwelcome visitor. But I was not expecting it for another week or so, and I wondered if it had arrived early because of the shock of the accident. At any rate, it was inconvenient and another fly in the soup of my life.

Having dealt with my 'situation', I emerged from the tiny closet and looked around while I washed my hands at the little basin. The first light of dawn was tinting the darkness with ghostly shapes so, instead of returning to my seat after drying my hands, I stood at the end of the carriage and stared out of the grime-streaked window at the real world beyond as it awoke.

Shades of black and grey sometimes coalesced into recognisable forms ~ trees flashing past close to the track, a hill defined on the horizon against a cloud, smeared pink by the hidden sun. Another small village, lit by a fading fire, appeared and was gone before any details could register.

Diary ~ Thursday 23rd August 1917 ~ evening

How disappointed I am with 'Anna Karenina'. At first I was absorbed in the book, amazed at the intrigue and deceptions in the lives of Oblónsky, his family and friends, to such an extent that many of the miles passed unnoticed. But as the book has progressed, I have found myself becoming increasingly frustrated with it. Tolstoy seems to treat Anna as just a device to stimulate the characters he thinks of as the important ones, the men. I want to read about Anna ~ she was a fallen woman, yet I admire her and my heart goes out to her.

The problem seems to be that all Russian literature is written by male authors. I remember going through the shelves of books at the palace and wondering why there are no female Russian writers. In England and America, women have been creating wonderful fiction; women like Jane Austen, the Bronte sisters and Mary Ann Evans. Is there something in the Russian psyche that prevents women from feeling that they can have something worthwhile to write about? Or is it that the publishing process is controlled by men, who are not interested in what women have to say? Perhaps that's why Mary Ann Evans had to publish under the name George Elliott.

Well, I plan to find out. I have kept a diary ever since I first learnt to write, and I have it all with me on the train, in a dozen or so exercise books. I will find a suitable starting point and begin to add more detail ~ turn it into a book. Then, if I live, I will try to get it published. In our present climate, that may prove to be hard, but maybe all this will pass; and if the Russian publishers don't want it, I will take it to England!

Diary ~ Friday 24th August 1917 ~ morning

The journey continues. Stations appear and slide to a stop by my window; sometimes they are in a city, with elegant buildings and busy streets; sometimes in little market towns, the domes of their pretty churches standing proudly over red roofs and painted walls; and sometimes the station itself is no more than an outpost, seemingly in the middle of a forest. Passengers get on or off, going about their lives as though it is not the end of the world. It all seems so normal, untouched by the hate and mistrust that has ripped apart society in Saint Petersburg and Moscow. I wonder how long it will be before these people, too, are killing each other.

When I gaze from my window at the relentlessly moving countryside, there are occasional small delights for my eyes ~ a flock of cranes gracefully making their way across the sky with slow wing-beats, heading for their evening roost, and an eagle, circling, climbing on warm air currents, eyes scouring the ground for prey. In different circumstances, I would be filled with joy to see nature like this, to be in the midst of it, to grab my sketch pad and reproduce it, but my heart is low, and though the sights bring a momentary little smile to my lips, they do not lift my spirits.

To pass the time, we read books, talk amongst ourselves or sit in quiet contemplation. Sometimes four of us will get together to play cards, including the family, and although Nicholas has never joined in with us, Alexandra sometimes does. Nicholas prefers to play a really complicated game called Bezique, usually with Doctor Botkin and Alexandra and Olga. I sit mostly with Rada and Polina, but sometimes with Tatiana who, I have noticed, when she is not close to her mother, often sits alone, deep in thought.

Chapter 22 ~ Day Three

Yuri visited me regularly to see how I was progressing, and I looked forward to seeing him. We chatted easily, as though we were old friends. I think we were able to be relaxed in each other's company because there was no attempt by either of us to make more of it than a comfortable friendship; neither of us was attracted to the other, neither sought romance or excitement.

I asked him about his family, and he told me how worried he felt at being sent so far away when they needed him at home. The last he had heard was that his little son had a cough, and that his wife had no money for food ~ she had to join the queues for soup and bread. He also explained to me why many of the soldiers were so rude to the royals, when it was their job to protect them.

"You see, Natalie, most common people like me sympathise with the cause. We have seen the Tsar and his family living in obscene luxury, while we go hungry, powerless as our families starve and freeze to death. And he has taken us into one stupid war after another, sending us away just when our families are most desperate. And for what? To satisfy his pretensions of being a great leader." He dropped his voice suddenly, realising that the whole family was around us and might overhear him. "The revolution will return the power and the wealth of the country to those who labour to create it," he whispered, "and my colleagues deeply resent having to risk their lives to protect someone they already hate, against people with whom they are sympathetic."

~ ~ ~

Luba's condition worried me greatly. When she was awake we were able to talk a little, but soon the pain would become too much for her, and the good doctor had to give her some more morphine. However, those few and short exchanges became important to both of us. A kind of friendship was formed ~ perhaps more of an understanding ~ and we were both relieved that the tension between us was gone.

I discovered that she was only thirteen years old and was born at the palace. Her father was a soldier who died fighting against Germany on the border with Ukraine, and her mother worked in the kitchens.

Her condition showed no signs of improving ~ quite the opposite. She developed a fever and become delirious, her poor little body was shivering and her skin turned as white as bone china and was beaded with sweat. Alexandra, Olga and Tatiana helped me to look after her, talking to her, placing cool towels on her forehead and trying to make her comfortable, and Botkin took her pain away with his elixir.

~ ~ ~

Another night arrived, and with the darkness we settled down again to try to sleep in that swaying, rumbling room that was our prison.

After a couple of hours, I was woken by Tatiana gently shaking me. She beckoned me to follow her to Luba's side. The doctor was just leaving her, his face grim, but she seemed to be sleeping peacefully.

I noticed that some of her long blonde hair was laying across her face, so I knelt at her side and carefully lifted it away. Her skin was cold, and I felt a sudden fear. I looked up at Tatiana, who nodded solemnly; Luba was no longer in pain.

It is hard to describe my feelings. We had only just begun to know each other, and there were few memories of shared times. It was often Luba who brought tea and cakes when Tatiana and I were working, and we had recently sat in silence, ignoring each other, on the little train to Petrograd. Then, of course, there was the crash ~ the grinding and splintering of the cab, the rolling and tumbling, bodies tossed around inside, and the screams. Then afterwards, for a short time, we had been close enough to see past the suspicion and hostility and wounded feelings to discover a real person. The tears that trickled down my cheek were for the poor child who, in different circumstances, might have been a friend. Perhaps they were also for myself and my fear for the future.

Tatiana and I covered her with a sheet, and sat side by side on the seat opposite the tiny body. I realised that not one single word had been spoken since she woke me. I took her hand, and we sat in pensive silence until dawn.

Diary ~ Saturday 25h August 1917 ~ morning

Luba died last night.

Would I have felt as sad a week ago as I do now? No, and it would be dishonest of me to say otherwise. I did not know her then, had not shared the fears and drama that brought us closer. Then she was just one of the people who resented me. If I can take anything from the events of the last few days, it is that the wall between Luba and me was breached, and we became friends. It is a lesson, of the kind that Myriam told me to be aware, and I must learn to apply it to other relationships, even those such as this in which I think I am the victim.

My wounds are beginning to heal, and they itch terribly. It is impossible to bathe, or even wash properly, because water is in such short supply, but I have been able to clean them by dabbing them with a towel dampened with a little of my drinking water. Tatiana or my friends help me redress them with clean pads, held in place by strips torn from the clothes I was wearing in the crash and are ruined. Some of my garments I have been able to repair ~ though my hands have puffed up from their battering, and it is very hard to hold a needle ~ but it is good to keep busy, and they will do for working clothes later.

I have started to expand my diary, to turn it into a story. After all, I have a good command of two languages, though I know nothing of the skills and techniques of an author (apart from what I have learnt from the books I have been reading). It seems to me that Myriam's first visit is a good place to start; before that, the record is rather boring. It is the first time I have re-read these passages; it is amazing to reflect on how much has happened since they were written, and oh what memories they are stirring as I add my commentaries!

Chapter 23 ~ Tobolsk

Just as the sky ahead was beginning to glow with the purple and orange haze of dawn, the train stopped and I awoke to the sound of shouting outside. There were whistles and blasts of steam from the engine, and a clanking of coaches as our carriage lurched forwards and back.

I opened a window and leaned out to see better. We were being uncoupled from the rest of the train, and there was another engine on the track alongside us. But before I could see more, one of our guards shouted at me, so I hastily closed the window and sat down again with my hands in my lap, trying to appear innocent. I looked up at him, and he shrugged. I wrinkled my nose, and he grinned.

Nicholas was deep in conversation with Lieutenant Izakov. When the noises from outside allowed, I heard snatches of their exchange:

Izakov:	"I will arrange for the body to be removed."
Nicholas:	"No, it is important that we keep her with us and give her a proper burial."
Izakov:	"I understand. I will get a coffin, somehow."
Nicholas:	"Thank you, Boris, you are a good friend."

After a while, following more banging and bumping, accompanied by huffing sounds from the engines, we began moving again, swaying against the points as we shifted to another track. As I watched from the window, I could see the main train puffing away around a bend and down the line towards Siberia and beyond. We had been separated from it, and were now being shunted onto a local line. As it vanished from sight, we began to move.

~ ~ ~

We travelled slowly over wasteland and through thick, gloomy forest. At one time we climbed a steep hill, the engine labouring so that each puff was accompanied by a small surge forwards, like tired footsteps climbing a flight of stairs. At the top, there were a few minutes of slow progress, then the train rushed down the other side with a long, wild whistle.

Soon after that, we crossed a road with a sign that read 'Tobolsk', and began to see buildings on both sides as we entered the city. I felt a hand grab at my heart, a sudden tightness in my chest at the thought that the first part of our journey, and our lives, was nearing its end. As the train slowed to a stop at Tobolsk station I shivered to think what might happen next.

All became busy around our carriage again. We could hear orders being shouted as the soldiers unloaded our possessions and transferred them onto the platform, and other men carried them out to horse-drawn carts lined up outside.

As we watched all the activity through the windows of our coach, Lieutenant Izakov entered with two of his men carrying a coffin. Nicholas nodded and smiled his thanks, and Alexandra crossed the carriage and spoke to him.

Doctor Botkin and Nicholas carefully lifted Luba's body into the coffin, and two soldiers carried it outside. Then, with a gesture of his hand, the lieutenant urged us all to follow. We trailed behind him, rather like a train ourselves, into the ticket hall, where a new escort was waiting for us.

Izakov introduced Nicholas and Alexandra to the officer in charge of the troop. The rest of us held back, but I could hear that this man's name was Captain Pashkov, a handsome man of about fifty, tall and slim, very smart in his grey uniform.

He called us closer. "Welcome to my city. I know you are anxious about your situation, but we will do all we can to make you comfortable and keep you safe. Over there are some vehicles to take you to the Governor's House, which has been prepared for your stay. Your possessions are already loaded, so if you would take your seats we will depart at once."

Outside, our departing guards once more formed a security corridor for us from the station to the waiting vehicles, although there were few people around, and they seemed more curious than hostile. We clambered into carriages and taxi cabs, remembering the last time we had done the same, and our new escort climbed into a brown van. After only a brief pause, Lieutenant Izakov approached the royal couple and saluted them. Then, with a nod to the rest of us, he and his men departed to rejoin the train for the long journey home.

As they turned and marched back to the station, Yuri waved to me, and I nervously waved back; I hoped he would find his family safe, when he arrived home.

The guards' van drove past us, and, one by one, the drivers of our various vehicles flicked the reins and off we all set, followed by a cart filled with our possessions and another carrying Luba's coffin.

The drive from the station to the mansion took about half an hour, so we had an opportunity to see something of the town on our way. Tobolsk was revealed to be a pretty place, with a white city wall, beautiful cathedral, wide, clean streets and smart shops and houses. When we reached it, the Governor's house was a comparatively large building that stood at the edge of the town, surrounded by a recently-erected, stout timber stockade.

Our convoy entered through wide, high wooden gates and stopped.

Stiffly, we poured from the carriages like termites from a hill, and stood, stretching, on the driveway, looking around us. The house was painted white, with a red tile roof and green-painted window frames and shutters. It was a pleasant-looking building, standing only two floors tall, in a simple square shape, like a dolls house, with steps leading to a columned portico.

A small gang of men emerged from the front door, and began to unload the carts, starting with Luba's coffin, which they respectfully lifted down and carried carefully into the house. As they started to work on the cart carrying the cases and trunks and bags, the royal couple was escorted inside by Captain Pashkov to inspect their new home.

~ ~ ~

We congregated into familiar small groups, talking quietly while we waited. I left my hand baggage on the grass beside the paved drive and took a slow walk around the gardens with Rada and Polya. Neat lawns were dotted with irregularly-shaped flower beds, and we discovered an enormous fountain with towering stone creatures, half man, half fish, fighting serpents with water gushing from their mouths. Streams ran from the four sides of the pool, containing large red-and-white fish swimming among water-lilies and reeds.

We heard voices, and saw that Alexandra had returned with Nicholas and Pashkov, so we rejoined them. She was shaking her head.

"It is much too small," she was saying to the officer.

"What do you mean 'too small'?" he demanded, astounded.

"Captain Pashkov," Alexandra began, in the condescending voice she sometimes adopted when negotiating, her German accent becoming more noticeable; she was quite unaware how irritating the effect was on those being addressed. "You know that Nicholas and I are not allowed to sleep together, so two bedrooms will be required for us. Even if my daughters sleep two to a room, that will add two more rooms for them, and there will be one for Aleksey and his companion. Where will my friends and staff sleep? And if, as I assume, you will want some of your men here at all times, there are just not enough rooms in the house for all of us."

He stared at her for a moment, bristling at her tone. "Madam, did you expect a palace? I am sorry, but we have to make do with what we have."

"But it is completely impractical, Captain, we cannot fit all these people into this house."

He looked at a loss, angry at her manner yet unable to counter her logic and unprepared for such a change in plans. Eventually he muttered: "Well, why did you bring so many people?" before, with a frustrated grunt, stamping off with two of his men to try to make alternative arrangements.

While he was gone, I decided to enter the house myself to see what it was like.

I was surprised that, as earlier when the twins and I had wandered around the garden unescorted, no-one seemed to be bothered by my curiosity. After the months under strict supervision at the palace, it felt liberating to be able to wander freely.

Downstairs there were four large living rooms, accessed from a broad, bright entrance hall. One room had a piano, a small table and chairs and a settee. Another was set out with big, leather armchairs and its walls were covered with bookshelves and huge, dark paintings. There was a spacious dining room, plus a bright garden room and a kitchen. Up a wide flight of carpeted stairs rising from the entrance hall, I found five bedrooms and a bathroom, and in the roof there were four smaller rooms which appeared to have been occupied by the governor's staff.

It was a pretty house, spacious, with many nice rooms, but I could see the point that Alexandra had made. There were more than twenty of us in total, and though the family was becoming accustomed to reducing circumstances, I could not imagine them coping with being crammed, along with their staff, into a house that was, after all, no bigger than any one of their individual apartments at the palace.

I returned to wait outside with Rada and Polya. We sat on the grass and chatted until Captain Pashkov returned, then we gathered nearby to hear what was happening. He informed Nicholas and Alexandra, in clipped tones, that the family and their friends could occupy this house, and that another property nearby had been requisitioned for the staff. In a voice that indicated he was retaking command of the situation, he told them to select whoever they wished to stay in the Governor's Mansion, and when she had done so, he ordered the rest of us to follow one of his men to the other house.

Chapter 24 ~ Funeral

We marched behind a sergeant of Captain Pashkov's troop to a small house, one of a row of similar properties on the opposite side of the road that ran past the mansion. Inside, it was cramped, just five small rooms plus a kitchen, for the six of us and however many guards would be on duty at the time.

"My men will have one upstairs room and one downstairs room," we were informed by the sergeant. "That leaves two bedrooms for you. You may go up now and choose where you wish to sleep."

One of his men led, and the six of us followed, forming a winding column up the narrow stairs, at the top of which he indicated the two rooms assigned to us. After examining them, we consulted with Ivan, and, by agreement, Rada, Polya and I selected the room with a double-size bed big enough for the three of us. The other room was slightly larger, but had two single beds, and Ivan had to somehow share it with his assistants.

Our bed seemed clean, and the room, though small, would be adequate. There was a wardrobe, a dressing table and a wash-stand with a neat porcelain bowl and jug. However, though we now had rooms and a bed, there was no bed linen, and we didn't have our clothes or any of our other possessions, apart from our hand-baggage.

Curious to look around, we three girls descended

the stairs. The soldiers seemed to have no interest in us, so we examined the small living room, then the kitchen, which was quite large, with a scrubbed wooden table in the centre, ringed by half a dozen chairs. There was a sink, and various cupboards hugged the walls.

A door from the kitchen took us into the rear garden, which was neatly laid out with rows of fruit and vegetables and pretty flower beds. My heart surged when I saw that there was also a bird-table, and I could hear the sounds of their singing and chattering in the trees all around. I would enjoy getting to know them.

We turned back to the house and retraced our steps along the little path.

"I suppose we will cope here, so long as it is just somewhere to sleep," I said as we joined the boys in the living room.

"Yes, I am sure we will," agreed Rada, "but I cannot think how we will do our duties."

"We will have to manage," said Ivan. "But my first concern is our bedroom; there are only two small beds in there, and I don't intend to share my bed with either of these two," he grinned at his assistants.

Shortly, Captain Pashkov arrived and consulted with his men. In a pause, I asked if I could speak with him.

"What do you want?" he grunted.

"Two things, sir," I said meekly. He was not an intimidating man ~ I had the impression that he was doing his best in a difficult situation ~ but we had no control over our lives, and we needed him on our side. "We have no sheets or blankets for our beds, and our bags with our clothes and possessions are still at the main house. Can we fetch them, please?"

After a moment's thought, he nodded. "Very well. I will arrange for some bedding for you."

He looked past me to the small group of servants who were standing in the narrow hallway.

"All of you, go into the front garden and I will have some of my men to take you across to the house."

"One other thing, please, Captain," Ivan said. "Can you possibly get us another mattress for our room? There are only two small beds for three of us."

"Very well," he replied, "I will see what I can do."

We waited outside the front door for a few minutes in the cool, late-afternoon sun, until three of the Captain's men appeared and escorted us the short distance to the house.

Once we arrived in the spacious entrance hall of the mansion, we searched through the heap of luggage to find our meagre possessions. Tatiana was also there, and I was able to ask what the family wanted us to do. She told me that she was happy for us to get unpacked and settled in, then get to bed, as they could manage without us for the remainder of the day.

Astonishingly, when we were ready to return to the little house, the men assigned to escort us helped to carry my bags, and Polya's and Rada's. It seemed that the atmosphere here was more relaxed than that to which we had become accustomed in and around Alexander Palace, and the men had some traditional manners. I concluded that it may be because the revolution had not yet really reached Tobolsk.

At any rate, we returned to our rooms to find that the Captain had kept his word. There were sheets and blankets for all of us, piled on the beds, and an extra bed had been installed for Ivan and his lads. While we were unpacking our bags in our room, we heard them rearranging their furniture to make the most of the limited space. We carefully hung our clothes in the wardrobe, and made our bed, then the twins and I sat together to talk for a little while. But tiredness soon overcame us and we put on our nighties and crawled between the sheets.

In our precarious position, it was good take comfort from small things. I was happy to be sharing a bed again with my friends; I had missed their warmth at night, and the simple knowledge that we were together was comforting. We clung to each other and were asleep in moments.

~ ~ ~

The family made arrangements for a funeral for Luba at the local church, The Church of The Angel Michael, a beautiful little building, painted blue and white, and with little steeples instead of the usual domes of most Orthodox churches.

Four days after we arrived in Tobolsk, the troops closed off the streets around the church, and we walked up the hill in two groups, the royal family forming one, we mortals following behind in the other. The twins and I entered the church together, each receiving a candle at the door, then stood respectfully silent, waiting for the service to begin.

This was not my first attendance at a funeral, I had endured one or two in Saint Petersburg, though they were normally much grander occasions ~ there was always someone dying in the extended royal family. I didn't accompany them when they travelled abroad to bury a relative in the English or German branches, but had been to a few interminable local interments.

To the sound of a pipe organ playing a dirge, Nicholas, Doctor Botkin, Alexei Trupp and Nagorny effortlessly carried the tiny coffin into the church and set it on a pair of trestles near the altar. When they had taken their places in the congregation, the priest entered, splendid in his long embroidered gown of gold, blue and red, and carrying a lighted candle, followed by chanting acolytes trailing incense. He approached Nicholas and Alexandra and lit their candles from his. They then lit those of their children beside them who, in turn, passed the flame to the people behind them. Row by row, the light was conveyed to the rest of us.

While this was happening, the lid was lifted from Luba's casket, and one of the clergy stood swinging a smoking urn of incense over it.

The priest began to chant prayers and psalms. There was nothing for the rest of us to do except listen and respond when instructed. We were passengers. This was a place for holy men and emperors.

As his voice droned on, I looked past him to the little box containing Luba's remains ~ the bones and flesh that were a vehicle for her while she served her time on Earth. The essence of Luba ~ her personality, her thoughts, the things she did, her loves and hates ~ were not in that box, I knew that much. She had departed her frail, damaged body on the train, and was now in whatever place awaits us after death.

The chanting ended and we shuffled out, past Luba's corpse, one by one, to pay our private respects as it lay in its velvet-lined casket. Some of those ahead of me kissed her face, some barely looked at her as they passed. When it was my turn, I stroked her cheek with the fingers of my right hand. That pretty, sad face was at rest at last, all pain gone. For me, it was as though I was finally doing something useful, saying goodbye to a girl who was not so very different from me and sending her on her way with a final gesture of love.

Afterwards, during the ceremony at the graveside, as the bells rang from the church and Luba's coffin was slowly lowered into the ground, I became aware of Myriam's presence within me, reminding me that she was there. I wondered what that place will prove to be. I felt comforted, though no more confident in my own precarious future.

Diary ~ Monday 22nd October 1917 ~ evening

The leaves on the trees are beginning to turn shades of russet and gold, and the first ones have fallen. It occurs to me that we are like those leaves ~ our glorious summer is at an end, now we are no longer required. Worse, we have become a liability, a burden to be shed. And, once on the ground, are we to be swept into a heap by the new gardener? And what then? Thrown onto the bonfire?

Our lives have become settled and really quite easy. Each day, we cross to the family's house to help them, but it is not arduous. For one thing, the family do not really need much help, now that their stuff is unpacked and put away. They no longer have any official duties, so they are able to pretty much take care of themselves, all we do is clean up behind them. And it hasn't taken us long before we have our little servant's house cleaned up and organised, so that is easier, too. My wounds have healed well, and I am glad to have done away with the last of the bandages.

Surprisingly, our guards are no trouble. We see little of them, and they are always polite to me.

We have been deliberately kept ignorant about events in the outside world, but yesterday evening I overheard Sergeant Malekov reading aloud to the rest of his troop from a newspaper; inevitably it was Pravda, the official propaganda sheet of the Bolsheviks. I listened at the door, and learned that the communists have seized power in Petrograd from Kerensky's Provisional Government, that Lenin is now in control, ruling from his headquarters in Moscow, and that fighting is taking place all over Russia between the Red Army of the revolutionaries and the remnants of the White Army that still support the old order. The news is of much ill-feeling within communities, with widespread killing and destruction, families divided, towns burned and citizens murdered.

When they had finished with the paper, they left it behind, so of course, I read it. I was shocked to learn that the revolution is much closer than I had realised, and that Tobolsk has already been taken by the Bolsheviks without a fight. A 'Urals Soviet' has been created, a regional command, enforced by a cheka, a local army of volunteers.

Chapter 25 ~ Exile

Two days after the funeral, while we were resting in our room, we heard a clattering din downstairs. I ran to the landing and looked down to the hallway, where I saw Captain Pashkov at the front door with some of his men, confronting what appeared to be another troop of soldiers.

One of those men announced that he and his company had come to assume supervision of the prisoners, and I heard Captain Pashkov refusing to hand us over. Cautiously, I descended two steps and sat down to obtain a better view. The spokesman of the group caught sight of the movement and for a brief moment held my gaze. He appeared to be annoyed, and I found his stare deeply unnerving.

"Captain," the stranger said, turning back to Pashkov, "I am Colonel Yakob Mikhailovich Yurovsky, the representative in Tobolsk of the Democratic Socialist Republic of Russia."

He produced a sheet of paper, and handed it to Pashkov.

"This letter is my authority from the new Government in Moscow, and this," he passed over another sheet, "is your instruction to relinquish command. Captain Pashkov, you no longer have any authority in this province."

The men behind Yurovsky did not look like trained, disciplined soldiers, they were for the most part dirty and unshaven. Most were dressed in rough, peasant clothes, but some had new-looking uniforms, consisting of brown tunics, open at the neck and pulled in at the waist with a leather belt, completed by peaked caps bearing a red star emblem, and a pair of black boots.

The Captain was clearly at a loss; his shoulders visibly sagged as I watched. He read the two letters, then handed one back to Yurovsky. "What do you want me to do?" he asked, simply.

Yurovsky nodded, curtly. "I'm glad you see sense, Captain. I would be grateful if you would accompany me to the other house and formally hand over responsibility for your protégés to me."

"Very well," Pashkov grunted. He turned to speak to his sergeant. "Bring down the servants at once."

Sergeant Malekov saluted grimly and turned to stomp up the stairs. I quickly stood, keeping my head down so as not to catch Yurovsky's eye again, and returned to my room to warn the twins.

~ ~ ~

By the afternoon of that day, Captain Pashkov had departed with his men, and the new order had been established. The twins and I were not allowed to see any of the family, we were locked in the downstairs reading room of the mansion, listening to the stamping of feet and shouting of orders, transmitted through the ceiling from upstairs.

That evening, the six of us were escorted across to our lodgings by two fierce guards. We went straight to our rooms. But we were not allowed to rest; one of the men from the new troop, wearing sergeant's stripes on the sleeves of his new, but ill-fitting uniform, threw open our door and told us to follow him. Puzzled, we did as instructed. As we emerged onto the landing, he barged into Ivan's room and shouted at the three men to come out, also. Anxiously, we all followed him down to the kitchen.

"Cook," he said, pointing to some meat and vegetables piled on the table. We looked in amazement at him, then at the food. "Cook!" he shouted, glaring at us with hate in his eyes.

"Now look here," Ivan began, but was halted by the soldier drawing his pistol and placing the muzzle on Ivan's cheek.

"You will cook for the men," he hissed, "or you will be sorry."

Ivan shrugged, and walked to the table, followed by his assistants. They began rummaging in drawers and cupboards for knives and pots.

But that was not all. The sergeant then turned to Rada, Polya and me and indicated a pile of dirty clothes that had been thrown in the corner. "You will wash clothes and clean house," he said.

Angry at his attitude, I glared at him, but received only a belligerent stare in return. We could hardly argue with him, he was the man with the gun, so we set to work. I heard him chuckle as he left the room, and noticed that he had left a guard lounging in the hallway, just outside the door. We found a gas-fired wash-boiler, and began filling it with water and soda crystals, working around Ivan and his boys in the limited space.

After a while, the smell of dinner cooking wafted around the house, and eight soldiers wandered into the kitchen for their meal. They ate carelessly and noisily, talking all the while and dropping food on the table and floor, and when they were done, they stood and abandoned their detritus for us to clean up. All but one departed. He stood guard while the twins and I helped Ivan and his boys wash the dishes and clean up the mess.

Diary ~ Thursday 1st November 1917 ~ evening

If life seemed hard at Alexander Palace under the Provisional Government, it was nothing to the way we are treated now. I have seen pictures of hyenas feeding on the living body of a freshly downed antelope ~ they converge on the helpless creature, pushing their muzzles into its flesh, ripping out chunks of meat, their faces covered with blood, and all the while baying their excitement. At least those animals have the innocence of their wild nature in their defence. The beasts, for they are nothing more, who now hold us captive, cannot be equally acquitted.

I have never been as afraid as I am now. It is eight months since Myriam told me I would be safe 'for a while' and I can't help thinking that my safe time has probably expired. There is a new tension in the air, a full octave higher than anything we have experienced so far. These men are contemptuous of the royals, and only slightly less so toward the servants. They address all of us in shouts, and if we are too slow to respond, they push us, or prod us with their guns to hurry up.

Chapter 26 ~ Imprisoned

Most nights we were awakened after midnight as the men returned drunk from the alehouses of Tobolsk, singing loudly and shouting obscenities at the royal family across the road. Their presence in our servant's house was disturbing, as they were so vulgar and wild. Each morning the place stunk of beer and vomit, and we often had some very unpleasant things to clean up.

But, strangely, our daily lives settled into a simple routine. In the mornings we first cooked breakfast for our guards and cleaned the kitchen, then we crossed the road and spent the day with the family, where some of our time was also devoted to providing for the soldiers there ~ cooking dinner, washing their clothes and cleaning up behind them ~ before returning to slave for the men in our house in the evening.

All pretence of exile had, by then, been dropped, it was made perfectly clear that we were prisoners. Yurovsky had installed himself in one of the bedrooms at the mansion ~ ejecting Catherine Schneider and relocating her in one of the tiny attic rooms ~ and he directed his men from there. During the day we were unable to leave the big house (apart from walking around the garden, under armed escort), and at night we shut ourselves in our rooms as soon as possible, to keep away from the guards.

As winter advanced, conditions of imprisonment became ever more difficult. The peasant guards were intoxicated with their power over the ex-Tsar and his family, and did everything their primitive imaginations could conceive to intimidate them. The sentries around the big house urinated in the gardens and scrawled lewd drawings on the fence to offend the women of the house, and laughed and jeered whenever any member of the family appeared.

Food became a major concern. The soldiers deliberately delayed bringing supplies to the mansion, so that sometimes the family had no food delivered for days, and had to make do with scraps and what vegetables could be harvested from the garden.

When not working, we all tried to find things to do to fill our days as pleasantly as possible, to mark a clear boundary with the hardships of our lives. Some of us read, and I had taken to pouring over my old diary entries, adding to them to begin building the book I was trying to write. There was also the piano, which most of the women could play, including Rada (but not me), so we sometimes had little concerts together. Nicholas and some of the male prisoners continued to play Bezique in another room, constantly watched over by their guards. Alexandra or Olga would sometimes be allowed to join them, if the guard was in a good mood.

~ ~ ~

Alexandra and the girls still wrote to their friends at home. They gave the letters to Yurovsky to post, but we were unsure how many were actually being delivered. I was sure he read all our letters, both outgoing and incoming. Nevertheless, Alexandra did occasionally receive replies, so some mail was clearly passing through the cordon.

I thought often about Frederick ~ heard again in my mind his quiet, sincere voice with its intriguing accent. It may seem strange to say, but though we had only met once, I felt a kind of yearning for his company. In his arms for that one dance I had felt safe, yet desired, a woman, not a girl. We talked, yes, but also much passed between us without words; our eyes were locked together from the first moment he took my hand until he was taken out of my sight, and my heart filled with happiness when I remembered that dance. Keen to hear from him again, and confident that he felt the same, I wrote another letter:

Tuesday 6th November 1917

My Dear Friend

Thank you so much for the photograph, which I was very happy to receive. Now I can keep you close to me, wherever I am. I think about you often, and do hope you are well.

I am sorry it has taken so long before I could write to you. The whole family has been sent into exile, and I have travelled with them. We are now in the Urals, at a little town called Tobolsk, at the foot of the mountains; I can see them towering above us as I sit in the drawing room, writing to you. Conditions here are very different from what we were used to at

Alexander Palace, but we are managing. I do not think we will ever return to Petrograd.

Do not be concerned, because I am well, but we experienced a frightening incident while travelling across Petrograd. Someone fired a gun and killed the driver of our cab. The horse bolted and we crashed. I was only hurt a little, but two of us were killed.

The Feast of St Nicholas is approaching; I wonder how we shall celebrate this year. Do you have Christmas, or something similar? I am sorry to show my ignorance, but I know very little about Sweden.

Well, I am afraid we are even further apart than ever, now, but I hope we shall meet again one day. I think of you very fondly, and look forward to your letters.

With my love, Natalie

The snow became heavy around the beginning of December; the garden was turned into a white desert, and the temperature inside the mansion plunged. We were promised logs, but they did not arrive, so we gathered what wood the men of the household could cut from the bigger trees in the grounds. But even though we managed to light a few fires in the two houses, they were both scarcely above freezing ~ we spent most of our time wearing coats. At night the twins and I huddled together in bed for warmth.

A few weeks passed, and a letter arrived addressed to me. I was briefly excited until I realised that the handwriting was not Frederick's. I opened it, and my eyes went straight to the signature; it was from his mother.

I sat staring at it with tears in my eyes. It was terse and brutal in its dismissal of all that existed between Frederick and me:

Young lady

I am aware that you have been writing to my son, tempting him into a relationship which would be quite inappropriate. I am instructing you to cease this nonsense at once. You are not a suitable companion for him, no more than a common servant girl, and I will not countenance any further contact. If you write to him again, your letters will be destroyed, and I may consider further action against you.

Isabel Froedor

Countess

This harsh letter left me stunned, not so much at her rebuttal, though that was hard enough, but at her distortion of the situation. 'Tempting' him indeed!

For a while after reading it the first time, I was so angry that all kinds of responses came to mind: I considered writing a letter to Frederick, telling him what his mother had written, or one to the Countess, correcting her misinterpretation of the relationship. But I swiftly rejected each idea, and eventually ran out of ways to respond. I would have loved to confront her and tell her to her face what I thought of her, but knew that would never happen.

Eventually, I calmed down, and my anger turned to sadness that I may never see Frederick again, although I had always accepted that it was unlikely, considering my predicament. Thoughts of revenge were lost in frustration at the unfairness of it all and finally into resignation. After all, it was just another example of my impossible life. It was true what she had written, I was 'no more than a servant girl,' for all my dreams of royal blood. It was the station I must accept.

There was no need to keep the letter, so. with a sense of satisfaction, I tore it up, and its envelope, and threw them on the fire ~ at least we could take a little moment of warmth from them. I could not forget it, but I refused to allow that woman to upset me.

Chapter 27 ~ Winter

With the first snows of winter, we busied ourselves preparing to celebrate the feast of Saint Nicholas. No matter how hard things were, Babouschka must still bring gifts for the children, even though those children were now adults. At difficult times like those, it was important to observe rituals ~ they provided a small semblance of normality in a world gone insane.

During the day I often had some quiet, private time, and used it to make little gifts for everyone for the feast day. I made little traditional peasant dolls in different colours for each of the four sisters, from pieces of fabric salvaged from some of my clothes that had been ruined in the crash (washed and ironed, of course). I knitted a bear each for Rada and Polya, with button eyes and a black nose, embroidered handkerchiefs for Nicholas and Alexandra with their initials in the corners, and for Ivan I knitted a scarf and some gloves.

Nicholas and his valet cut down a small tree to serve as a yolka, and the women made decorations for it. It lifted our mood, and we all pitched in, chattering and giggling. No meat is eaten on the eve of the feast, so the four sisters prepared a traditional sparse supper of kutya, which everyone, including all the staff, shared before we crossed the road to our little house.

Then, on the day of the dinner, we all sat together in the chilly garden-room, where our combined body heat soon raised the temperature, and Ivan produced a meal, seemingly from nothing. It was quite unlike the feasts he had created at the palace, when privileged guests from all over Europe would pitch into multiple courses of game and exotic foods from around the world, but in our reduced circumstances it seemed almost as luxurious. Afterwards, we distributed the little gifts we had made for one another, and even had a small glass of wine each from two bottles that Nicholas had kept for the day.

Everyone knew that it was a pretence, that life for all of us would most likely never be normal again, but while there was life, there could still be a little hope. For a few hours, the room was full of laughter and our bellies full of food, and we all retired that evening with cheerful calls of 'goodnight'. I trudged across the road with the others to our little prison, lifted by the pleasantness of the day, but deeply aware that it was no more than an oasis in a deadly desert of oppression.

~ ~ ~

After Christmas, our lives returned to the variety of 'normal' to which we had lately become accustomed. Day followed tense, cold, hopeless day. When the last night of 1917 arrived, we were not allowed to gather to see the transition, so we quietly wished each other well before parting that evening. In all truth, we could hardly celebrate the arrival of a new year, which held only the promise of more hardship and danger, and perhaps worse. So, when we woke the following morning, 1918 felt no different from the year that had just ended.

But, for me, for one reason only, it was a significant year. In different circumstances, this would have been a time for rejoicing, the year I reached adulthood, I would be eighteen. I would not exactly have 'come out', with a great ball, as the duchesses had, because of course my heritage could not be acknowledged, but nevertheless it would be important to me.

On the morning of my birthday ~ as was usual every day ~ my first action after completing our chores for the guards, was to feed my birds. Each evening, I would save any good scraps of food left from the men's dinner, and before doing anything else in the morning, would take them out to the bird table. My little friends had soon learnt to expect my arrival, and would be gathered in the trees and shrubs all around, waiting for their breakfast. That winter was not as bad as the previous one had been, although there were frequent heavy snow storms, and the temperature was perpetually many degrees below zero. But there were periods when it was possible for me to watch them for a little while from a distance as they flocked to the table.

When I had finished taking care of my protégés, I re-entered the house and found that everyone else had already left. Even the guards were gone. I assumed I had been overlooked, so I quickly ran alone across to the mansion.

On my arrival, I was surprised to find that no-one was around, and not a sound could be heard. There was a bored guard in the hallway, half asleep in a chair, but no sign of anyone else. I looked in the kitchen, and through the window into the garden, but without a sign of them. I was about to climb the stairs to look in the bedrooms when Tatiana appeared from the garden room, with a serious expression on her face.

"Nata, I have something important to show you," she said, gravely, beckoning me to follow her into the room. I followed her, curious and somewhat anxious, through the door which she held open for me.

The room was in darkness, with the curtains all closed. I turned to switch on the light, but, at that instant, the curtains were thrown open and there was a great din of voices shouting "Surprise!"

"Happy birthday," said Tatiana's voice behind me, echoed from around the room.

Alexandra stepped forward and kissed me on both cheeks, then, with a smile, handed me a small package wrapped in tissue paper. "This is from Nicholas and me, Natalie. Happy birthday."

I carefully removed the tissue, automatically handing it to Tatiana for re-use, then opened the small blue box within. Inside, sitting on a velvet cushion, was a silver and garnet pendant on a silver chain. I recognised it immediately as one from Alexandra's own collection. The stone was a large deep red rectangle, set in a mount of silver filigree. For a moment I was speechless, it was so unexpected.

"It's lovely," I said emotionally, at last, looking from Alexandra to Nicholas. "Thank you so much. Garnet is my birthstone."

"I know," she said, "that's why we have given it to

you, to symbolise your passage into womanhood."

It was my turn to embrace her, and I also went across to Nicholas and kissed him on both cheeks. I would never have dreamed of such a thing when he was Tsar, and even now I was anxious in case I had gone too far, but he smiled and tenderly took my hand. "Happy birthday, Natalie," he said, warmly. How things had changed in the last twelve months.

But that was not all. One by one, every person in the room came forward and gave me something, a gift or a card. Most were simple things, nearly all handmade, but in our circumstances it showed that every gift came from the heart, and meant more to me than riches.

Eventually, we all settled down to chat and relax; the twins brought tea and cakes from the kitchen, and the men shared a bottle of brandy. For once, we were unsupervised; there was no sentry in the room, just that one bored man in the hallway. Perhaps Alexandra had managed to persuade Yurovsky to allow us some privacy. At any rate, when I look back on that day, I remember how the mood slowly changed, with an inevitability that later seemed ordained, from relaxed to tense, as the conversation drifted to our predicament.

"The revolution will fizzle out. The people need to know that there is the stability of a monarchy to lead them," declared Nicholas with a slur to his voice.

"It seems to me," said Botkin over his spectacles,

"that the citizens are behind the revolution, and it is against the monarchy that they are revolting."

"That is the illusion the Bolsheviks are creating," Nicholas replied, pacing the centre of the room with his brandy glass cupped in his palm. "In truth, it is a few power-hungry men like Lenin who are orchestrating the whole thing."

Alexandra looked unhappy at the way the conversation was going. "I do not think we can achieve anything by arguing about the causes, or what may or may not happen in Moscow. The fact is, we are imprisoned and at their mercy; we can do nothing."

"Perhaps we ourselves are powerless right now, but we have strong families in England and all over the continent, and one day soon they will rescue us. I have heard that, already, soldiers loyal to us are fighting their way here." He swirled the brandy in his glass and downed another swig.

"Nicky, be careful. If you are overheard by the guard there could be serious repercussions."

"Oh, I am fed up with cowering before these peasants, Sunny. Yes, they have the upper hand at the moment, they strut around making life difficult for us, but the tide will turn and then the shoe will be on the other foot." He plonked himself down into one of the big, stuffed leather armchairs.

Despite the tension, or perhaps in an attempt to relieve it, Alexandra grinned. "I think you have somewhat mixed your metaphors there, Nicky dear."

Nicholas was not deterred, and ignored her attempt at levity. "That doesn't matter. I am saying that we must be prepared to be rescued at any time. We should be alert to any signs and must have our most precious possessions ready to take at a moment's notice."

"Nicholas," (we all noticed the change in Alexandra's tone, and her use of his full first name), "this is not the time or place to discuss such things."

"Then when should we discuss it?" he retorted, becoming red in the face and waving his arms. "When our saviours are at the gate?"

She glared at him. "Please do not be belligerent towards me, that was uncalled for."

He jumped to his feet. "What else is left to us but hope of rescue?"

"Nicky, please."

"I've had enough of this." He gulped the last drop of brandy and banged his glass down on the table then stormed from the room.

Alexandra's friend, Catherine Schneider, went over to her and sat beside her. "He will calm down, Alix, then he will be filled with remorse and will apologise to you."

"Trina, I don't want an apology, I want him to see sense. There is no hope of a rescue, he is deluding himself. We are trapped here and I fear we will die here."

Silence fell upon the room, but for the soft sobbing of young Anastasia and the echoes of the words that had been spoken and could never be withdrawn.

Chapter 28 ~ Polina

Life under Yurovsky's *cheka* was tough, but mostly bearable for the servants in the little house, and after a while the security in our dormitory became lax. There seemed to be fewer guards around, and we could come and go almost as we pleased. Usually, one man slouched in the hallway at the front entrance of our house, his rifle propped against the wall, and there was never anyone at the back. After all, if we had wanted to escape, where could we go? We would die from the cold before we could travel very far. And as long as we kept them fed, they paid us little attention, apart from some crude flirting, which we always treated with disdain, to their great amusement. Nevertheless, it was a tense relationship ~ their barbarism was barely restrained ~ and one night everything changed.

It was close to midnight. Rada and I had just retired to our little shared room, and were chatting wearily, waiting for Polya, when we heard a commotion in the corridor outside ~ running footsteps on the bare, wooden stairs and loud sobbing. As we stood up to investigate, Polina burst into the room and threw herself into Rada's arms, in obvious distress.

Rada cast me puzzled look over her sister's shoulder that showed she clearly knew no more than I, and Polina was sobbing hysterically, quite unable to speak. Her dress was torn at the bodice, and, oddly, she had a tea towel knotted loosely around her neck.

"Now, now Polya, dear," Rada whispered tenderly, holding her close and rubbing her back with gentle circular movements. "You are with Nata and me, don't worry."

She guided the helpless girl to the bed, and they sat on the edge, side by side.

Slowly, Polina's breathing settled a little, and between sobs she managed to begin to explain:

"After you came up, I stayed in the kitchen for a while, tidying, putting things away. I was just finishing when one of them came in from the hallway." She stopped again, biting her lip, panting, trying to control the emotions, but unable to continue as she recalled that moment.

I sat on the bed beside them, so that Rada and I were one on each side of Polina, and I put my arm around her waist and a hand on her arm.

Eventually, she was able to resume: "He seemed agitated, I could smell on his breath that he had been drinking, and he began to say suggestive things to me. At first I thought he was just flirting, and I told him to behave. But then he suddenly grabbed my arms and pushed me backwards against the table and started to force his lips onto mine. I kept twisting my head away from him, and he angrily picked up a tea cloth, and quickly twisted it in his hands.

"While he was occupied with that I tried to squirm free, but he flipped the cloth over my head, crossing it over my face, forcing it between my teeth and tying it so that the knot was filling my mouth. Then he began pulling at my clothes, ripping open my blouse, forcing his hands inside and groping at my breasts. He was panting, rasping, like a raging animal, and saying filthy things, calling me a whore, and saying that he wanted 'his share', whatever that meant.

"He turned me around, pushing me down onto the table, so that my face was pressed against the surface, holding me down with one hand, while he lifted my skirt with the other."

She moaned in distress at the memory of that moment, and her lips began to quiver as she tried to hold back the tears.

"I could feel the cold air on my legs, and the roughness of his uniform, scratching against my skin. He was too strong for me, Rada. I could not fight him off, I did try, but he was so strong. And I could not cry out because of the gag in my mouth."

She began to cough, and I jumped up and ran to the washstand, where I poured some water from the jug into a glass and brought it back to her. She accepted it gratefully with shaking hands, and sipped at it, taking deep breaths to try to control her emotions. Rada gently stroked her sister's cheek with her fingers as I sat again beside them, holding one of Polina's hands in mine.

After drinking a little of the water, she continued. "I felt his hand grab at my knickers, and his nails raked my skin as he ripped them away. Oh Rada, I could not stop him, he was like someone possessed, and so strong!" She paused, gasping for breath.

"Oh my poor love," Rada murmured. I looked at her face, it was set like a mask, her anger tightly under control while she tried to console her sister. I, too, felt rage inside me at this beast of a man.

As her breathing settled, Polya resumed. "I felt his hand roughly grasping at my bottom. I tried to press my legs together, but he kicked my feet further apart to open me up, then began to push his fingers inside me. It ... it ... oh God it hurt!"

She paused, panting, but carried on quickly, as though it was important to finish telling, so she could lock the memory away and never have to look at it again.

"For a moment, he stopped, and I thought he was going to leave, but suddenly I felt his penis thrusting into me, and his hips pounding against my bottom. I screamed with the pain, but my voice was stifled by the gag. He stole my virginity, Rada! I can never have a husband now, he has defiled me! It would have been better if he had killed me!"

Her shoulders were jerking as she tried to breathe, and her whole body was shivering. I felt helpless in the face of her misery. I sent an angry message to Myriam: *why Polya, the gentlest, most innocent person I know? Why?*

After another sip of her water, she inhaled a deep breath, and when her lungs were full, slowly let it out again.

Then, with a tearful look at each of us, said quietly: "As though that were not bad enough, when he was done, he started swearing and laughing and saying dreadful things about me. I felt his weight lift off me, but before I could run, he grabbed my hair and hauled me across the kitchen, towards the door. I tried to keep my feet, but my legs would not support me, and I stumbled and fell to the floor. He tried to drag me by my hair, but I held onto a leg of the table, and he gave up. He stood over me, looking down with disgust on his face and vile, filthy words pouring from his mouth, then he started to kick me. I rolled into a ball to protect myself, and he eventually stopped and walked off."

Again she sunk into sobs and violent shivering. Rada gently stroked her hair and whispered softly to her, wiping her sister's eyes and face with her own skirt, even though tears were also pouring down her own cheeks.

"We must tell Alix," I said, angrily. "He cannot be allowed to get away with such a terrible thing, even in our current situation. Surely she will speak up for us."

"Alexandra has no power, Natalie dear," Rada answered through tight lips. "And if she dared to speak out, which I am sure she would, she could make her own situation even worse."

I had to agree, we could not add to her already heavy burden. "Then I will confront Yurovsky myself," I said, more boldly than I felt.

"No," said Rada, quickly. "You know that they will not deal with it. They are all men together, we mean nothing to them. We must take care of this ourselves."

I nodded, she was right, though it seemed impossible that we could achieve anything.

"But what am I going to do?" Polina wailed. "He will tell everyone and I will be disgraced."

"No!" said Rada, a certainty in her voice that I did

not feel at that moment. "He will not. Don't you worry, little sister, you will suffer no more from that beast." She wrapped her arms around the shivering girl, and held her close. "Polya, tell me, which one of the men was it that did this thing?"

"I do not know his name. He has a scar here, across his mouth."

"Ah yes," said Rada, pensively, "I know the one; he is tall, but rather overweight?" She looked at me as she said it, and I nodded; I knew the man.

"Yes, that's the one," Polya whispered.

Rada put both her arms around her sister and held her tightly. "Very well, dear one, do not worry, you are safe now, with Natalie and me. Nothing more will harm you, I promise."

Polina was clearly exhausted, and, as she relaxed in our company, so her eyes became heavy.

We helped her to get ready for bed and tucked her in, kissed her lightly on her cheek and whispered "goodnight," then sat quietly beside her until her breathing became soft and rhythmic. She was asleep.

Chapter 29 ~ Retribution

Rada turned to me and tilted her head slightly. Somehow I knew what she was thinking, and it sent a cold shiver through my body. It was crazy, impossible, yet it had to be done. "Now?" I asked.

"Yes," she whispered, grimly. "No time must be lost. But we will need disguises, in case we are seen."

"Uniforms," I said, simply. "From the guards room."

She nodded.

We slipped silently out of our bedroom into the corridor, where we paused and listened. There was not a sound in the house. Either the guard on duty on the landing was asleep, or he had gone with his friends to the tavern.

The third room on the landing was the one used by the guards, and we knew from our cleaning duties that some spare uniforms were kept there, hanging in a closet. The door was ajar, and I carefully, soundlessly, pushed it open enough to peer in. The room was empty. I turned to Rada and beckoned with a twist of my head, and together we entered.

Wordlessly, we quickly grabbed some trousers each and put them on, then a greatcoat. We checked each other over. Rada's hair was short, and presented no problems, but mine was too long, and had to be tied up and stuffed into a cap. Finally we picked up some socks and boots and, carrying them, tiptoed past Ivan's room, past our own, where Polya slept, down the stairs and along the hallway to the kitchen.

There, we each took a knife from the drawer and wrapped it in a towel. This was the moment at which it all became suddenly, frighteningly, real. But it was not the time for second thoughts, with our weapons hidden under our greatcoats, we hurried to the front door and looked out.

All was quiet. The night air had a smoky smell to it, mixed with the heavy dampness of a mountain mist. Mounds of snow persisted against walls and hedges, though there had been no fresh falls for a week or so. We sat on the step, putting the socks and heavy boots on; they were too big, of course, but essential if we were to pass the casual glances of anyone we may meet.

Rada pointed down the hill. "That's the direction I see them go every evening," she whispered in a cloud of steamy breath. We set off, clumping uncomfortably, trying to look like soldiers heading for a night's drinking.

~ ~ ~

The tavern proved to be just a couple of streets away, about ten minutes walking. We found it by following the sound of bawdy singing and the sickly, acidic smell of large amounts of beer. As we approached it, the door was suddenly opened from the inside, and light sliced across the pavement ahead of us, spit by the shadow of someone about to leave. We slipped into a passageway that ran beside the building, where the smell was even worse, and we tried not to breathe as we groped our way into the darkest corner.

The silhouette of a man appeared in the half-light at the street end of the alley. He took a few lurching steps towards us, and I feared that he had seen us, but he stopped and turned to face the wall, groping in his trousers for his penis. He stood there for what felt like an eternity, steam rising from the wall and around his feet, made into a luminous cloud by the glow from a gas lamp outside. Eventually he was done, and after fiddling again with his fly, set off to resume his drinking.

"Would you recognise the man we are looking for?" Rada whispered, when he had disappeared around the corner.

"Oh yes, without a doubt," I replied tensely.

"Right," she hissed. "You hide across the street and watch for him; I will stay here. When he staggers out for a pee, you come back, and we will have him cornered."

I gave her a quick hug, then walked nervously to the entrance, stepping carefully around the still-steaming puddle. At the opening, I paused to check that no-one was in sight before hurrying across the road and blending into the shadows opposite, where I could see the tavern without being observed. Then the wait began.

Several times the door opened, and I tensed, but each time it was the wrong man. They all went to the alley to relieve themselves, then returned to continue drinking. Poor Rada must have been suffocating in the stink of their urine. As the men emerged onto the street, I noticed that they did not bother to put on their coats, nearly all were wearing only their trousers and shirts in the cold night air; it was probably hot inside. I was shivering in my greatcoat, but perhaps that was from fear.

Then, with a surge of anticipation, I recognised the man we sought, as he almost fell out of the door and blundered along the front of the tavern towards the alley, steadying himself against the wall with a hand. When he turned into the black hole of the passage, I hurried across the road towards his disappearing back, the big boots slopping awkwardly on my feet.

As I entered the passageway, he was already peeing, and his head came up when I blocked the light. "Oh, hello, comrade," he slurred. "Here, there's room for another," and laughed.

I caught a slight movement behind him as Rada moved into position. With my heart thumping, I drew the knife from under my coat, holding the handle with the towel, twisting it in the air between us, so it glinted in the pale light.

"Hello, comrade," I said, and heard a surprised intake of breath when he saw the weapon and heard my female voice. Then all the air in his lungs was suddenly expelled in a gasp of pain as Rada plunged her knife into his back.

The pounding of my heart in my chest was like machine-gun fire, and I was panting. I knew that it was adrenalin, from the anger and fear, but there was something else: a realisation that this was the moment

I left my past behind and took responsibility for my life.

"Did you feel like a man, when you raped my friend?" I hissed, stepping closer, my face inches from his. I saw his eyes, white in the shadows, bulging with pain and terror, his mouth moving, wordlessly, his arms moving sporadically. "Not feeling so brave now, are you?" I said, thrusting my knife upwards through his belly and into his chest, watching dispassionately as he doubled over and slumped to the ground, his last breath bubbling from his mouth.

Until that moment, I was not sure that I could do it ~ kill a man ~ but anger gave strength to the arm that drove the knife home, and hate for all that he represented dissolved any misgivings I may have felt. And then, from that moment, there was no time to waste on satisfaction, or any soul-searching at what I had just done; we must escape. I stood for a few seconds, carefully wrapping the dripping knife in the towel, as Rada stepped over his body to join me, then we hurried to the end of the alley to begin our flight back to Polina.

Expecting to hear an outcry at any moment, we walked briskly to the end of the road and turned towards the hill leading to our house. Though every second was precious, I had to get rid of my weapon, and I paused to quickly dig a shallow hole behind the garden wall of a house, using the blade as a trowel, then threw the knife in and pushed the soil back with my boot, finally treading it down firmly.

"Damn!" Rada swore quietly, "I left mine in his

back."

"Well there's no going back for it," I whispered, feeling a nervous giggle rising in my voice.

We hurried on, seeing the familiar palisade of the mansion up the hill ahead. A small stream ran beneath the road, and I tossed the blood-soaked towel from the bridge into the blackness of its rushing waters, seeing it vanish quickly. We knelt to wash our hands, in case any blood was on them, then pressed on up the hill.

Minutes later, we were slipping our boots off at the door of our house, and hurrying quietly inside. There was still no sign of anyone. In the guard's room, we removed the uniforms and carefully hung them back in the closet, hiding the muddy boots on the floor at the back. Then we tiptoed into our room and closed the door behind us.

I never expected to be so glad to see that tiny room. Rada and I looked at each other and smiled, nervously, then hugged. I had been aware of shivering the whole time, and I could feel that she was shaking too, but we had succeeded, we had avenged our sister and had prevented her assailant from gloating to his friends about his filthy deed. We held each other tightly for a little longer, then undressed and climbed into bed. Polya was still sleeping peacefully, blissfully unaware of what had just transpired.

Chapter 30 ~ Reaction

After a short and restless night, we were woken before dawn the next morning by an uproar all over the house. Gruff, angry, male voices shouting, orders being given, a slamming of doors and the drumming of many boots on bare floorboards and stairs. Very shortly, one of the soldiers threw open our door.

"Downstairs, now!" he barked, grabbing Rada, who was nearest to him, by the arm and pushing her out of the door. Obediently, with apprehensive glances between us, we followed him down, still in our nightclothes.

In the kitchen, we found Ivan and his lads, plus Yurovsky, the chief of the *cheka*, and some of his men. Yurovsky was not a huge man ~ with his thick, curly brown hair and pointed beard he looked more like an intellectual ~ but his face was red, and he was clearly furious, making him unpredictable and frightening. He was wearing his brown uniform tunic, pulled in at the waist with a leather belt, into the front of which he had thrust a revolver.

"What do you know of this?" he demanded, pointing to a bloody knife on the bare, wooden table and sweeping us with an intense glare. It was, of course, the one Rada had taken, a chef's knife, large and pointed, one that Ivan and his assistants used every day for preparing food. We stared at it in silence. Of course, the others had no idea of the significance of it. "Well?" he shouted, raising his arms and glaring at us.

No-one was inclined to say anything, but one of the soldiers poked me in the back, pushing me forwards a step. Thrust into the limelight, I was forced speak. "Is it a kitchen knife?" I asked, shivering, aware that one wrong word could mean death.

"Of course it's a fucking kitchen knife, you stupid girl!" Yurovsky screamed, spluttering and waving his hands in exasperation. "It is also a murder weapon. This morning we found it in the back of one of our comrades, lying dead in an alley. What do you know about that?"

"Nothing, sir" I muttered, querulously, my head lowered, accompanied by similar sounds from the others.

"Well, someone does," he said, "and I intend to find out who." He turned to the two soldiers with him, while simultaneously pointing at us. "Take them to work!" he shouted. As we were about to leave, he added: "I will speak to each of you when you return tonight. Be under no illusions, I intend to find out who did this, and that person will be punished. The penalty for murder of a serving soldier is immediate execution by firing squad."

And so we were pushed from the kitchen at gunpoint and escorted, first upstairs to dress, then across the road to join the family for our day's duties. There we found that security was heightened, the soldiers were irritable, and the royals were rarely without a guard, but in one solitary moment, I asked

Tatiana if she had heard anything about the killing.

"Yes," she whispered. "It was like a fox had been loosed in a hen-house here early this morning; everyone has been interrogated. Apparently, some of the soldiers went out drinking last night, and one was found later, behind the inn, with his penis out of his trousers, lying dead in a pool of urine and blood." She hesitated, looked around, and smiled wryly, "I can't think of a better end for him, and all the rest of them."

Despite the situation, I had to grin, but quickly suppressed it as her guard returned.

Most of my work at the Governor's house had, by then, become more domestic than in the last year, like washing and ironing clothes, but I didn't mind ~ I had started as a lowly maid, and much of it was familiar to me. Sometimes, as that day, there may be needlework to do, altering and mending clothes or curtains; I always enjoyed that, and the time did not drag. I saw the twins once or twice, but could not find a chance to be alone with either of them.

And so the day passed, amidst even more intense scrutiny from the wary and watchful guards, with their filthy hands and faces and their stink of stale beer and body odour. Then, as evening fell, we were marched back to the servant's house. My heart was pounding as I anticipated the interrogation to come. I had to be on my guard not to let slip anything incriminating. I stole a quick glance at Rada, who looked as tense as me. We had to wait together in silence in the little living room, watched by two scowling thugs, then were dragged, one by one, into the kitchen.

Polina was taken through first, then Rada. Once called, no-one returned to the room; I hoped it was not a bad sign. It was my turn next, leaving Ivan and his boys till last. The soldier who accompanied me gripped my arm tightly with one big hand, and roughly shoved me through the kitchen door. I stumbled, and, as I recovered, I saw Yurovsky sitting at the table, waiting to quiz me, with the knife, still coated with dried blood, before him. He indicated with his hand that I should stand on the opposite side of the table, so I obediently took position facing him.

He began to fire questions at me, and I tried to act innocently, as I would if I were not really the guilty party he was seeking. No, I did not know for sure if I had seen that knife before. Yes, I had seen similar knives in that kitchen. No, I did not know if any were missing. No, I did not kill the soldier.

Actually, I snorted rather convincingly when he asked that question, and answered before I had thought about what I was saying. Did he think that I, a young girl, could manage to slip out of the guarded house and kill one of these huge men, then sneak back in again without being caught? It was preposterous, I said, and although he shouted at me to be more respectful, I think he agreed, because he did not press the point.

He glared at me for a moment, then became sly. "This chef of yours, he's a big strong man, wouldn't you say?" he said, almost casually.

"Ivan? Well, yes, I suppose he is," I answered, puzzled at the sudden change.

"And good with a knife?"

"Oh," I said, realisation dawning, "I see where you are leading me. Of course he is very skilful, but he would never harm anyone, he's the gentlest man I know."

"Nevertheless, he could have done it. At the moment he is my prime suspect, and you could make life easier for yourself and everyone else if you tell me what you know."

I was shaking my head. "No, it's just not possible. What motive could he have? And when could he have done it?"

"Ah, you know about motive and opportunity," he grinned. "A detective, are you?"

"No," I retorted, "but I read a lot."

"Well, let me tell you something, Miss Well-educated Lady's Maid: friends of the murdered man have told me that he was bragging that one of you girls seduced him. What do you have to say about that, hah? Was it you? Perhaps your chef was jealous, or defending your honour!" He laughed out loud.

So, the man had been talking, lying, but it seemed that he had not said which of us it was. After a moment's thought, I said, very carefully: "Captain, he was fantasising. I can assure you that none of us would want to have sex with any of your men."

"Oh," he grunted, still chuckling, "and why not?"

"Because they are ugly, arrogant, ignorant, violent and smelly," I answered, vehemently.

His face became shrewd. "Too good for honest working men, are you, Miss Lady's Maid?"

That touched a nerve. I do not consider myself

above anyone, I was just repulsed by the crudity of these rebels. Before I could stop myself, I retaliated: "Not all of them, only those I have met so far!"

I bit my lip, scared I may have angered him, but he just laughed again. "Well, we don't get to choose who volunteers for the *cheka*," he said, surprisingly. Then he leaned forward, his elbows on the table on either side of the murder weapon, his hands clasped under his chin, and fixed me with a stare. "Who do you think committed the dreadful dead, then, Miss Detective Lady's Maid?" A smirk lingered on his lips.

I could tell he was trying to antagonise me into letting something slip, and the realisation helped me to relax a little. He was blundering in the dark. He had no idea, and no clues. "A jealous husband, perhaps?" I answered, "or one of his colleagues? Someone he owed money to? I really have no idea, Colonel."

He stared at me for a long minute, then, with a twist of his head towards the door, suddenly ended the interview, saying: "That's enough for now. Go to your room." I lowered my head to hide my relief, curtseyed, and scurried out of the kitchen to join my friends.

"Anyone would think he was a saint, the way Yurovsky is going on," Polina said as I entered our room and threw myself onto the bed.

"It was no less than he deserved," added Rada.

I smiled nervously at them both. By common, unspoken consent, we did not talk about it in the house, but I knew that, of course, Rada would have briefed Polya during the day, and it was with a thrill that I thought once again about what we had done.

Somehow, she and I had slipped from the house undetected, avenged her sister, and returned, leaving not a trace of evidence by which we could be linked to the man's murder ~ no bloodstained clothes or skin, and no witnesses. I did not feel satisfaction, because I would never be able to reconcile my actions with my conscience, but neither could my sense of justice have allowed me to let his attack on an innocent girl go unpunished. Since he and his friends chose to live by violence, it was appropriate that he should meet a violent end. The only remorse I felt was that I had compromised my own standards.

And these thoughts did not leave me when we slipped into bed. I lay awake, listening to the gentle breathing of the two people I loved most, while I replayed my interrogation again in my head, checking for any slip-ups. One by one, I heard the three men arrive in the next room from their interrogations, then some activity downstairs and voices outside. Eventually the house settled down, and in the silence that ensued I must have finally fallen asleep, because suddenly, unexpectedly, it was time to get up again.

I joined Ivan and the boys in the kitchen, where they were preparing breakfasts, and when they turned to greet me, I was stunned to see that they all had bruises and cuts on their faces. "Oh no," I exclaimed, "did they beat you?"

All three nodded. "Yes," said Ivan through puffed lips, "they seem to think I am their murderer, and that my friends are hiding the truth from him." He tried to smile, but the pain twisted his face.

"I'm so sorry," I said, hugging each of them.

"They searched our room, yesterday, while we were at work," Ivan revealed. "It looked like Crimea after the Cossacks had ridden through."

"Well, you know you have nothing to hide," I said. "Though no doubt they will make all our lives unbearable while they try to find out who did it." I shivered as I thought of what they were capable of doing if they discovered it was Rada and me.

Chapter 31 ~ Rescue

For a week or so, the house and mansion were like a termite's hill after being poked with a stick, and Yurovsky made everyone's lives as difficult as possible. But despite his determination to track down the killer, he was unable to find any evidence to solve the mystery of his murdered henchman, and he eventually gave up trying. It seemed likely to me that he may have decided that the assassin could perhaps have been one of the townspeople, a jealous husband, as I had suggested.

And he had other things on his mind. Life was becoming harder for all of us by the day, as food supplies dwindled still further, and the winter dragged on through March and into April. If our plight had seemed tough before, now it was desperate ~ it had become a matter of survival. It was no longer the case that any of us were being denied supplies, because conditions were now obviously just as bad for the guards. There were few provisions to be obtained in the town, and no edible vegetables left in the gardens. We salvaged every scrap, wasting nothing, even picking up any wild creatures we found, killed by the harsh weather. Mouldy vegetables and evil-smelling meat were carefully cleaned, trimmed and cooked with herbs and spices to make them palatable. All of us ~ the guards, the family and the servants ~ were losing weight. Our faces were drawn and our clothes hung like sacks on our bodies. Colds were commonplace and we all became weak, but, as far as I could tell, all survived.

There was rarely much left that I could salvage for the birds, though I always tried to take something for them ~ it was my only remaining pleasure. No-one was officially allowed in the garden without escort, but the soldiers were reluctant to venture outside unless necessary, and I spent as much time alone in the little patch behind the servant's house as possible, watching and drawing all the little feathered visitors, with a guard peering at me from the relative warmth of the kitchen. I could not stay out there for long, as my fingers became numb with the cold, but I enjoyed that rare private time.

April passed into May, then crept into June, and gradually the weather began to improve, food supplies became slightly better and our health and mood improved.

~ ~ ~

In early June, whilst in the garden, I began to hear the sounds of distant explosions. The following day, it seemed to me that it was becoming nearer and, at around dawn the morning after that, as we were getting dressed, we were startled by intense exchanges of gunfire not far away. I was about to look out of our window when one of the jailers burst into my room, a pistol in his hand. "Come!" he shouted, waving his free hand in a sweeping motion.

The twins and I ran to the door and followed him

through to the middle room, Ivan's room. "What is happening?" I asked the guard.

"Fighting," he replied, "very close; it is very dangerous." He remained to guard us, but we heard the rest of the men clattering out of the front door.

After that it became extremely noisy, not only with gunfire, but also the roar of heavy machinery and the thuds of nearby explosions. The sounds of battle drew so close that we knew the fight was happening right outside, and suddenly the front of house was showered with machine-gun fire. I heard the window shatter and bullets ricocheting around the walls of our room. We all crouched on the floor, but thankfully no shots reached the room where we were and, eventually, the conflict outside faded into the distance.

We breathed sighs of relief that we were safe. Even so, we were held under guard for much of that day until, about the middle of the afternoon, we were ordered out and escorted across to the Governor's mansion.

There were signs of battle everywhere. The heavy wooden gates had been demolished, smashed aside like paper toys. Most of the windows in the house were broken, lines of bullet-holes were sprayed across the walls, and the front door had been battered down. There was a row of dead bodies lined up on the lawn, the snow around them stained with blood.

We were gathered in the entrance hall and addressed by Yurovsky, who paced up and down before us, his boots crunching on the broken glass. He looked extremely tense and drawn.

"You see all this?" he spat, gesticulating. "As we expected, the Whites attempted a rescue; they circled the town and attacked from the west, the side we were least able to defend. My men resisted gallantly, and killed many of them, but we also lost some good and loyal friends. The rest of the Whites escaped, taking with them some of the blood-sucking family. But I promise you, they will not get far."

I did not know how to feel. Part of me was glad that something had at last happened, but without knowing who had escaped and who remained, it was just an event ~ significant, yes, but I had no way of knowing how it affected me, or the others. Yurovsky had also omitted to mention whether or not any of the family had been hurt, or even killed, in the attack, and I was certainly not going to speak up and ask him.

"My men will be busy burying the dead," he continued, "and now that I have fewer of them, I cannot be bothered with providing security in two houses for the bitches who remain. Therefore, you servants will all gather your personal possessions from across the road and will move in here for the night. Then you and the bitches will decide amongst yourselves which of you wish to return home, and I will arrange to put you on a train. I do not want more than ten people left in this house after tomorrow, including the bitches. Do you all understand?"

We nodded and muttered, and were escorted back across the road to collect our things.

Three times he had used the word 'bitches'. I knew he was referring to the duchesses, or some of them.

Did it mean that Nicholas had been rescued? Perhaps also Aleksey?

~ ~ ~

When we returned to the mansion from our little house, laden with our bags, a carpenter was already at work repairing the front doors, and soldiers were loading the dead bodies onto a cart, its skin-and-bone horse snorting and stamping and giving off clouds of steam in the cool evening air.

Our guards took us upstairs and into one of the bedrooms, where we found a small group huddled together. Tatiana was there, and Aleksey. I also saw Doctor Botkin with his son and daughter. Anna Demidova was also there, as were Pierre Guillard, Alexandra's two friends and Alexei Trupp. The doctor was attending to Aleksey, who was laying on a couch.

Their heads raised as we entered, and Tatiana immediately came over and hugged me. I was surprised, but pleased that she was so glad to see me, and it's true that I was also relieved to see her safe. I noticed that she had been hurt, and had a rough, blood-stained bandage on her upper arm. That became my first concern. "What happened there?" I asked, pointing to the wound.

"It's nothing," she shrugged. "I tried to push past a guard to get to my parents, and cut myself on his bayonet."

"Your parents, are they alright?"

"I'm not sure," she said, her face downcast. "The rescue seemed to be well planned, and I saw

Lieutenant Izakov amongst them, so I suspect he helped to organise it. They took papa and mama and my sisters. They tried to reach me and Aleksey, but the guards fought them off. I don't know what happened to them after that. Why are you here?"

I pointed to my things, which I had dropped when she embraced me. "We are to move in here with you tonight," I explained. "Then tomorrow, some of us will be sent home."

"That settles it," she said at once. "You must leave while you can. I do not want any of you to remain here, risking your lives. Aleksey and I have no choice, but this is your chance to get away."

"Well, we will see ..." I began.

"No we won't," she interrupted. "I will not hear it. You are going, and that's final."

"All right," I conceded. "But we need somewhere to sleep tonight; will you show me which room the twins and I could have? And the boys, too, will need beds."

As we carried our things into the room which had been Olga's, Tatiana revealed to me that Nagorny had been killed in the battle. "He tried to snatch a gun from one of the guards who were keeping Aleksey and me in Aleksey's room, and one of the others shot him at point-blank range. Then they threw his body out onto the landing."

Poor Nagorny, loyal and brave, had given his life for Aleksey. How many more would die before this dreadful time was over?

Chapter 32 ~ Captivity

At dawn the next morning, I made my way to Tatiana's room, feeling strange that my old routine had decided to assert itself, though now it was by choice. As soon as I arrived, I noticed that her face was white and drawn, and she was unsteady on her feet. I insisted on checking her wounded arm and, when I took off her bandage, I could see that it was not the trivial wound she had made it out to be. The padding was soaked with blood, and fresh blood poured out of a huge gash as soon as I removed the protection. I quickly pressed the wound closed, as she had taught me, and asked Rada to find the doctor, who came at once.

He cleaned the wound and applied stitches to close it over, before wrapping a clean dressing around it. As he did so, he scolded her. "You told me it was a scratch!"

"I didn't realise it was so bad," she said, humbly.

As the day progressed, she became delirious, and was crying out with the pain, so I ordered her to bed. The doctor gave her a drop of his magic syrup, then, with a shrug, showed me the bottle, which was nearly empty. He frowned at Tatiana. "The wound is infected. It was a dirty cut, and left unattended for too long. You should have told me."

Turning from his patient, he said to me: "She has a fever, and must stay in bed for a few days, Natalie. She will need constant care."

"Yes, doctor. I will stay and look after her."

"No!" she cried, weakly, but it was my turn to be adamant, and I enjoyed my moment of power.

"I am your nurse, now, madam, and you will do as I tell you," I said sternly, unable to suppress a wicked grin.

~ ~ ~

Soon after this, Yurovsky arrived at the house and called us all together in the entrance hall again. "Well, who is going and who is staying?" he demanded, peremptorily. "Stand over here if you are leaving."

The doctor pushed his son and daughter towards Yurovsky. "These two can return home," he said, with finality. It was clear they did not wish to leave him, but he had evidently decided it was best for them.

I had discussed the matter with the twins the previous evening, and we three had decided to leave together, but my discovery of Tatiana's illness meant that I could not go. Nevertheless, I nodded to them when they looked enquiringly at me, and was relieved when they crossed to stand with the others.

Alexandra's friends, Anastasia Hendrikova and Catherine Schneider, also joined those electing to return home, as did Guillard and Ivan's two assistants.

"Is that all who are going?" Yurovsky demanded, glaring at the seven of us remaining. "Right, before I take you to the station, I have some news for you all. Your precious royal family has been recaptured." He looked around the room with a smirk. "I told you they would not get far."

"Are they alive?" asked Anna Demidova.

"I don't know why I should tell you that," he replied brusquely, "but, yes, they are all alive, which is more than can be said for the pathetic band of children and old men who were sent to rescue them; they are all dead, including the officer leading them. They were ambushed near Yekaterinburg, and your former employers are now being held there by my good friend Alexander Avadeyev of the Urals Soviet."

So poor Lieutenant Ivanov had died trying to rescue his friend. I was saddened at the news; he was a good man.

Anna broke into his gloating. "Then may I be allowed to join them? My place is with my mistress."

Yurovsky was clearly amazed, and lost for words for a moment. Finally he found his voice. "Are you mad, woman?" He stared at her for several seconds, but she held his gaze and, when she did not answer, he said: "As you wish; I can arrange it. God! You people! Right, get your possessions and join these others here."

She walked quickly off towards the stairs, and he turned to the small crowd in which stood my two best friends. "Do you all have your luggage ready? Right, get it and wait outside for me."

He turned back to us, six now, looking up and down our pathetic little line. "I don't understand it; why are you staying?"

When no-one answered, he pointed to Alexei Trupp, a young man I had never given much thought to before. He was always with Nicholas, and we had scarcely exchanged more than a dozen words in all my time with the family. "You, why are you staying?"

Trupp shuffled nervously, and spoke with his chin in his chest. "I am an orphan, sir, I have no family but this one, no home to go to. The Tsar is like a father to me."

Yurovsky bristled visibly. "He is not the Tsar!" he shouted. "You must forget all that old nonsense. The people run their own affairs now, we don't need a self-appointed ruler to live in luxury while we starve. If he means so much to you, why do you not join him like that mad woman?" He waved his arm towards the stairs where Anna had just disappeared.

Quietly, so softly that I hardly heard him, Alexei said: "Yes, please."

"What?" screeched Yurovsky, "I can't believe what I'm hearing! You want to risk your life for those bloodsuckers?"

Alexei nodded, but said no more.

In the long silence that followed, I saw myself for the first time. I had been resentful all my life, feeling deprived, angry at the injustice of it, thinking I was the only one, when all the time this young man had been content with what he had. How many others were stoically facing their problems, each overcoming their personal challenges and carving new lives? I felt ashamed and humbled.

Eventually, Yurovsky grunted and waved his arm towards the stairs. "All right, get your things. And the rest of you, go to your rooms and stay there until your friends have left."

Alexei ran ahead, a smile on his lips, and the rest of

us followed more soberly. I waved nervously to Rada and Polina, who waved back, then I returned upstairs to take care of Tatiana.

The twins and I had talked long into the night about whether to stay or go, and I was, at that time, sure that we should all leave. But that was before I discovered the true state of Tatiana's health. Our original plan had been to stay together and go to Azov, the town where they had been born, to start a new life together, somehow. I hoped they would still do that, and perhaps I could join them later.

I watched from an upstairs window as the cart took them off to the station. I was still standing there, lost in tearful memories, long after they had disappeared from sight.

Across the road, workmen were replacing the windows of the little house that had been my home since we arrived in Tobolsk. I wondered where the Kornilov family had been staying while their home was occupied, and what they would think of the mess they would find on their return.

~ ~ ~

Nothing much happened for a few days. Those of us left behind ~ Ivan, Tatiana, Dr Botkin, Aleksey and I ~ made do as best we could, and apart from two sentries on the gates, we were left alone by the soldiers. The weather was beginning to break; the remaining snow that lingered in sheltered corners was melting, and green shoots had begun to appear on the trees. Food was not quite such a problem as it had been, as there were fewer of us to feed. It felt like luxury to eat a full meal occasionally, as we had all become accustomed to being frugal with everything.

Tatiana's health slowly improved, and I was pleased to see that her wound was closing up nicely, though still oozing horrible yellow stuff.

While she was incapacitated, it fell to me to act as nurse and maid to Aleksey, also. In truth, he required little real care ~ he had been unhurt in the skirmish to rescue him and his health was as good as any of us ~ but that did not prevent him from expecting ~ demanding ~ attention.

After checking Tatiana, I entered Aleksey's room. He was sitting at his desk, writing.

"You're late," he grumbled.

I ignored him, and placed his breakfast on the table.

"In future, you are to come to me first," he said over his shoulder.

I crossed the room to sit in an armchair near his desk, facing him. "Aleksey," I began.

"Stand in my presence," he demanded, hotly. "And you will address me as 'Sir'." This from a boy scarcely fourteen years old.

"No," I answered, mildly.

Bristling, he leapt to his feet and took a step towards me, raising his hand, as though to strike me. I stood up and glared at him, and he hastily dropped the hand. But I did not stay; I turned my back on him and walked to the door.

"Come back here!" he shouted.

"Learn some manners," I replied as I closed the

door behind me.

Later, when I returned to collect the breakfast tray, I found him in bed.

"You are insolent," was his greeting.

I stood at the foot of his bed, with a hand on my hip in a deliberately insolent pose. "Your sisters know how to treat me with respect," I said calmly. "So do your parents. And in return, they get respect from me. I am only here because Tatiana is my friend and needs me. You are not my master, Aleksey, and the sooner you accept that the better we will get along."

"Get out!" he spat.

I shrugged, picked up the tray and left.

~ ~ ~

A few more days passed. Then, one afternoon, with only one hour's warning, we were called together and informed by Yurovsky that we were to be moved again, to rejoin the rest of the household in Yekaterinburg. Our little party of five was loaded like cattle into a cart and driven to the railway station. There we found a small train waiting, consisting of a grubby little engine and a single carriage. Inside, it was a simple affair, with six rows of four seats across ~ three facing the front, and three the back ~ and space at the front and back for luggage. We had few bags, having been restricted to what we could carry ourselves, so we were quickly settled on board, accompanied by a single guard.

I was nervous. Each stage of our captivity had signalled tougher times and more danger, and I could not imagine that life was going to become better; most likely it would be worse. Still, it was good to be travelling through the countryside again. Russia's road system was primitive, and transportation slow, which is why the railways were such a major component of travel, and I found the whole process of speeding through open fields and forests exciting.

As we rumbled along, I found myself studying our two guards, idly wondering if it would be possible to overpower them. One of them saw me looking, and glowered, menacingly. I turned my head away and, instead, watched through the windows as we passed tiny hamlets and farms, enjoying the sight of nature in the wild. It had been a crazy idea. What if one of us was hurt or killed? And where would we go if we succeeded but to join the family?

After several hours, the train stopped and we were ordered to disembark. I gripped Tatiana's hand and we stepped out onto the wooden boards of the platform, followed by Botkin and Ivan, flanking Aleksey. We stood waiting to discover what would happen next, a forlorn, lonely group of exiles, with our sullen guards watching over us.

Chapter 33 ~ Avadeyev

Beyond the station fence, I could see the rooftops of a small town, indistinguishable from hundreds of others in Russia. It rose lightly on a hill, revealing narrow streets crammed with simple buildings. There were plain shop fronts and rows of similar little houses, and the occasional minaret of a church or public building.

We waited for about half an hour in the cool spring-evening sun, until we heard a motor car pull up outside. A solitary figure marched through the ticket hall and emerged onto the platform. He was tall, well over six feet, and very slim, about fifty-five or sixty years old, with a fine head of long, grey-white hair and a matching moustache, stained yellow. He wore a military officer's uniform of green/brown material, open at the neck, and with red insignia on the shoulders and breast pockets. A black leather belt was buckled around the middle of his tunic, with a holster attached, and I could see the silvery, rectangular hand-grip of a pistol protruding from under the covering flap.

He paraded up and down in front of us, his hands behind his back, looking each of us up and down as though choosing which to eat. In his right hand he carried a riding crop, which he periodically slapped against his black leather boots with a twist of his fingers. His breath, as he inspected me, was rancid.

When he reached Aleksey, he paused for a moment, glaring menacingly down at the child, who managed to stare challengingly back.

Eventually he stopped pacing and stood before us with a sardonic smile on his face, drawing a cigarette from a packet and lighting it.

"Well, my little pretties, welcome to my party." He bared a row of brown teeth. "Don't you recognise me? Oh dear, I am disappointed. I am your host, Alexander Avadeyev, beloved of royalty throughout Europe. Oh come now, don't look so glum, you are about to be reunited with your dear murdering royal family."

I heard a cart pull up behind us, and instinctively looked around. "Yes, your carriage awaits, madame," he said, sarcastically. "Off you all go then, there's good children, jump into your coach."

The guard nearest me pushed me towards the exit, and the others followed. We climbed into the back of the cart, sitting on wooden seats attached to each side. I saw Avadeyev climb into his motor car and roar past us, then we too began to move.

After a short ride on rough roads through the small country town, we arrived at a large, detached house. It was the kind of house favoured by professional families: red brick, wide-fronted, with generous windows protruding in bays on either side of a central door. Avadeyev's car was already parked outside.

The guard ordered us to jump out, and we stood anxiously outside the front door. Suddenly it was thrown open and Avadeyev shouted: "Well, come in then, don't stand there making the place look untidy."

We trooped inside, looking anxiously around at the heavy brass gas-lamps, the pretentious carved wooden bannisters and the florid wallpaper.

"Upstairs, if you please, ladies and gentlemen. You mustn't keep your royal masters waiting," Avadeyev chipped. His sense of humour was already becoming irritating. I followed Botkin, Tatiana and the others up the stairs. At the top we were confronted by several men in uniform blocking our way. They lounged casually against the walls or sat on the floor, but their eyes and their guns were trained threateningly on us.

"Well go on, go on!" urged Avadeyev's voice behind us. I felt his hand push hard against my back, and I was propelled into Tatiana, who stumbled into the doctor. Nervously we edged past the men and through an open door. As soon as I, the last of us, had passed through it, the door was slammed shut behind us and I heard a key turn. We were in a short hallway, with doors off both sides, one of which was open. Through it I saw familiar faces looking up to see what was causing the disturbance, and we entered a large room to join them.

Of the twenty-five of us who had started our journey from the palace, nine months earlier, the few who remained were now reunited in that room. Nicholas and Alexandra, along with Olga, Maria and Anastasia, were already there, accompanied by Anna Demidova and Alexei Trupp. All of them looked extremely tired and ill. In my small group were Tatiana, Aleksey, Doctor Botkin, Ivan Kharitonov and me. Twelve of us altogether, just half of the original party still together. I wondered what would become of us.

Tatiana ran to her parents and embraced them, and soon the family was in a huddle, talking, talking, talking. The doctor escorted Aleksey to a bed, then sat with him. I saw that young Trupp sat alone on a chair aside from it all, with his head down, so I went over to join him, and Ivan came with me. Alexei smiled as we sat beside him, glad of the company.

"How are you?" Ivan asked.

Alexei considered for a moment.

"Scared," he said, shyly, with surprising honesty, then shrugged and smiled wanly.

He had summed up all our feelings in one meaningful word.

After a long silence, Ivan added quietly: "Me too ... me too," and I nodded agreement.

He turned to me. "Are you alright, little one?"

I tried to nod again, but gave up, and shook my head, tears filling my eyes. "Why are we here, Ivan?" I didn't know if I meant 'why have they brought us here?' or 'why have we stayed with the family?' or 'why have our lives come to this?' Perhaps all of those things.

Ivan put his big arm around me, and I rested my head on his shoulder. Alexei leaned closer and gently placed his hands on mine.

The room in which we were gathered appeared to have once been a good-sized bedroom, with two doors at one end and a window the other. The door through which we had arrived was in the centre of one of the longer sides, and there were two beds, a couple of battered armchairs, a table with four wooden chairs, and a chest of drawers, arranged around the walls. A large, threadbare rug covered the centre of an otherwise bare wooden floor.

After a while, I rose and restlessly drifted around to inspect our current prison. One of the doors led to a lavatory, with a flushing toilet and a wash basin; the other was a cupboard. From that end, I walked the length of the room to the window ~ a distance I counted as fifteen paces ~ hoping to look out onto the town, but the glass had been smeared over on the outside with white paint. I tried to open the window, but on closer inspection found that it had been nailed shut.

Aware that I was pacing like a caged tiger, I wandered out of the communal room into the hallway, where I found doors leading to four bedrooms. One, the smallest, appeared to be unused, but was stacked nearly to the ceiling with boxes. I cleared the bed, piling the boxes in any available space, and lay down on it, staring at the ceiling, counting the cracks. I fell asleep almost at once.

~ ~ ~

The sound of the hallway door being unlocked woke me. When it opened, Alexander Avadeyev walked past my bedroom, accompanied by two of his men. I could see his back as he stood in the doorway of the communal room.

"Oh, how touching," I heard him say as he looked

around at the little groups in the room.

I slipped through the door, past the three of them, and rejoined Ivan and Alexei. Avadeyev watched me, disinterestedly. Then, like a curtain dropping at the end of a scene, his expression became hard and cold and he glared at Nicholas and Alexandra.

"You need not expect to be waited on while you are under my care. Your days of luxury and privilege are over. Here, you will all work, and you will look after us. There is food to be cooked and cleaning and household chores to be done, and every one of you will do your share. Follow me."

He turned away, but then stopped and looked back over his shoulder. "Except the boy and the doctor."

Compassion? I doubted it; that was not an emotion in his vocabulary. Aleksey was incapable of any kind of work, and Botkin was probably more useful in his professional capacity.

We followed Avadeyev downstairs, along a hallway past some closed doors and into a modern kitchen, with a gas cooker, a deep sink with a water tap, and a row of neat cupboards. "Two of you will cook," he said, looking at us with a raised eyebrow.

Ivan stepped forward, and was joined by Tatiana.

"Good," Avadeyev smiled, sardonically. "You are learning."

He turned back to the rest of us. "Follow me, children."

He led us through the hallway, and proceeded to a small scullery, with another large sink, a table and a wash boiler.

"Three people to wash and iron clothes," he stated, simply, again with that raised eyebrow.

After a moment's hesitation, Anna, Olga and Alexandra walked into the little room.

"Splendid! The German Bitches know their place. I can see we are going to get along just fine," he beamed, happily oblivious to the glares from the family.

Back along the corridor we traipsed, and out into a small courtyard, about twenty paces square, with overgrown borders, a vegetable patch, and a small, dry fountain.

"Two people here!" Avadeyev barked.

Several soldiers were lounging in the garden, smoking. They had leapt to attention as Avadeyev entered the courtyard, but soon relaxed again when he flapped a hand at them, except for one. He stood staring right at me, an expression almost of shock on his face, as though he thought he recognised me. He was taller than all the rest of them, and looked much smarter and more professional. I glared back, belligerently, but he did not drop his gaze, and eventually it was me who looked away.

Nicholas took Anastasia's hand and stepped forward.

"Well, well," said Avadeyev, "how keen you all are. Splendid! The remainder of you will clean rooms and make beds." He turned, and was gone, leaving us standing there.

So, my life had turned full circle, and I had returned to my original trade of housemaid. I smiled, wryly, and re-entered the house with Maria and Alexei. We went from room to room on the ground floor, knocking at each door in turn, checking the contents and tidying up as we went. Maria was quite useless, standing with a confused expression on her face; housework was not one of the skills she had been taught. I suggested that she might like to help the doctor with her brother, and she gratefully headed upstairs while Alexei and I pitched in. The time passed quickly; it was good to be working again.

Alexei became quite talkative, not the reticent boy I had become used to seeing. He told me, as we worked, that the place of our imprisonment was the home of a military engineer, Nikolay Ipatiev, and that the guards here were mostly recruited from the nearby factory and railway yard. He also warned me that Avadeyev was a ruthless man, dedicated to making a place for himself in the new Bolshevik hierarchy, and that he hated the royals passionately; he called the former Tsar "Nicholas The Blood Drinker."

Chapter 34 ~ Yekaterinburg

Occasionally through that day and the next I saw that soldier again, the smart-looking one who kept staring at me. On the third morning, he approached me when I was sitting alone in the courtyard, taking a break from my labours.

He was good-looking, with wild blonde hair and a weathered face, and unlike most of the guards, he was clean and his chin neatly shaved. Also, he did not have their arrogant swagger, but seemed to be respectful. I could not resist feeling an attraction to him. Despite a rush of excitement, however, I was apprehensive as he came near, fearful that he intended something similar to what had happened to Polina.

"Excuse me for speaking uninvited," he said. His voice was deep, but soft and cultured, and although he spoke in Russian, he had a slight accent that I found it hard to pinpoint. "Please do not be alarmed; I intend no harm. Your name is Natalie, yes?"

I nodded, tensely, avoiding eye contact.

"I hope you will not think me forward or insane," he continued, "but I have to tell you about a dream that is bothering me."

As a chat-up line it was original, and I suppressed a smile. He had removed his cap, and was nervously feeding it through his hands, like rosary beads.

Once he had started, he seemed to rush on, as though afraid he would lose his nerve. "It was a strange dream, which came to me the first night after I was posted to this house, before you arrived. A mysterious woman spoke to me, about you. She told me your name."

He paused, embarrassed, and I was intrigued by what he had said. I raised my eyes to meet his, and was surprised to see an unexpected warmth in his expression.

His mouth lifted in a little, lopsided grin. "Yes, I am sure you think I am quite mad. Perhaps I am; it is a mad world right now. Would you prefer that I go?"

I softened to him, and smiled back. "Perhaps not. Please tell me more."

His grin broadened. "Not completely mad?"

I nodded, amused. "Not completely."

"A little progress, already." He hesitated, collecting his thoughts, but visibly more relaxed.

"Very well, I will tell you some more. My name is Maksym Mikhailovich Drubich. My family moved to Yekaterinberg from Ukraine when I was six years old, so that my father could work in the cement factory." He paused. "May I sit beside you? It feels uncomfortable to be towering over you like this."

I nodded, and moved along the seat to make room.

"Thank you." He smiled again, taking the space offered, careful not to touch me. "Now, the dream. A woman appeared to me. She said that her name was Myriam, and that she had a message for me. She placed an image of you in my mind, and said that I must speak to you. She told me your name is Natalie Tereshchenko ~ is that right?"

I was stunned. Until this moment I had nearly convinced myself that Myriam was most likely a figment of my imagination, yet here was a complete stranger who had also met her. Somehow I managed to nod my head in answer to his question.

"Tereshchenko, that name is also from Ukraine," he said. "Natalie, I do not understand this. I could not have known your name, could not have imagined it, yet she spoke it clearly to me. She said she is an angel, and her purpose is to protect you. Is such a thing possible?"

I felt I had to tell him about Myriam, to ease his confusion. "Maksym, I have also met Myriam in a dream. She visited me about a year ago and warned me about the dangers I would experience. She also told me that I would meet a man who would help me."

For quite some time we looked at each other, taking it what all this meant. He had a kind yet strong face, with blue eyes, a strong, noble nose and a wide mouth. His hair was blonde, long and straggly ~ he looked a little like a Viking. He was tall ~ even as we sat side by side, he was a full head taller than me ~ and muscular, with broad shoulders and strong arms. Unlike most of the soldiers I had met in recent months, he had a clean smell about him ~ a hint of honest sweat, but not rancid as so many were ~ and there was something I could not define, something that drew me to gaze into his eyes.

He smiled again; we were both more relaxed knowing that we shared this incredible secret. He shook his head, his long hair flying. "This is amazing," he said, then laughed. "I am a soldier, I do not dream of angels." After a few moments of silence, he asked: "Shall I tell you some more about myself?"

"Yes," I said sincerely, "I would like that."

"Well, I was conscripted into the army at the start of the war against Germany, three years ago, and it seems as though I have been fighting ever since. Then Lenin won control of the government, and declared an end to the war. They sent me home to Yekaterinberg, to rejoin what remains of my family; I am relieved to be home again in one piece. But, as you can see, I am still a soldier, except that now I am in the Red Army."

At this moment, I saw Nicholas enter the courtyard with Anastasia, accompanied by a soldier, to do their daily gardening. Maksym rose, seemingly automatically, and stood to attention, although he did not salute, and I noticed a grim expression on his face, which had a few seconds earlier been so warm and relaxed. When the royals had started work, he turned back to me.

"I will walk you to your room," he said, with an almost imperceptible raise of his eyebrow. I stood beside him and we began to walk to the door. He nodded to his colleague and the former Tsar; I automatically curtseyed to Nicholas, and we re-entered the house.

"I have to return to my work," I told him, once we were inside.

"Yes, of course," he replied, "I'm sorry, I was not thinking. Which room?"

He suddenly seemed tense, and I was puzzled at his

change of mood.

"I am finished with the bedrooms, so now I just have the downstairs rooms to clean." I smiled, nervously, and was relieved when he returned the gesture warmly.

We stopped in the entrance hall, and I could see Alexei through an open door. "I'm glad you have spoken to me, Max. It has been very pleasant," I said, not sure if he had any thoughts of continuing our chat.

"You have no idea how relieved I am that you did not laugh at me," he grinned. "It took me two days to pluck up the courage to tell you." He gazed into my eyes for moment before continuing, as though trying to read my mind. "I am on escort duty this afternoon; I have to meet a special visitor at the railway station. But I would like to see you again soon, if I may ... if you don't mind ... that is. Do you mind?" Before I could answer, he rushed on. "May I see you again tomorrow?" Bless him! He was nervous.

"I would like that very much, Max" I smiled, and with a small bow and a large grin he departed.

~ ~ ~

Alexei and I worked well as a team. I had grown to like and respect the young man; he was quiet, yet cheerful, and laboured steadily. We stayed together for safety; I could never forget what had happened to Polina, and the atmosphere in this house was intimidating in the extreme. So we finished each room together, before moving on to the next. The afternoon passed unnoticed as we swept and dusted, collected rubbish and cleaned up vomit.

The room at the front of the house was the last, and whilst there we heard vehicles pull up outside. Curiously, we looked through the lace curtains at the window and saw Avadeyev getting out of his motor car. Behind it was a truck, from which were climbing four soldiers, one of whom was Max. Then I noticed that there was a passenger in Avadeyev's car, and, as he swung his legs out of the door and stood stretching beside it, I recognised Yurovsky, our captor at Tobolsk.

The men approached the front door, so Alexei and I returned to work, trying to be inconspicuous, yet looking busy, and at the same time also keeping the open door in view. In a clatter of boots and weapons, the party spilled into the hallway, talking animatedly, unaware of our presence.

" ... Hungarians or Latvians. It cannot be our men," Yurovsky was saying.

"You have that arranged?" asked Avadeyev.

They passed our room without looking in.

"They are on their way," I heard Yurovsky declare as a door closed along the hall and their voices were lost.

I look at Alexei, puzzled, and he shrugged. We returned to our cleaning.

Chapter 35 ~ Max

It was a glorious summer, and the next day was exceptionally hot. I normally enjoy the sun, but the sweltering temperature indoors was making physical work very tiring. I looked for Max as Alexei and I went from room to room, but saw no sign of him, and there seemed to be fewer guards than usual about the house.

When our chores were done, Alexei went upstairs to our room, and I wandered out into the courtyard, hoping Max might be there. But he wasn't, though several other men were lounging in a group in the shade at one end. *So that is where they all are*, I thought, *lazing in the sun*. I felt their eyes on me as I sat on the bench to wait for Max, expecting him to join me at any moment.

Time passed, and the sun beat down into the enclosed yard, turning it into an oven; I was glad of the little shade on the bench from an apple tree behind it, and my hat, which I had found in a box in my bedroom. The group of men in the corner changed gradually as I waited ~ one arriving, another leaving. I felt uncomfortable under their scrutiny, but eventually they all dispersed, ogling me as they passed. I heard them muttering, conspiratorially, and there was a sudden burst of laughter, but nothing transpired.

I stayed for another half an hour, baking in the glare of the sun, until it seemed certain that he would not be coming. But as I began to stand, sadly contemplating returning to my duties, he at last appeared. I smiled, and moved to make room for him on the bench, but instead of taking the place he stood in front of me, his rifle held at readiness across his chest.

"What's going on?" I asked, anxiously.

"Pretend you are not pleased to see me," he said, tensely, his eyes scanning the yard. "We must not appear to be too close." Before I could speak again, he continued: "Can we talk in your room?"

"Certainly," I said, mystified. "Now?"

"Yes, I will escort you."

Puzzled, I stood and re-entered the house, hearing him fall into step behind me. I could hear voices from one of the downstairs living rooms as we passed, but, unusually, there was no guard on duty at the top of the stairs when we arrived. In the communal room, we found Ivan and Alexei playing cards. I introduced Max to the boys, then told them that he and I needed privacy in my room. They looked surprised, and knowing looks crossed their faces.

"It's not like that," I chided. "But we do need you to keep any visitors out, if possible." They agreed, and I led Max into my little bedroom and shut the door. There was no space to stand, so we sat side by side on the edge of my bed, the only furniture in the room.

"I'm sorry to have behaved so strangely," he said at once. "Something is happening; I don't know what it is, yet, but it is making me nervous. They are bringing in some new men, and I think they may be planning to move you all again. At any rate, if they see you and me together, it could make things very difficult. I had to wait until Avadeyev went out before I could do anything, and then I took over duty on the landing. Imry was glad to be relieved, so he could get outside in the sunshine."

"I understand," I whispered. "We can meet here any time you like ~ my friends will be discreet. How long can you stay now?"

"Only about an hour, perhaps less. Natalie, this is all very dangerous for you, are you sure you want to be mixed up with me?"

I shrugged my shoulders. "I don't see that we have much choice; Myriam has thrown us together, and I'm sure she knows best."

~ ~ ~

We talked and talked, until it felt that we must know every detail about each other. Words flowed easily between us. I told him everything about my past and he told me about his.

"My parents came to Russia from Ukraine in nineteen-hundred-and-one, when I was five," he said. "My father had found a good job in the cement factory. Soon after we arrived, my mother set up a little café in Yekaterinberg. They were not rich, but comfortably off. My sister, Yulia, and I had a nice home and a good education. But my father was not happy living in Russia, and one day he ran off with the wife of the factory owner. I was only thirteen. Our mother raised us and taught us, and managed to build up the café business, until she died of pneumonia in the winter of nineteen-fourteen. By then, I was old enough to be called up for the army, so Yulia was left to run the café on her own."

Somehow, we began to hold hands as we sat together. It seemed natural, but when it happened I nearly jumped. It felt as though a spark had passed between us, and my whole body was suddenly awake to new sensations. I may have shivered, because he stopped talking and looked intently at my face. "Are you alright? You are not cold, surely."

I could not help it. As I gazed into his eyes, my own felt as large as soup plates. I raised a hand and stroked his cheek. He took my fingers in his own huge hand and kissed them. At that moment I remembered Myriam's words: "You will find love, I promise you, and you will know beyond doubt." I understood at last.

He lowered his head and gently kissed me on the lips for the first time. Despite the disquieting passions raised by Petr, and the warm glow of my memories of Frederick, I realised that I had never before felt as I did at that moment. I trusted him completely; he could have led me to walk barefoot across burning coals, and I would have gladly followed. I felt a yearning for him that I knew I could not control. I returned his kiss, clinging to him, aware that tears were running down my face.

"What is wrong, little one?" he asked, suddenly concerned as he felt my tears on his cheek.

"I love you, Max," I whispered. "I don't know if you love me, and I don't care, I just know I love you, and I want you to know it."

His arms tightened around me, and he kissed me again. Then he pulled away and looked at me intently. "You may not love me if you knew my dark heart," he said softly.

I felt icy fingers of dread against my skin. "Why, Max, what is in it?"

He pondered for a moment. "Natalie, I have known love before, and seen it snatched from me. I cannot help it, there is a man I hate. I know I should forget it, but I cannot."

Puzzled, I studied his face. "Who? Who is the man you hate so?"

He could not hold my gaze, and lowered his head. "He is your employer, Nicholas," he said, softly.

His answer was so unexpected that it took a moment to register in my mind, and when it did, I could not grasp the meaning. "Nicholas? But why? What has he done to you?"

He looked away, across the tiny room. "I know it is wrong to hate, especially when the person you so detest has no comprehension of what he has done. But it is that disregard of consequences that is so callous, a man in his position of power should be aware of the effects of his actions."

"Max, darling, what did he do to you?"

For a moment, he was pensive, then he began:

"It was January last year. I was fighting for the Tsar against the Germans; I had been at the front for nearly a year without leave. I was married in nineteen-fifteen, just before the Germans invaded, but had not seen my wife, Esther, since our honeymoon, because of the war. She was here in Yekaterinberg, working for her father in his grocery shop. The winter was very hard, as you know. Many people were unemployed and starving, because the nation was being stripped of all resources to keep the war going. In December, I received a message that Esther had been killed by robbers who were stealing food from the shop. Of course, I applied for compassionate leave to return home for the funeral and to be with the family, but the Tsar refused to sign the authority for my leave ~ he told my commanding officer that nobody could be spared from the fighting. I was risking my life for a country that was starving to death, and a Tsar who did not care."

He paused, studying my reaction. "I am sorry, Natalie, I am bitter and I hate him and I know that is wrong. When I see him, I want to kill him. Oh, I would not do it," he added quickly, seeing my shocked expression. "I could not. And I do not approve of the way the other guards here speak about the family, or the way they treat them, but I am consumed with bitterness that he can swagger around, playing with people's lives as though he has the authority that only truly belongs to God, and be oblivious to the tragedy of it all."

He fell silent, his head bowed, his eyes turned away from me. I took one of his hands in both of mine, and stared at his down-turned face; he was a picture of misery. Squeezing his hand with my fingers, I said, quietly: "Please look at me Max."

He lifted his head and anxiously met my eyes.

"I cannot begin to understand the loss you have suffered," I said, "and it would be wrong for me to judge you. All I know is that you are an honourable man, and I trust you completely; you have told me about it, and that reveals much about you. It seems to me that your hatred is not without cause, it is understandable. All my life I have known only the royal family and household ~ they are the nearest thing I have known to a family of my own. I have had little to do with Nicholas; or rather, he has had nothing to do with me, it is Alexandra who has been my employer, and she has been almost like a mother to me, though always remote. But I can say this: I, too, have seen the casual arrogance that comes from their position of wealth and power. Alexandra and the girls have always been good to me, but they are a class apart, detached and aloof from everyone, convinced that they have been given authority by God. But, Max, they are no longer in control of the fates of others, it is the other way round now."

I leaned over and kissed him, and he surprised me by taking my face in his hands as I went to withdraw, and returned my kiss with passion, moving his head so that our noses pressed against each other's cheeks. When we finally parted, breathlessly, he gazed into my eyes and said "I love you too, Natalie Tereshchenko."

We stayed, holding hands and smiling stupidly at each other, until Max, with a deep breath, said that he had to get back on duty, before anyone noticed he was missing. We stood and moved to the hallway door, where we loitered for a while, not talking, just looking at each other in amazement at what was happening, then parting with another lingering kiss.

Diary ~ Wednesday July 17th 1918 ~ evening

How perverse it is of fate (or God?) that I have finally found the love I hoped for, just as my life is hanging in the balance. Max is all I dreamed of, the man who completes me as a woman.

I can see now that the fairytale romance of Frederick's letters and the animal passions aroused by Petr were like pictures drawn using only a black pencil on white paper, whereas my love for Max is painted in bright shades of every colour from the rainbow.

Myriam was right: I fell in love with him from the start, and I knew at once that he was the one. What a pity she neglected to tell me that we would have only a short time together. For I am sure we are all to die. We are moving inexorably closer to whatever destiny has been ordained for us. These people hate us so comprehensively that I cannot imagine what has prevented them from killing us already. Sometimes it feels that it would only take one little incident, a careless word or look, to set one of them off.

My friends are as terrified as I am. All of us are losing weight ~ our cheeks are drawn, our eyes are pits of darkness, our lips thin and white. There is an air of resignation, an acceptance that we are just waiting for the inevitable. All hope of rescue is now gone, there is no prospect of reprieve.

Part Three

~

И наименее вступает наибольшей

And The Least Shall Become Greatest

Chapter 36 ~ The Final Chapter

There is a great commotion, people are moving around, lights flashing. It is about two o'clock, and we have been awakened by the guards and told to dress. They say that we are to be moved for our own safety, that anti-Bolshevik forces are approaching, and the house may be fired upon. I am reminded of the night in Tobolsk, when the Whites tried to rescue the family. We grab what possessions we can carry, then are led down the stairs in two groups ~ the family at the front, the rest of us following.

There are six guards; one is Max. He has a grim expression on his face, and has positioned himself somewhere behind me. Torches flicker as we shuffle through the house and out into the courtyard, which is in darkness but for a dull light shining above a door in the far corner. We cross the yard and pass through that door into a gloomy passageway and down some more steps.

Suddenly I feel strong arms grab me roughly from behind, and I scream as my feet are lifted off the floor. The others turn to look back, but are angrily pushed onwards by the guards towards the end of the passageway. I am terrified. I can tell that everything had reached a dreadful turn, and I fear we are being taken to our deaths. I pull at the hands that grip my body and cover my mouth, twisting in an effort to free myself, but without success. My feet are still off the floor, so I swing both my legs backwards, hard, to kick him in the shins, and I hear a satisfying grunt of pain.

He effortlessly twists me round in the darkness and pushes me into a doorway, slamming my back hard against the closed door. I feel his hand groping clumsily at my breast, his hot breath on my face. Again I cry out in anger and fear as a pistol appears beside my cheek, cold and hard against my skin. But in the darkness, the voice that hisses in my ear is Max's.

"It's me! Don't stop struggling, fight as though your life depends on it."

Suddenly the door gives way, and I would fall backwards into the small cupboard beyond but for Max's strong hand around my waist. He rams my body against the open door and begins kissing me, brutally. I feel his hand grasp my buttocks, squeezing with his fingers and pulling me closer, so our hips are pressed together. A part of me finds it incredibly arousing, knowing it is Max, while at the same time I am terribly afraid. I wriggle and make muffled squeaks of protest, beating futilely at his shoulders with my fists.

One of the guards in the corridor flashes his torch on us, and I hear him say something. Max stops kissing me, waving his gun with his huge hand as he laughs and replies to the man, who chuckles and continues on his way.

Then everyone is gone, and Max releases me and cautiously leans out of the doorway to look along the corridor in both directions.

"Max, what is happening?" I ask.

"Everyone is to be killed," he whispers, bluntly. "We have to get out, fast!"

Before I have time to absorb the meaning of his words, he grabs my hand. "Follow me, quickly."

We run quietly out into the courtyard, across it and through the silent house to the front door.

Thankfully, we see no-one the whole way.

As Max opens the door to the street, I hear the muffled sound of a gunshot from behind us, then two more, then a whole volley.

"This way!" he says huskily, urgently, leading me out into the dark streets of Yekaterinberg.

~ ~ ~

Threading our way through unlit, deserted streets, walking quickly, sometimes running to keep up with him, I follow Max, clutching his hand. He turns down a dark alley. I have to trust his knowledge completely in the total blackness.

Another turn, and we come to a stop.

I hear him tap lightly, and a door is quickly opened by a strikingly beautiful woman. In the pale light of the candle she carries, I can see that she has light brown hair, like Max's, dark eyes in a pale face, and a figure that is not diminished by the drab clothes she wears.

Max gently pushes me ahead of him through the door, and closes it quickly behind him, before embracing the woman. Then, with one arm still around her, he reaches out to me and, taking my hand, pulls me closer. "Natalie, this is my sister, Yulia," he says.

I am shaking with fear, and she feels it as she hugs me. "Poor child, come through; I will give you some hot soup."

We pick our way by candlelight along a dark, narrow hallway into a warm back room. Yulia places the candle in the centre of a table, and I see by its light that that we are in a kitchen. All the windows are covered with thick blankets and sacking.

We sit down at the neat, clean table, and Yulia brings a bowl of soup and some bread for each of us. It is a mild night, and am not cold or hungry, but I sip at the soup and find it soothing.

It is then that my mind begins to assemble and comprehend what has just happened, what Max told me as we began our escape.

"It's happened, they have all been murdered, haven't they?" I declare.

Yulia looks at her brother for confirmation.

"Yes, my darling, all of them," Max replies, gently.

"All of them, dead?" I know it is true; there is an inevitability about it. I had expected to die with them, yet still I cannot grasp it as a fact. My voice is quavering, I am fighting to hold back an explosion of grief.

"Tatiana? Alexandra? Ivan? My beloved Ivan, who never hurt anyone in his life? And poor Alexei Trupp, that sweet boy!"

"I'm sorry, Nata." He puts his arms around me and speaks softly. "We received the order at midnight. Lenin decided that none of the family could live, as they might inspire rebellion against the new government. And there must be no witnesses. Avadeyev knew it was going to happen; it was just what he was waiting for, hoping for. That is why I had to take desperate action to snatch you from the execution, it was the only way I could think of to save your life. There was an assassination squad of Hungarian mercenaries waiting for you all in two rooms in the basement. I wish I could have prevented it, but I was only one man."

He pauses for a moment to consider what more to tell me. In those few seconds, I think of the swirl of events as he whisked me away from what would have certainly been my death, too, and my imagination conjures up dreadful, lurid images of what must have happened to the others. I press my lips together to suppress the desire to burst into tears.

Seeing my face, he quickly continues.

"Remember the man in the corridor, the one who spoke to me when I grabbed you?"

I nod my head, numbly.

"What he said to me was 'Make sure you take care of her when you have had your fun.' Meaning that I should be sure kill you."

I look from Max to Yulia, and back. My mind is filled with the memory of the silent, ragged procession that had meekly followed those horrible men down the stairs to their deaths. That forlorn little group of people have been part of my life for as long as I can remember, now they are gone forever, every one of them ~ the only family I have ever known, murdered in cold blood.

And yet, my perverse, ungrateful mind does not stay for long on those poor people who have just died. Instead, my heart leaps as I remember that Rada and Polya were not with them, have gone to safety before this terrible event occurred. It is shameful that I can accept so quickly the deaths of the people who had been good to me, but I cannot help it, I feel a rush of relief that the twins were not with them. At this moment, if there was such a thing as a God, I would be thanking him for saving my friends' lives.

I tell Yulia about Rada and Polya. I describe our years together as junior maids to the Empress and the family ~ how we grew up together, the freezing nights when we kept each other warm, and the times we giggled hysterically at some silly thing. Never once, in all those years, had a single harsh word been spoken between us. Yulia listens intently, sometimes nodding, but mostly just giving me her full attention, making me feel that what I am recounting is important to her.

I realise that I am babbling, but I cannot stem the flow of words, for to stop talking now would allow me to start thinking again.

"I never had friends like that," she says when I have finished. "We were mostly kept apart from other children when we were young, because our father was foreman at the factory, and he didn't want us to get too friendly with the kids of the workers, but Max and I were very close, like you were with the twins. Quite often our parents were too busy to look after us, so it was up to me to take care of my little brother."

She looks at Max and smiles. Although she is quite

tall, several inches taller than me, her 'little' brother is now a full head above her. Max returns her smile with an affable little grin.

"She used to bully me," he tells me.

"I so did not!" she retorts, throwing a piece of bread at him. "He was always getting into fights, or falling from trees or something equally silly, and it would be me who had to patch him up."

Max catches the missile effortlessly with one hand.

"It's true," he agrees, gazing affectionately at his sister. "Yulia was like a mother to me a lot of the time, especially after our father ran off. Our mother had to work hard to support us, and she had little time to spare."

"After she died," Yulia continues, "I took over the café. And shortly after that, Max moved away to get married. Then I heard that he had been called up into the army. Now life has taken a circle and he is home again."

We know that we are talking about simple things from the past to insulate ourselves from the awful events of the present, for to think too much about what has just happened would be opening a window into hell. It is like an unspoken agreement between us, to avoid acknowledging what we all know and fear.

Chapter 37 ~ Sleep

But even though thoughts of the past can be suppressed, the future still lurks, shadowy and threatening. "What will happen now?" I ask Max.

He becomes serious again. "We are not out of danger yet," he says, grimly. "Avadeyev and his mob may be busy for a little while, disposing of the bodies, but they will soon notice that you and I are missing, and Imry saw us together. We have to get as far away from here as possible, as soon as possible."

"How, where?"

He leans closer to me across the corner of the table, and takes my hands. "Before all this happened, I had been planning to return to Ukraine. It is the place of my birth, and I think we could be safe there. Will you come with me?"

"Ukraine? But it is so far, and I do not speak the language."

"You will have me with you. We have to get out of Russia, Nata, or Avadeyev will surely find us and have us killed."

I know he is right, but too many things have happened to me, too quickly, and I cannot get my head around it all. He sees my confusion, and touches my cheek with his fingers.

"You need sleep," he whispers. "We can talk some more in the morning."

I nod, aware that I am only putting off the

inevitable decision, but too tired to think.

Yulia stands and takes my hand. "It is good to have you here, Natalie," she says, "if only for a short while and for the saddest of reasons. I have made up a bed in the spare room for you."

Max has also risen to his feet. He puts his arms around me and kisses me gently, before picking up my bag and moving towards the door. "I will show you to your room."

I follow him up a narrow flight of wooden stairs and along a short hallway. He opens a door and stands back to allow me to enter.

I pause in the doorway, looking into the pretty little room with a bed and a small chest of drawers. "Max, I don't want to be alone," I stammer, turning to face him, tears suddenly filling my eyes. "The memories ..."

Quickly he puts down my bag and takes me in his arms. "You could have my bed, if you like. I will sleep in the chair beside you."

His big body, close to mine, is reassuring. I nestle my head against his chest, feeling the warmth, hearing his heart beating, inhaling the comforting smell of him. "Yes, please," I whisper.

He picks up my bag again and I follow him to his bedroom. I am surprised to find it tidy and spotless, unlike the disgusting state of the rooms that I have been forced to clean at various houses in recent months. I wonder if, perhaps, it is his sister's doing.

As well as the bed (neatly made) there is a small cabinet, a large cupboard and a wooden chair. On the floor is a rug, and a fire has been laid in the grate. He puts my bag on the bed and leaves me to undress and scramble between the covers. I have no nightdress, but the night is warm, and the sheets are soft. When he returns, he leans over and kisses me. "Goodnight my love."

I cling to him, unsure of myself, yet certain of my need. "Max?" I whisper.

"Yes, my angel?" He sits on the side of the bed, studying me.

"Sleep with me, please." My heart is pounding. It is more than the fear of being alone. I want him, need his body close to mine.

He looks at me, seriously. "Are you sure?"

I smile, nervously, for this is unexpected. Will he think less of me for asking? "Yes," I whisper. "Absolutely certain."

Quickly he undresses and slips into the bed beside me. I lift my head as he puts his arm around my shoulder, and we gaze into each others eyes. I have never shared a bed with a man, have no idea what to expect or what to do, but my heart knows that this is right. I run my fingers through his wiry chest hair, and as I look up at his face he plants a kiss on my nose. Despite the drama we have so recently experienced, I feel safer with Max than I have ever known in my entire life, and a wave of emotion washes over me. "I love you, Max."

He smiles. "Oh, I love you too, Natalie."

I feel his free hand slip around my waist and up my back, and I squirm with pleasure at his touch as he pulls me tightly to him. Slowly, lightly, he strokes my skin in little circles and lines, watching my face the whole time; it is exquisite torture. His hand glides down my back to my bottom, and he squeezes, pulling me closer, as he had in the corridor, except that this time, with the fear removed and only the memory of it to torment me, I relax and enjoy being held.

Without thinking, and though I have little idea what to expect, I move my hand down from his chest, seeking a way between our hips, easing my body away from him a little until I find what I am seeking. I do not even know what to do with it, but I want to please him and, yes, I am curious and excited.

Max starts to sing, softly: "Oy u Hayu, Pry Dunayu;" in a deep and resonant baritone, gazing adoringly down at me.

"What is that song?" I ask him.

"Oy u Hayu ... 'In A Forest Glade' ... it is a love song from Ukraine," he says. "Like all Ukrainian songs, it is sad." He laughs, then touches my face with his fingers. "Come here."

I return to his arms, and he kisses my lips, then my cheeks, then my neck. I close my eyes and rest my head back on the pillow as he resumes his song, murmuring the words while kissing my shoulders: "In a forest glade near the river, there is a nightingale singing."

His lips move down a little further, to my chest. He rests his head there, laying on one cheek, his long hair tickling my belly, watching his hand as he begins to caress a breast, stroking and pinching my nipple, which rises to meet his touch.

"He sings to gather his loved ones," Max sings. I find myself humming along to the tune.

Then he cups the breast in his huge hand, and lowers his mouth to it, sucking, drawing my nipple between his lips. When it is as hard as a cherry stone, he moves to the other. "I want to fly like a bird, to where my lovely one is now," he sings before his mouth is again busy. His face is unshaven, a day's stubble; the roughness against my skin is exquisite, and I writhe under his sensuous touch.

I feel his weight move on top of me, his chest hair gently rough against my breasts. I want more, I wrap my legs about his waist, pulling him to me with my feet; my whole body quivers and I cry out with delight. Unexpected waves of ecstatic pain flood me from head to toe, again and again, until I collapse exhausted.

Chapter 38 ~ Changes

I awake to a room filled with sunlight, and the smell of cooking wafting through from the café below. Max's side of the bed is empty, but as soon as I become aware of that fact he appears in the doorway carrying a tray. "Some kasha and a cup of tea," he says, circling the bed and resting the tray on the chair beside me. Then he kisses me and sits on the side of the bed, grinning.

He is dressed in loose trousers and a traditional cotton tunic, secured at the waist with a leather belt. His feet are bare. It is the first time I have seen him wearing anything other than military uniform, and I like what I see. I stretch for a moment, then sit up to eat, wrapping the sheet around me.

Max helps by raising the pillow to support my head, and transfers the tray onto my lap. Kasha is a porridge made of buckwheat, and he has added some honey to sweeten it; it tastes good. As I eat, he outlines his plan for the day.

"Yulia has been to the railway station and bought tickets for us to Voronezh. From there, we could cross into Ukraine, or return to Petrograd, if you would prefer, although I think it will be very dangerous ~ Lenin has complete control in that area. But, whatever we do, we must act quickly and get away from here as soon as possible. They are bound to start looking for us around the town, if they haven't already."

My subconscious mind has been mulling over the options since our discussion, and I have made a decision. "I will go with you, Max, wherever that may be."

He smiles and plants a big kiss on my mouth. Then, tasting the honey, he licks my lips with the tip of his tongue, pushing with it until I open my mouth and let him in. I squirm to move the tray aside, then twist my body and slide my feet out onto the floor. As I turn and lean over the bed to steady the tray, I feel him move close behind me, his hands on my hips, his groin pressed against my bum. I straighten, and he wraps his arms around me and holds me close from behind, breathing heavily against my neck, his hands on my belly and my breasts. Through all the longings of my years before meeting him, I could not have imagined the feelings that overpower my mind and body. I love, and know that I am truly loved. Despite our dangerous situation, I feel happy and secure, that somehow we will always be together.

He holds me tightly, and I can feel that he is becoming aroused again. I turn to face him, and stand naked before him, my arms extended above my head, for him to admire all that he now owns. That he is dressed and I am naked makes me feel wanton and wicked, I can feel his clothes brushing against my skin. As I turn, he traces his finger tips across my body, gazing at me like someone who has just bought a priceless painting and cannot believe it is his. We kiss again, his hands caressing my back, then my bottom and hips, pulling me closer.

Like a woman possessed, I frantically remove his belt and trousers, while he lifts his tunic over his head, and we embrace, naked, lost in the rising storm of passion within us. Even when the storm is spent, we stay locked together, gazing into each other's eyes, panting, smiling, kissing, until he finally, gently, lowers me so my feet touch the floor again. Then we stay a while longer, lost in reverie, absorbing the incredible moment that has just taken place.

~ ~ ~

Eventually, reluctantly, we part. I climb back into bed and watch as he dresses. I notice huge bruises on his shins. "Did I do that yesterday?" I gasp, pointing.

He looks down ruefully; not only are his legs bruised, but the skin is broken. "Yes, my love. You can be a wildcat when you choose to be." He grins as he finishes putting on his trousers.

I feel a strange mixture of remorse to have hurt my loved one, and satisfaction that I fought so hard; I cannot suppress a small smile.

"Now," he says, purposefully, ignoring my smirk, "there will be a train heading west this afternoon, so we have a little time to make preparations. What do you need in the way of clothes and things?"

I am acutely aware that I have nothing to wear but what I arrived in last night. All I was able to carry down to the basement was my small portmanteau containing a few personal things and my diary.

"Everything was left behind," I tell him, "I only have the clothes I put on when they woke us."

Suddenly, the memories come flooding back, smothering me, and I stop speaking, fighting back the tears. He quickly sits on the bed beside me, sensing the reason for my silence. Without speaking, he holds me tightly. I feel myself become calmer, controlling the emotions that threaten to overcome me. I look up into his eyes and smile wanly.

"Ok, now?" he asks.

I nod.

"Right, Yulia will help you with clothes or other stuff you need," he continues, all business again. "She can also shop for anything else you want, if she can get it. It will be good to change our appearances as much as we can. I will cut my hair and wear my smartest clothes and shoes." He grins. "Even you will not recognise me."

Glad of the distraction, I respond eagerly, grabbing a handful of my hair and examining it. "I think mine can be chopped off too. Perhaps I could disguise myself as a boy?"

He stares at me, apparently serious for a moment, then laughs. "No, my love, you could never pass as a boy." He leans forward and kisses my forehead, running his fingers through my long hair. "But if you really want to change it, Yulia could cut it for you. She is very good; she used to do our mother's." Decisively, he stands and picks up the tray. "Now, finish your breakfast and get out of that bed, you lazy trollop."

"Cheek!" I exclaim. "I'm not coming out from behind this sheet until you leave the room, Mr whatever-your-name-is. I may be a trollop but I'm not a tart!" He laughs again, shaking his head, and waves casually as he disappears through the door.

With only a few hours to plan and prepare everything, our morning is busy but very pleasant. Yulia cuts my hair into a short bob that changes the shape of my face dramatically, and she has raided her wardrobe for simple, childish clothes. By the time we have finished, I look four or five years younger, and I giggle when I see myself in her mirror. "When I was thirteen I wanted to look older, now I am trying to become young again."

"You could easily pass for thirteen, now," she chuckles, then stops and studies me for a moment. "Oh how I would love to be thirteen again; I had no worries in those days, everything was so much simpler, then. Seeing you in my clothes brings it all back to me."

I take her hand. "Thank you for all you are doing for me, Yulia. I am lucky to have you as a friend."

She smiles. "We are lucky that you have come into our lives, Nata. When Max's wife died, I thought I would never see him smile again. But, despite all that is happening around us and to us, he is happier now than I have ever known him."

"We were made for each other," I say, simply. "Myriam told me I would find him. I thought it wouldn't happen, but she knew." I expect her to be amused at my belief that I have been visited by my guardian angel, but instead she shows a genuine interest. She tells me that Max told her of his encounter with Myriam, and that she had initially been sceptical. But she knows he is not a fool, and now I am here, proof enough.

We resume our clothes party, picking light items to take with me. "At least you won't need any heavy, winter things," she says, pulling an assortment of stuff out of her cupboards and passing them to me to choose from. I quickly try on the garments as she hands them to me, then we pack the ones I like best into a small, old suitcase Max has dug out of the loft.

Eventually, I am ready, and we join Max downstairs. His appearance, too, is dramatically different. He has aged himself with a careful choice of slightly old-fashioned clothes and a short haircut. I notice that he has shaved carefully, except for his top lip, where the beginnings of a light brown moustache are already giving him a distinguished look. He looks at me and smiles. "You look perfect," he says. "I have been thinking of a story we should tell, if asked. You shall be my niece, and I am returning you to my brother after having you to stay for a while with Yulia and me ~ a week, perhaps?"

"Yes, a week is enough, otherwise people would expect to have seen me around." I change my voice to that of a little girl: "Fank you uncle Max."

Chapter 39 ~ Flight

Just before noon, with a packed lunch, two suitcases, several tearful hugs and kisses, and much trepidation on my part, Max and I leave the café to go to the station. We exit by the rear door, the same way we arrived. At the gate, Max checks up and down the alleyway before gesturing for me to follow. Now, in daylight, I can see that the café is part of a row of twenty or so similar buildings, each with a back yard leading onto the alley.

My heart is thumping, and I am glad that there is no-one in sight as we make our way out onto the quiet side street. At the end of that street, however, we emerge onto a busier thoroughfare, and mingle with the flow of people going about their daily lives. I hold Max's hand, to help with the image of a child out for a walk with her uncle, and try not to look nervously around.

What worries me most is his height ~ he stands a full head above everyone else, and could easily be seen by anyone looking for us. However, peering under my eyelashes it seems to me that we are not being noticed; everyone is continuing on their way without paying us any attention; people are walking, shopping, talking, and carriages are passing, the horses raising dust from the unpaved road.

We thread our way through the little town, our confidence growing as we remain unchallenged. After a little while, however, Max stops suddenly and turns us around. "Army patrol," he mutters through clenched teeth, dragging me into a narrow passageway between the shops. It is gloomy and smelly, with heaps of rubbish piled against the walls, from which rats scurry at our approach. A short distance down is a doorway, and we squeeze into it, peering back up the alley.

A few minutes later, we see a group of six soldiers pass the end, without looking in our direction. They are carrying rifles with bayonets fixed, and are wearing full combat uniform, including steel helmets.

"They may not be looking for us," Max whispers.

But I am not convinced, and I can tell that he is just trying to reassure me.

We resume our journey, but have hardly merged again with the crowd than we encounter another patrol. Once more we hide in a gap between the buildings.

"Avadeyev wants us badly," I say as we wait for them to pass.

I realise that I am shaking with fear, and Max must have felt it, because he wraps his arms about me and pulls me close. I rest my head on his chest, comforted by the bulk of his body and the knowledge that he will defend me.

"Once we are on the train, we will be safe," he whispers. "There, they have passed, we can continue." He leans down and kisses me gently on the forehead, then takes my hand and leads me back out onto the street.

This time we get a little further, but it is not long before he spots some more soldiers. We dive into a shop, a milliners, and begin to browse the displays while watching the window for the patrol to pass.

I find a display of hats for men. "Here's an idea," I say, holding up an English bowler hat, grinning. "You could pretend to be a banker." I am trying to be light-hearted, though my voice has a tremor to it and my smile probably looks more like a grimace.

He responds by putting the hat on and pulling a face, which has the desired effect of making me giggle.

A voice from behind Max makes me jump. "Do you have any intention of buying that hat, sir, or are you just here to play games?"

Max turns, and I can see a smartly-dressed salesman beyond him, glaring at us.

"I'm sorry," Max apologises, taking it off. "We were just looking. It's not quite what I want, though."

"Very good, sir," responds the man, snatching the hat from his hands and looking at him over his spectacles. "Perhaps something else?"

"No, thank you. Not today," Max replies, struggling to keep a straight face. He gropes beside him to take my hand. "We have to be getting along now," he explains, weakly, leading me away, back through the door with its tinkling bell and out onto the street.

~ ~ ~

At last we reach the end of the high street, and, on the opposite side of the narrow road that crosses before us, we can see the railway station. We pause, in the slight concealment afforded by the corner of a bank building, to study the building. As we feared and expected, there is a group of soldiers guarding the station entrance, checking everyone who tries to get in. Max risks a peep around the corner. "Eight of them," he reports over his shoulder. "We'll never get in that way. And one of them is Nagy."

"Who is Nagy," I ask.

"He's Avadeyev's right-hand man, a sadistic killer, completely ruthless." he replies. As we stand, undecided, we hear the whistle of a train, and with a grimace, Max looks quickly back at the station. "Oh wonderful!" he groans. "The train is in, we will have to act fast."

"Is there any other way into the station?" I ask.

"No, this is it," he says, shaking his head. "The only chance for us is to board the train as it pulls out. There is an incline, so it will be moving fairly slowly. We need to get up the line a bit."

We turn back and retrace our steps a short way until we reach a side road. Max breaks into an easy trot as soon as we slip into the narrow lane, and I follow suit, my bag and portmanteau swinging clumsily. Although he is carrying both the cases, I find it difficult to keep up with him, and I am becoming tired by the time we reach the end and stop briefly to check that all is clear.

This is a quieter road; there are no shops, and few people, just rows of small houses, and at the bottom I can see the railway tracks. As quickly as we can without attracting attention, we walk down to the corner and Max nervously peers out.

"It's clear," he says, visibly relieved. "I'll cross first and wait by that tree. You follow on my signal. Ok?"

I nod and, after another check, he briskly crosses the road, carrying our two cases, and takes position on the far side. I see him look again along the road towards the station, then he makes a 'come on' sign with his hand.

My legs are tired and, struggling with my bag, I stumble part way across the rough road, but manage not to fall. When I reach him he holds me tightly for a moment. But we have no time to spare, for the train gives another hoot on its whistle, and we hear the familiar *shoof! shoof! shoof!* as it begins to move.

Beside us there is a low fence, and beyond that the land down to the track is overgrown with weeds. Max helps me over the fence, then throws my bag to me, followed by the cases. As he begins to climb, he shouts to me to start making my way to the line. I grab my bag and push my way through the coarse undergrowth, thorns tearing at my skin and dragging my clothes.

I reach the track just as the great engine is passing, towering over me as big as a house, with great puffs of steam and smoke shooting from all over it. The huge wheels, each taller than me, turn slowly, while long, green-painted rods between them push and pull. I look up at the driver's cab and see him leaning out, staring ahead up the track, his eyes white in his coal-blackened face. If he saw me he gives no sign.

Then the carriages begin to clatter past, and I turn around to check that Max is all right. He is just emerging from the scrub, and stands beside me, our clothes blowing in the wind stirred up by the passing coaches. "Here comes the last one," he shouts, and points to the metal platform on the back of the rear coach. "You will have to run and jump up there as it passes. Can you do that?"

"I'll try my best!" I yell back.

He grins. "Good girl, you can do it."

I begin running beside it, and as the end of the carriage passes, I throw my bag up onto the platform. With my hands free, I am able to grab the handrail and swing myself on board. I can hear Max's feet pounding on the gravel a few steps behind me. As soon as my feet touch the bottom step, I drag myself up onto the little platform, to clear the way for Max.

There is the sound of a faint but distinctive crack from behind, and I look back down the line to the dwindling station. Soldiers are running onto the platform to join one who is already there, his rifle pointed at us. A puff of smoke appears at the end of his gun, and a second later I hear the sound of another shot, while at the same moment the wooden panel of the carriage splinters beside my head, leaving a rough, round hole. I look back again, and see the others reach his side and begin to take aim.

Max is running faster and faster on the uneven gravel beside the track as the train gathers speed. He hurls first one suitcase, then the other, and I catch hold of them, hauling them up to the top. There is a faint volley of shots from the station.

"Max!" I scream in panic as he stumbles and nearly falls; I fear he has been hit by a bullet. But he manages to grab the handrail with one hand, and, with an amazing effort of will and strength, swings his whole body round and up, landing with both feet on the metal steps. Then he stands and gives me a bow and a cheeky grin.

For some reason, I am angry. "This is not a game!" I shout. "I thought I had lost you!"

He joins me at the top of the steps and I point out to him the tiny figures of the soldiers on the station platform, still shooting ineffectually at us. He waves to them, cheekily, then puts his arm around my shoulder, pulling me close to him.

We stand panting for a few moments. Then we gaze at each other and I begin to chuckle. He too starts to laugh, then gives a great yell and grabs me in a bear hug, lifting my feet off the deck and kissing me. The platform is swaying, and the wind is swirling around us, carrying with it the smell of smoke and steam. We are on our way.

Chapter 40 ~ Nagy

The train surges forth, but we stay on the little metal grille for a while, resting, leaning on the handrail, watching Yekaterinberg station vanish into the landscape behind us, feeling the cool breeze on our faces. Max puts his huge arm around my waist, and I snuggle close to his chest, feeling safe for the first time since ... when? The abdication? Perhaps even before that. Somehow we have made it, we are free. Amazingly, we have escaped a gang of ruthless murderers and are heading for a new life together.

After a while, we open the door and enter the packed carriage. Every seat is filled, and people are standing in almost every available space. The air is thick with the smell of tobacco smoke and many unwashed bodies. Heads turn briefly to study us, then immediately lose interest and resume whatever they were doing.

We find a space at the rear and put our cases on the floor. I open a window to let in some air, partly because it is so hot and I am still flushed from running to catch the train, but also to relieve the awful smell of compressed humanity. I stand for a while, watching the trees close to the track flash past, and the countryside beyond slowly rotate as the miles rattle away, then I return to Max and sit on a case beside him.

As the afternoon passes easily into evening, we eat some of our food. We know this will have to last us for several days, so we limit ourselves to just a little bread and cheese and a few sips of our water. There is little else to do, and we cannot talk freely, so we mostly sit or stand side by side, holding hands ~ so comfortable in each other's company that no words are necessary, just an occasional look and knowing smile.

The train hurtles on, chasing the fading day as it moves westwards, but losing the race with the pursuing night. When the last pale glow has gone, we take turns to sleep through the almost total darkness, while the other holds guard over our meagre possessions, each wrapped in our thin blankets against the chill of the night air. We can take no chances, for these are hard times, and many people would not think twice if they should see an opportunity to steal something, no matter how trivial, for themselves or their families.

Eventually, a misty dawn breaks and an uncomfortable day begins. Our cases were not designed to be seats, and soon we find ourselves standing again, swaying to the broken rhythm of the wheels as they bounce on the joints of the tracks. Sometime around mid-day, the train stops at Perm, and we gaze across the town while people get on and off. Perm is an attractive and affluent-looking place. From the station we can see the river that winds through its centre, with wide greens on each side and, beyond that, wide avenues packed with carriages of every kind.

No seats have become available nearby, so Max and I stay with our cases, and, once the train begins to move again, we eat a little more of our food ration. I stand up to stretch my limbs, wandering over to the window and gazing out as I eat my apple, fascinated as always by the tapestry of nature that is drifting past. I can still see the river, branching off to the south, glistening in the bright afternoon sun.

~ ~ ~

As I turn away from the window, I notice that a man in military uniform has entered the carriage through the door at the far end. He walks slowly along the central aisle, pushing past the people standing there and studying every face as he passes. He seems familiar, though I cannot place him. I quickly drop my gaze when he looks in my direction, but I saw his eyes fix on me. A short while later he arrives at the rear of the carriage and speaks to Max in Russian, distorted by a thick accent. Suddenly I recognise him as one of the guards at the house at Yekaterinburg. As Max rises to greet him I bow my head and sit down on my case, hoping he will not see my face properly.

"Drubich," the soldier says, tersely.

"Nagy," replies Max, wary and tight lipped.

Nagy! The ruthless killer, Avadeyev's right-hand-man. How did he get on the train? I can only think that he must have boarded the train just before it left Yekaterinburg. Does that mean they know where we are, or did he join the train on the offchance? How many more of them are also here?

Despite the fact that he is shorter than Max, who stands taller than just about everyone in the carriage, Nagy's appearance and demeanour make him seem menacing. He is stockily built, with skin that is quite dark, like polished oak. His face is puffy, with high cheekbones, and he appears to squint through eyes that are no more than thin lines between prominent lids. "You are not in uniform," he accuses.

"No, I am on leave," Max replies, carefully. We are unprepared for this development, and Max is clearly defensive.

Nagy is staring past Max at me, and he points. "That is the servant girl from the house!"

"You are mistaken," says Max evenly. "This is my niece. I am returning her to my brother in Kordon."

The man is unconvinced. "Show me your papers," he demands of me.

"What are you talking about?" laughs Max, nervously. "Stop being ridiculous."

This seems to inflame Nagy, and events begin to happen very fast. I see him reach for the pistol that is in a leather holster on his belt, and I jump to my feet, a cry on my lips, but stand transfixed as Max steps quickly forward and grabs the wrist of Nagy's pistol hand, pushing him towards the rear door. Nearby passengers move out of their way, while the rest watch the sudden activity curiously, though no-one seems inclined to help either man.

Max slams the soldier's gun hand against the wall, but he does not drop the weapon. The door falls open and they stagger out onto the iron platform, still locked together, struggling, twisting, grunting. There is a muffled crack as Nagy's pistol goes off, a puff of smoke carried away instantly by the swirling wind, then Max gives a shove and the man tumbles down the steps and off the speeding train, his gun clattering behind and bouncing after him. Max stands breathing heavily and clutching the handrail. I run to his side and we look back at Nagy as he picks himself up and waves his fist at us.

~ ~ ~

We re-enter the carriage, aware of the curiosity of the people staring at us as we return to our cases. It is only when I put my arm around Max's waist that I notice a huge red stain on his shirt.

"You are hurt!" I blurt out. "Let me look."

We retreat into the corner of the swaying coach, and he takes off his jacket, wincing as he twists his body to slip it off his shoulders. When he unbuttons his shirt I can see that he has a small but deep wound in his side, from which blood is pouring. After a moment's thought, I quickly open my handbag and take one of the pads I have made for my periods. I place it over the hole, pressing gently, but as firmly as I dare, to stem the flow of blood.

"Hold it there while I make a bandage to keep it in place," I order. "Press as hard as the pain will allow."

"Yes nurse," he replies, trying to grin through clenched teeth.

I tear strips from one of our blankets, the only thing I can think of that will be long enough to wrap around him. Eventually we have a serviceable dressing held in place, and his blood loss seems to be under control.

A man who is sitting on one of the wooden seats

nearby and has been watching us, stands up and offers his seat to Max. He is quite old, about fifty, and at first Max refuses to take it, but the man insists and I tell Max that it is the best thing to do. It is such an unexpected and kind gesture that I am overwhelmed and thank him profusely as he helps Max lower himself gingerly onto the hard seat.

"It is nothing," the man replies, "there are too many brutes like that," he waves his arm in the direction by which Nagy has just ignominiously departed. "No better than savages who suddenly have power over us. I am glad you disposed of him."

Max smiles wryly. "Thank you, my friend. My name is Max, and this is my ... niece, Natalie."

"Pleased to meet you, Max, I am Dmitri."

He turns to me. "Now, young Natalie, you must get your ... uncle to see a doctor with that wound."

He raises an eyebrow knowingly as he utters the word 'uncle', clearly not taken in by Max's attempted subterfuge, and I find myself blushing. I quickly agree with him about the doctor, and look sternly at Max until he nods.

"Good," Dmitri smiles, "In a few hours we will arrive at Nizhny Novgorod, which happens to be my destination and my home. I know the doctor, and will be happy to take you to him."

Chapter 41 ~ A Doctor

It is late afternoon when the train stops at Nizhny Novgorod. Max is now looking very ill, and I am seriously worried. Even in the smoky gloom of the railway carriage I can see that his face has turned a shade of yellowy grey, and his eyes reveal the pain that he is otherwise concealing from us. As we disembark, Dmitri insists on carrying our baggage, and helps me to steady Max as he climbs carefully down the steps from the train. A man is waiting to greet Dmitri at the station exit, and they talk briefly, before the man leaves.

"It seems that I am required urgently," he explains to me, "and will have to leave you."

He raises a hand, and a cab moves to our side. He speaks to the driver, and hands him some money.

"This man will take you to the doctor's house," he tells me. "I am sorry I have to leave you. Good luck."

Max weakly shakes Dmitri's hand, managing a wan smile, and I give him a grateful hug.

We climb into the cab, and are taken into a residential suburb, where we stop outside a smart house. I jump out and position myself to be a leaning post for Max as he painfully lowers himself to the pavement, while the cab driver unloads our bags. Max seems now to be semi-conscious, barely able to control his muscles, and stares at the ground before his feet, as though confused.

As the cab disappears around the corner, I look up at the doctor's house. The low sun casts long shadows from high, spiked iron railings ranged across the front, giving it the appearance of a fortress. Four stone steps rise to a black-painted door, framed on either side by ostentatious, white, Grecian-style pillars. A polished brass plate on the door declares it to be the residence of 'Dr N.V. Kuznetsov M.D. (London)' and above it a heavy, brass knocker in the shape of a lion's head with a ring hanging from its mouth, stares mutely over my shoulder at infinity.

I lift the ring and let it fall, creating a thud that echoes inside the building. After a minute or so, the door is opened by a large, elderly woman encased from chin to toes in an enormous, black gown. Pale light from a single small gas lamp on the far wall barely lifts the gloom of the entrance hall behind her to a shade of maroon. "Yes?" she hisses.

"We have been attacked by robbers," I say, reciting our agreed story, "and my uncle has been wounded. We need to see the doctor."

She tutts and lets out a heavy sigh, as though we have brought all the burdens of the world to her door. "The surgery closes at six o'clock; come back tomorrow." She begins to close the door.

"He will be dead by then," I say, quickly. "Can you not see how ill he is?"

She pauses, sparing Max a cursory glance.

"If I had known we would miss surgery, I would have asked the robbers to wait until the morning, but they seemed to be in a hurry." I add, glaring at her.

"You had better come in," she snaps, looking anxiously past us for accomplices. She waits impatiently while I fetch each suitcase and struggle inside with it, then quickly shuts the door as soon as we are inside.

She leads us to a small room and holds the door open for us to enter. "Wait here!"

The room appears to be the doctor's surgery, for there is a long, scrubbed table in the centre, with a rack of metal implements beside it. Around the walls are cabinets containing bottles and other containers of all sizes, colours and shapes. I lead Max to a chair and help him to sit.

~ ~ ~

Shortly a middle-aged man arrives. He is plump, with a red nose and flushed cheeks, and is dressed in a maroon velvet jacket. Brusquely he points at the table and addresses Max, ignoring me as though I did not exist.

"I am Doctor Kuznetsov," he declares in a businesslike manner. "Lay on there so I can examine your wound." He reaches above the table and pulls a thin, brass chain connected to a large reflector hanging low from the ceiling. An intensely bright electric light floods the area below it in a blue-white glare.

Max is leaning heavily on me, scarcely able to stand. I manoeuvre him onto the table, struggling while the doctor watches, unhelping, seemingly uncaring. When I have Max sitting on the edge, I remove his jacket and bloodstained shirt to reveal the wound, then, as gently as possible, lower him into a prone position, finally lifting his feet onto the hard surface.

The doctor takes my place beside him, not quite pushing me aside, and begins cutting away the bandage I had made and examining the hole in Max's side. Unexpectedly, he suddenly inserts his finger into the cavity, and Max bellows with pain.

Kuznetsov straightens up. "The bullet is lodged deep in your intestine, I can feel it with the tip of my finger. If it stays there it will cause further damage which could be fatal. My fee to remove it will be ten rubles, payable in advance."

"Ten rubles!" I screech, incredulously, "that is more than a working man could earn for a month's hard labour."

"We have escaped one robber, only to face another," Max growls, glaring at the doctor, who shrugs, nervously.

"It is my price, you are free to leave if you wish."

We are at his mercy. Max needs to be treated at once, and the man knows it.

"You are well aware that we are not in a position to haggle," I say to the doctor, turning away from him to produce the payment from the bag concealed under the waistband of my skirt, where all our money is hidden. The doctor, bristling from Max's comment, takes the money, checks it, then, after pushing it into a pocket in his jacket, dons a large apron, rolls up his sleeves, and begins to assemble some metal instruments from the rack onto a small trolley beside the table.

I stand beside Max, on the opposite side to Kuznetsov, and watch as the doctor cleans the skin around the bullet hole then pokes inside with various long, shiny metal tools. Max cries out as the doctor probes deeper, and squeezes my hand so hard I feel that my bones must crack, before he passes out from the pain.

Eventually the doctor triumphantly holds the offending projectile aloft for me to see, then drops it with a clink into a small china dish. He continues to probe and peer into the wound, withdrawing several strands of cloth with his tweezers.

"These were carried into your uncle's flesh by the bullet," he explains. "If I had not removed them they would have caused severe infection." He fills a rubber bulb with some liquid, and attaches a nozzle. He then inserts the tube into Max's wound and squeezes, flushing out a brown fluid that he captures in a dish. After wiping the skin dry, he deftly applies several stitches to close the wound, then covers it with a new dressing and yards of white bandage wrapped several times around Max's middle.

As he works, I see Max's eyes flicker open, and he manages a small reassuring smile for me; I lean over the table and kiss him gently.

When the doctor is done he stands back. Despite the tension between us, I am grateful for what he had done, and I thank him.

He gives a small bow, nothing more than a slight leaning forward at the waist, then turns back to Max. "Avoid exertion for a few days and eat little ~ soup is best. Good day." With another little bow he leaves the room.

I rummage through Max's case for a clean shirt, and while I help him put it on, the housekeeper returns. She watches, dispassionately as I ease Max into his jacket, then, when we have collected our things, which I carry, to spare Max, she shows us to the door.

"Which way to the railway station?" I ask the woman as we stand in the fading daylight on the doorstep.

"Down the hill," she replies, curtly, shutting the door behind us.

"Lovely woman," Max grunts.

Shadows are beginning to stretch across the pavement, the sun sits benevolently on the roofs and spires to our right, washing the sky with magenta. I look up. The moon is already out, and the first bright stars are visible, and I realise that I have no idea of the time.

"How long do you think we were in there?" Max asks, as though reading my thoughts. He seems to be rather more alert, now that the bullet is gone and the wound is clean.

"No more than an hour, I should think."

"Ten rubles for an hour's work," he grunts. "Perhaps I should train to become a doctor."

I manage to grip the cases and my bag in such a way that I can carry them all, and we begin to walk down the hill. Max tries to take one, but I refuse to allow him. "We cannot risk you opening the wound again, Max. That is a bad injury you have."

"Stubborn woman," he grumbles.

"I'm glad you realise it. Now, for once in your life, do as you are told ~ walk!"

~ ~ ~

The part of the town where the doctor lives and practises is elegant and residential, with an air of wealth. But after about half an hour of slow walking down the hill, with frequent pauses for Max to rest and for me to put down the cases and flex my shoulders, shops and cafés begin to replace the houses. Here there are a few lights, and we begin to meet groups of people.

At the bottom of the hill, the road reaches a junction on a busy commercial street, and we stop. I put down the heavy cases as we look around for a sign of some kind indicating the direction of the railway station.

"Which way now?" Max ponders aloud.

"I will have to ask someone," I suggest, stepping forward to speak to a woman as she passes.

She points down the road to our left, and I thank her, turning back to Max, but find him in conversation with two men. With a shock I realise that they are police officers, and I desperately look about me to see if there is some way we can escape, but it is hopeless, so I return to Max's side.

"These gentlemen believe we are escaped criminals, Natalie," he informs me, nervousness clear in his voice.

"We simply want you to come with us to the police station," says one of the men.

Max gives a resigned shrug. "It's best we do as they wish."

The officers help me with the cases, bless them, as they lead us to a black carriage that stands nearby, its two horses waiting patiently. Effortlessly, they lift the cases with which I had been struggling into the large trunk on the rear of the vehicle, then one rides with the driver while the other sits inside with us.

"What crime are we supposed to have committed?" I ask him as we move off.

"I don't know, miss," he says. "We were just told to look out for a tall, injured man and a girl, and to bring them in."

The remainder of the short journey is completed in silence, and shortly we arrive at the police station, a grey building, in typical municipal style. We are escorted inside, and taken along various corridors, eventually arriving at a door with the words 'Captain Dmitri Lebedev' on a china plaque screwed onto its plain wooden face. One of the officers opens the door and steps back to allow us to enter, saying: "Are these the ones, sir?"

A familiar voice replies from within the room: "Ah yes, these are they. Hello Max, hello Natalie, it's good to see you both again. Come in and sit down."

We must look quite hilarious, standing there with looks of amazement on our faces.

Chapter 42 ~ Dmitri

"You're the captain of police?" I stammer.

Dmitri laughs. "Yes, I'm afraid so. Come on in, you're with friends."

Max steps towards the desk. "But why are we here?"

"Ah, well, I found reports about you waiting for my attention when I arrived, it seems some people are anxious to see you again."

"Are you going to hand us over?" Max asks, grimly.

"Good Lord no," Dmitri exclaims. "Certainly not. I imagine you will be anxious to resume your journey, so I have been making enquiries. There are no trains westwards over the weekend, I'm afraid, so you are stranded here until Monday. I could not see you sleeping on the streets ~ who knows what could happen to you ~ so I want to invite you to join me for a meal, then I will help you to find somewhere safe to stay. You must remain hidden until you are ready to travel."

He laughs again and gestures towards two chairs by his desk. "Max, Natalie, please sit down, you are making me tired just watching you."

Max grins nervously as we sit. "So, we are not under arrest?"

"Oh, no-no-no, you are here as my friends and my guests."

I lean forward. "Dmitri, I don't know what to say. Why are you being so kind to us?"

He becomes serious. "That man, the one on the

train, the soldier, I have seen too many people like that in recent times. There is a group in this area, calling themselves 'The Urals Soviet', claiming to represent the new government, demanding this and that. Do not get me wrong, I agree with the need for change, for the old monarchy to be replaced with a fairer system, but what I have seen so far worries me greatly. Have you heard of a man called Avadeyev?" Max and I exchange glances, and Dmitri nods. "I see you have. He called me this afternoon on the telephone device," he gestures towards the shiny, new, black machine on his desk, "ordering me to look out for two fugitives, a tall man and a girl, instructing me to arrest them and report to him if they appear in Nizhny Novgorod. What did you do to upset him?"

There is a pause. When Max speaks, his voice is tense. "We witnessed a murder, carried out at Avadeyev's command."

By revealing the reason we were on the run, he could be risking our lives, and he knows it. He is placing great faith in his judgement of the chief. It is a brave action, based only on our short association with him. For all that Dmitri is being nice to us, we do not really know him, it could just be an act to trap us. Understandably, Max has not said who the victims were.

Dmitri nods again, slowly. "I thought it must be something like that."

Suddenly he stands, decisively, the smile back on his face. "Are you hungry? We could eat now if you would like."

We are indeed, very hungry, having had nothing since our sparse breakfast, half a day earlier. He walks with us out of the rear of the police station, and down an alley to the back door of a nearby café. There, in the kitchen, the proprietor, clearly an old friend of Dmitri's, sets a table and brings three glasses of beer.

I look around the busy room, tentatively sipping my ale. Two cooks are hard at work, and the air is warm and heavy with the smells of cooking. The man returns with a menu, and Max chooses a bowl of mutton soup with vegetables; I have the same. We watch the man ladle it from a large pan, and in moments it is before us, proving to be so thick as to be almost a stew. Afterwards, when we try to pay, Dmitri will not allow us, telling the proprietor to put the bill on his account.

~ ~ ~

As we walk slowly back into the police station, and re-enter the captain's office, Max asks Dmitri if he knows any more about Avadeyev. Dmitri becomes serious again. "He and Yakob Yurovsky created the Urals Soviet about a year ago, under Lenin's personal guidance. Yurovsky is Lenin's man, and heads the whole region; Avadeyev is in charge of the local division of the army ~ some people say he led a gang of bandits before that. He came here to see me in March, after the Bolsheviks took power in Saint Petersburg and Moscow. Max, Natalie, watch out for him, Avadeyev is ambitious and ruthless; he is also cunning, and means to impress the party leadership in any way he can."

"What did he tell you about us?" Max asks. He looks tired, washed out. I wish we could have a few quiet days to allow him to recover.

"Just that you are wanted for questioning," Dmitri answers. "He said we were to look out for a tall man, who is pretending that the young woman with him is his niece. He described what you are both wearing. I assume the man you threw from the train managed to report back to him."

Max is pensive, and I can see that he is struggling to make a decision. "Dmitri, what is your opinion of the Tsar?" he asks, finally.

"I'm afraid I think he is an idiot," comes the blunt reply. "He has ruined Russia with his wars and his bad judgements. It's no wonder he fled the country when the revolution started. I don't think he's a bad man, just stupid."

"Where do you think he is now?"

"Oh, probably in England. He has family connections over there."

"Would you believe me if I told you he is dead, murdered by Avadeyev, along with his whole family and their friends and servants?"

The captain is visibly shocked. "Oh, dear God! Are you sure?"

"Quite certain, Dmitri, we were there when it happened." He glances at me; I nod, nervously, and he continues. "Natalie was part of the royal household, she only just escaped the same fate. That is the real reason Avadeyev wants us captured; we know too much and we will be killed if he gets his hands on us."

Dmitri is shaking his head in amazement. "You really need to get out of the country, there is nowhere in Russia that will be safe for you."

"We were planning to head for Ukraine, I have family there," Max says.

"Forgive me, Max, but that would be unwise. Ukraine is embroiled in its own revolution, and the Bolsheviks are at the heart of that, too."

"Is the war still raging in France and Germany?" I enquire.

"Yes, very much so," Dmitri replies, gravely.

"What about England?" asks Max.

"England is still in the war, but it may be the safest place for you, if you can get there." He stands up, suddenly. "Look, you must rest tonight ~ longer, if possible ~ to recover your strength from your injury. I can take you to an honest guest house, and we shall resume in the morning. But listen, you should avoid being seen out together; you do not know who may be watching out on behalf of Avadeyev."

He helps us gather our luggage, then takes us in a police carriage to a lodging house near the river. "You will be safe here, the beds are clean and the cost is reasonable," he assures us as we wait for someone to answer the bell.

~ ~ ~

The door is opened by a small woman, dressed in a simple, full peasant dress. Her face is a shade of copper, and when she smiles in greeting to Dmitri she reveals a piano-keyboard of black and white teeth.

"Captain!" she screeches with delight.

"Good evening, Mrs Novikov, I wish to introduce my two friends, Max and Natalie. Would you please be so kind as to provide them with a good room for tonight?"

"Of course!" she beams. "Come in dears and let me show you."

The three of us follow her up a flight of stairs and into a small but neat bedroom with a double bed. She has clearly assumed that we are married, and none of us chooses to disillusion her. The room does not compare with the luxury I have enjoyed for most of my life, but neither is it as bad as I have endured over recent months. The furniture is old, but cared for, as is the bedding. I wander over to the little window, with its pretty floral curtains, and look out, but all that can be seen are a few twinkling lights in the distance, and the pale glow of street lamps below.

Dmitri deposits our cases, then departs, after an emotional hug from me at the front door and a warm handshake from Max.

"Mrs Novikov," Max says anxiously, after Dmitri has gone, "may I enquire what you charge for the room?"

"Ooh, as you are friends of the dear captain, it will be 10 kopecks a night, lovie, includin' breakfast." After the dreadful price charged by the doctor, we breathe sighs of relief that the rate is so reasonable. We pay her for our first night, and retire to bed.

Max, though weak, looks less pale than earlier in the day, and I hope that a few day's rest will see him return to his former self. As for myself, exhausted after a busy and eventful day and worried about the future, I want nothing except to sleep in the arms of the man I love.

Chapter 43 ~ Vadim

Soon after dawn, I slip from our bed and gaze out of the window of our room upon a wonderful scene. The front of the building looks across a wide green to the river beyond. Small boats, with their brown sails flapping, are weaving intricate patterns over the water, and on the green a travelling circus is an artist's palette of vivid colours in the bright early sunshine. Elegantly-dressed people are walking along the pavement beneath our window, and carriages glide past on the road, their horses beautifully decorated with plumes and ribbons.

After breakfast, ignoring Dmitri's admonition, we take a gentle stroll together down towards the river. The late-July sun is already hot, promising another fine day; I hope that we will have time to stay for a while and enjoy this lovely town. The circus is preparing to move on, and we walk curiously between the rows of busy labourers, stepping over ropes and giving a wide berth to cages of snarling wild animals. One man is hitching a trailer to a gigantic steam engine, which broods like some pre-historic beast, hissing ominously. Then a blast of noise, like a trumpet played badly, heralds the passing of an elephant, led by a young girl. Max holds my hand, and we drift happily through the fantasy world.

When we return to our lodgings, Mrs Novikov informs us that we have a guest, a gentleman, who is waiting for us in the garden. Curious, we follow her through the house, and find the man sitting at a wooden table on a small patio area. He stands politely as we emerge from the house.

"Vadim Konstantinovich Ippolitov at your service," he says formally, with a slight bow.

He is short, balding, wearing clean but worn clothes and little, round spectacles. He looks nervous, his head is gleaming with perspiration. As we sit down with him at the table, Mrs Novikov returns, bringing a bottle of wine and some glasses, then leaves us.

"Captain Lebedev asked me to speak to you," the man begins. "He said that you are being pursued, and need to escape from Russia, perhaps to England. He has also explained some of the details that have made you fugitives."

He pauses to sip his wine, raising his head and looking over the top of his glass at Max as though expecting a response. He has a small moustache, which he regularly brushes with a fingertip, left, then right.

Max nods. "Yes. Dmitri told us that he would speak to someone on our behalf. But, forgive me for my bluntness, Mr Ippolitov: how can you help us?"

Ippolitov's tension is apparent; I cannot decide if we should trust him or not.

"I have contacts who may be able to arrange cover for you," he replies. "But first I must understand how you came to be in this position, and find out if you have any information which may be useful to us."

Max leans towards the other man, his elbows on the

table. "This is a very dangerous situation for us," he says quietly. "And for you too, if you help us."

It is the man's turn to nod. "I will be direct, as I think it is best for all of us." He turns to me. "Dmitri told me that you gave your name as Natalie, and said that you worked for the Tsar; could you be Natalie Tereshchenko?"

I am amazed. Someone else who knows my name before I have met them! For a moment, I half expect him to say that he has been told it by an angel. I look at Max for guidance. "May I ask how you have that name, and why you think it may be important?" he says, carefully.

Ippolitov smiles. "Word is spreading. If the young lady is who I think she is, she could hold the future of Russia in her hands."

He sits back in his chair, apparently reassured and rather more relaxed than earlier.

"Max, Natalie ~ you are the sole surviving witnesses to a horrific murder, a crime of enormous proportions, with implications that are hard to estimate. There is something more that you probably do not yet know: on the day of your escape from Yekaterinberg, Bolshevik soldiers swept the country, rounding up any remaining members of the royal family and killing them all, every single one."

Max and I both inhale sharply at this news ~ it so unexpected, so obscene as to defy reason. Even the events we witnessed have not prepared us for this.

"I am sorry," says Ippolitov quietly.

I am shaking my head in disbelief. The scale of this

pogrom is beyond anything I had expected, beyond all reason. Max, in contrast, is nodding, as though it confirms something in his mind. "Lenin," he says, pointedly.

"Yes," Ippolitov replies, "he wants all trace of the Romanovs wiped from the records. No-one with royal blood must live to become a possible focus for opposition forces."

He looks piercingly over the top of his spectacles at me. I blink. Is he hinting that he knows my secret? I look down into my wine glass, twisting it between my fingers on the table, avoiding his gaze.

"Avadeyev is dreadfully embarrassed that you have escaped," he continues. "He has men scouring the countryside looking for you. It is my job to make you disappear." He studies Max, then me. "One thing is certain; if we are to get you to safety, you must travel separately. As a couple, you are just too easy to identify."

"You are not the first to tell us that," Max says, shrugging. "What have you in mind?"

"Ah, well, we are lucky. There is a circus in town ~ an excellent place to hide you; there are people of all sizes, many strong men like you."

"He must not do any physical work for a while," I interpose. "He has a serious bullet wound in his side."

Ippolitov looks with surprise at Max, who nods.

"I'm sorry, I had not realised. But it need not be a problem, you do not have to work, just look as though you do; I will take you to meet the circus owner, to see what can be arranged."

"And Natalie?" Max asks. I can see that he is becoming tense again.

"We have a small convent, here in Nizhny Novgorod. I have already spoken with the Abbess, who is willing to help. She is arranging for a small group of nuns, perhaps four or five, to travel to Moscow, to visit the Marfo-Mariinsky Convent. You, Natalie, will be one of those nuns."

I cannot help grinning; me, a nun!

"No!"

I jump as Max suddenly erupts. His face is red, and his eyes are tight slits as he growls: "Natalie needs me near her, now more than ever. I will not leave her, will not allow my love to travel without me. Think of something else." He turns away and slumps back into his chair, breathing heavily, looking down at his arms, which are folded across his chest.

"Max, our options are limited, and we cannot delay," Vadim replies carefully. "There are informers everywhere. If you stay here, it is absolutely certain that Avadeyev will find out, and the net will quickly close around you. He may already know. Unless we act now, I may not be able to do anything for you, and if you travel together, you will be spotted as sure as the sun that crosses the sky."

Max shrugs, sulkily, and refuses to look up. I understand his reluctance, I feel the same. He is my strength, even injured as he is now, and my comfort. But together we are a magnet to the eye of anyone on the lookout for us.

I rise from my chair and crouch beside him, looping

my hands through his big arm, resting my head on his shoulder and looking up into his eyes. "I think we have to take this opportunity, my darling," I whisper. "We will be together again soon." I look over to Ippolitov for confirmation.

He nods his head. "Yes, about a week. The circus has its own railway train, and will be travelling indirectly to Moscow, arriving next Sunday."

Max's lips are pinched tight in resistance; his instinct to protect me is battling with his desire to get me to safety. Eventually, he looks up at Ippolitov and nods once, tensely.

Vadim smiles. "Good. I will go at once to talk with the circus owner. When I return, you must both be ready to travel."

He stands, and we rise to follow him to the door. "I should be back within an hour," he tells us over his shoulder as he heads down the path towards the circus. "Stay indoors until I return; no more foolish excursions like this morning."

I close the door, and we join Mrs Novikov in the kitchen to discuss what will be happening.

~ ~ ~

It is an hour later, and we are in our room, sadly closing our cases and talking softly, when we hear a familiar, chilling sound outside. We run to the window to look out, just in time to see Avadeyev's motor car passing on the road beneath us; we cannot see how many people are inside it, because the canvas roof is up, but the car is unmistakeable. The expression of shock on my face must mirror Max's, because he takes me in his arms and holds me tightly. I cannot help thinking that we were standing beside that road only a few hours ago; if he had passed then, he would have seen us.

"What is he doing here?" I ask, knowing, of course, that Max has no more idea than I do.

"He wouldn't travel this far without some motive," he answers grimly. "Someone must have seen us. He probably has spies everywhere, or perhaps someone on the train reported us getting off."

"Is this to be our lives: forever running, in perpetual fear of that man?" I am close to tears.

He kisses my forehead, and we stand thoughtfully looking out across the green.

"Perhaps it's not him!" I realise, suddenly. "In fact, the more I think about it, I don't think it can possibly be him. We didn't arrive here until late yesterday, after a full day's travelling on the train; even if someone contacted him at once, he couldn't have made it here so quickly."

"That's true," he grins. "And he would have had to put his car on the train, there's no way he could drive here from Yekaterinberg. It must have been someone else, with a similar car to his; I suppose there must be others about."

"Yes, of course." I smile up at him, relieved, and he puts his arm around my waist.

Shortly, we see the small figure of Ippolitov crossing the road towards us, accompanied by two, bigger men. We pick up our bags and carry them downstairs, where Mrs Novikov meets us and leads us into her drawing room. Ippolitov arrives almost at once, with the other men. They are muscular, unsmiling and intimidating.

As I look at them, I feel a rising fear that we have allowed ourselves to be trapped.

Chapter 44 ~ Yelena

Mrs Novikov puts an arm round my shoulder. "Don't look so worried, dear," she says quietly. "We are all on your side." She guides me to a settee, and sits beside me. The men also find seats.

Ippolitov waves a hand to indicate the two men who arrived with him. "These gentlemen work at the circus. I asked them to come over because they are tall and strong, like you, Max. When you walk back with them, you will not be quite so conspicuous; and they have brought you some labourer's clothes, to change your appearance a little. All these things will help you to blend into your surroundings."

I am hugely relieved, and I can see Max relax a little, too. One of the men gives him the bundle of clothes he is carrying, and Max accepts it with a small nod of thanks.

While he is out of the room, changing, Vadim turns to me. "The Abbess wants you to spend the weekend at the Convent, to provide you with appropriate clothes, and to teach you as much as possible, so that you can behave correctly."

Mrs Novikov interrupts: "I will take you there after Max has departed."

I am glad it is to be her; I have grown fond of the old lady. I smile my thanks. "How will Max and I be re-united?"

Vadim resumes. "The circus is making its way to

Moscow, to perform in the permanent arena there. It has its own train, which it is packing at this moment, and will set off tomorrow for Kirov, where it will stay for two days. Then it will travel to Moscow, to arrive next Sunday. In the meantime, you will make your way to the Marfo-Mariinsky Convent, where you will stay as a guest of the Abbess."

Max returns to the room, looking very different in worn, workman's clothes; Ippolitov and the two circus men stand and join him at the door. Tears suddenly fill my eyes as I run to hold him once more, and he wraps his big arms around me. We can't speak, and just cling to each other for one last time.

Then he is gone, walking down the road, indistinguishable from the other two. I stand at the front door watching until he disappears into the crowds milling around the circus, wondering when I will see him again. Vadim remains with us for a while, then he too slips out quietly, leaving just we women ~ Mrs Novikov and me.

"Ready dear?" she asks.

Wiping my tears from my face with my sleeve, I nod. She puts on her coat and we leave the little guest house and begin to walk up the hill.

"Mrs Novikov," I begin.

"Call me Yelena, dear," she interrupts with a reassuring smile.

"Yelena, there is more to you than I know, isn't there?"

"That depends on how much you have worked out," she answers cagily.

"Well, I can't help noticing that everyone seems to know you and respect you, and they all come to you when things need organising."

She laughs. "I'm a popular lady alright. Yes, you are right, I like to help people."

"And you have done this kind of thing before?"

She nods. "A few times, yes."

"But why Max and me? We can't give you anything in return, yet you are risking your life for us. And so are these other people, Dmitri, Vadim, the men from the circus. Why, Yelena?"

We have reached the gates of a park, and Yelena leads me through to where some seats have been provided beside the path. There, we put down my bags and sit in the mottled shade of a tree. She looks around. The park is nearly deserted; a young couple stroll hand-in-hand a short way off, eyes only for each other, some children are playing in the open, watched by their mothers or nannies, but there is no-one nearby.

"You underestimate your importance, my love," she says, thoughtfully. "You are not only a witness to a terrible crime, you are also the sole survivor. Avadeyev cannot allow you to carry word to the outside world about what has happened ~ and he has the whole structure of the Bolshevik machine to help him find you and silence you." She looks at me, gravely. "But, Natalie, you are not alone. All over Russia, there are people who are loyal to the old ways, and they will do anything they possibly can to restore them. You have a responsibility to them: they deserve to know what has happened."

"What do they expect me to do, Yelena? I can hardly go around street corners shouting about it, Lenin would have me killed before I uttered ten words. And who would hear me?"

"The word is already spreading, Natalie," she says, softly. "Remember, there is a strong underground network."

"Oh great," I sigh, "I can feel the net tightening around me already."

"We will take care of you. Lenin doesn't hold all the cards, not by any measure." She stands. "Come on, I must get you to the convent." I rise to my feet, but before we move off, she puts her arms around my waist and hugs me. "Don't worry, you are in good hands," she whispers.

~ ~ ~

The convent is not, as I have been expecting, an ancient building with centuries of dusty history floating in cold, stone corridors, but small and modern. When Yelena turns from the pavement and rings the doorbell of an ordinary house, I assume that she is perhaps visiting a friend on our way. But the door is opened by a young nun, and Yelena turns to me, saying, quietly: "Goodbye, young Natalie, and God be with you." She kisses me on each cheek, and is gone. I raise my hand to wave as she turns the corner, but she doesn't look back.

The nun at the door smiles.

"Hello, Natalie. My name is Alice," she says, stepping back to allow me in. She is tall and thin ~

gaunt, even ~ but pretty. She is a little older than me, with dark hair which is cut very short, almost shaved.

She leads me to a warm office, where I met the Abbess, Mother Mary Magdalene. The Reverend Mother is a small woman, who could be any age from sixty to eighty, it is impossible to tell ~ her skin is dark and wrinkled, but her eyes are bright and sharp.

"Our convent here in Nizhny is just a small outreach of the provincial monastery in Makaryevo," she explains to me, after the introductions. "There are five of us here, offering help to the poor and homeless of our little town. Sister Alice," she indicates the nun with a nod of her head, "will help you to prepare, and will accompany you on the train on Monday. You will be joined by more sisters at Makaryevo."

"Thank you for helping me," I say. She is an easy person to like: natural, warm, motherly. Dressed in her black robes, she looks almost saintly.

She smiles. "I'm glad to. But there is much you have to do for yourself; by Monday, you must look, sound and think like a nun. False papers are being prepared for you in your new identity; I hope to receive them tomorrow. Now, go with Alice to begin your training." She stands and circles her desk to shake my hand. I notice that she walks with difficulty.

Alice holds the door open for me, and as I reach it, Mother Mary, echoing Yelena's words earlier, says simply: "God be with you."

I smile, grimly. I need a miracle, but I don't expect to see one.

Chapter 45 ~ Sister Ephraimia

In a comfortable little bedroom, Alice shows me the clothes I will be wearing. As I undress, so she can show me how to wear them, she insists that I remove everything.

"You must not have anything from your former life," she tells me. Alice is about eighteen years old, with a clean complexion and sparkling brown eyes, though her skin is tight on her cheekbones, and her lips are thin. She, too, has the calm air about her that I noticed with the Abbess.

"But I am not really becoming a nun," I say, "it is just a pretence."

I begin to undress, placing my clothes in a pile on a chair.

"I know," she replies seriously. "This is not for ascetic or devotional reasons, but for your safety. We hope that none of us will be searched, but suppose you are; what will they find?"

I grin. "Ah, silk French knickers. That could be incriminating, I suppose."

She returns my grin. "Right, so take them off. And that necklace will have to go, too." She points to my silver chain with my birthstone.

"I suppose the same applies to everything in my suitcase," I say, as I put the chain on the pile and remove the last of my undies. "The clothes given to me by Max's sister, Yulia?" I know what the answer will be, of course.

She nods, handing me some cotton pants. "Shall I give them to the poor?" she asks.

"Yes, please," I answer, quickly pulling on the knickers, feeling self-conscious in my nakedness. "I would like that. But what about my diaries? I cannot bear to lose them."

"Sister," she says, gently, "you must not have anything with you that could link you to Natalie Tereshchenko. I could keep them here for you, if you wish; then you can contact me when you are safe, and I will send them to you." She starts to help me into a black robe.

"Yes, look after them, please," I reply. "One day, they are to become a book about my life."

She arches her eyebrows. "That will be quite a book," she exclaims as she begins tying a black scarf around my head. "I will put them in the safe until you can send for them. Now, the robe you are wearing is called an Isorassa," she explains, "and this scarf is the Apostolnik. You must learn to tie it yourself."

She removes it, and guides me as I practice tying it.

"Right," she says, "now you look like a novice. You would remain one for the first, oh ... three years in the convent. If you came to us here at, say, thirteen, you would have probably have taken the next step by now and become a sister." She holds up another black gown. "You would then receive this, the Exorassa, the outer garment."

As she helps me into it, she asks, casually: "How well do you know the Bible?"

I cough. "Rather well. Alexandra pumped it into us every day." At the mention of her name, I feel my voice fade as the memories flood back.

"Good," Alice says briskly, seeming not to notice. "That may come in handy if you are interrogated."

"Do you think that's likely?" I ask, anxious at the thought.

"I sincerely hope not. But don't be under any illusion, Natalie, your life is in considerable danger. The Communists want you eliminated, and they are combing the country for you."

She holds me at arms length and studies me briefly, then turns me towards an old, scratched mirror.

"There! You look the part, now."

I see, not the girl I know, but someone who looks just like a nun. It is amazing.

"Even Max would not recognise me," I mutter.

"Is he your man?" Alice asks, gently.

I nod, too emotional to answer. I turn to face her, tears in my eyes, and she gives me a hug.

When I am composed, she steps back and studies me.

"One final touch," she says, holding up a veil, and loosely tying it for me. "This is the Epanokamelavkion. You must wear it at all times when outside the convent."

I have to admit that, as a disguise, it takes some beating.

As we leave the room, and while Alice's back is turned for a moment, I reach into the pile of clothes and extract my necklace, slipping it into my robe.

~ ~ ~

Six o'clock the next morning, and Alice wakes me for prayers. How strange it feels to resume the practice that was the routine of my whole life at Alexander Palace. We dress in our inner robes and tidy our beds, then go down to the little chapel in the basement. After prayers with the Abbess, and the reading of a gospel, the service ends with a psalm.

Alice then takes me into another little room that proves to be a library, where we sit at an oak table and she waves a sheet of paper she was handed by the Abbess after prayers.

"The Reverend Mother has been given the name by which you are to be known," she says, as soon as we are seated. "Your papers will be here later in the day, but we have to spend our time getting you familiar with your new identity."

I can hear the voices of a small choir intoning a chant, rising from the chapel below. It adds to the sense of unreality that is making the whole experience like a dream.

"Who am I to be?" I ask, with some irony.

"You are Sister Ephraimia," Alice grins, reading from the page. "You are aged fifteen. You were born 17th June 1903 in the Perm region, although you remember nothing of that place because you were made an orphan at the age of six, and taken in by the sisters of the convent at Makaryevo."

Through the morning, we systematically pick our way though my former life, and I memorise all the details, aware that one little mistake could mean death, and perhaps not just for me. At mid-day, we stop for lunch with the other nuns in the small dining room ~ bread, fresh salad vegetables and a little wine ~ accompanied by a reading of the life of Saint Peter, intoned by one of the sisters.

All afternoon, Alice grills me on the morning's work, until every detail is deeply embedded in my brain. Then, at about five o'clock Mother Mary interrupts with the documents that have been forged for me. They are impressive little pieces of paper and card, some that look as old as I am supposed to be, some almost new.

Later, after dinner, we attend evening prayers. I am aware that, in all things, I must be convincing in my portrayal of a nun, so I watch everyone carefully, and try to carry myself as they do, speak as they do. I feel like an actress, learning a new role. Afterwards, we retire to our bedroom, where we talk quietly for a short while. I ask Alice if she does not find the restrictions and rules of chastity and obedience all rather arduous.

"Oh no," she smiles, wistfully, "it is my life. I am giving back to God what He gave me. Without the sisters, I would have died. I am happy to dedicate myself to serving Jesus."

"How different our lives have been," I comment. "And yet, here we are, thrown together."

Alice extinguishes our candle, and we climb into our beds. With a thrill, I realise that, tomorrow, we will begin our long journey across the heart of Russia. At the same moment, my mind, as it does at every opportunity, returns to thinking about my dear Max. I cannot imagine what his life is like, and, instead, dwell on our times together. I fall asleep with memories of his face before me and his strong arms around me.

~ ~ ~

The next morning, feeling very self-conscious in my new clothes, and naked without my diary, I set off with Alice and Mother Mary Magdalene to catch our train. I am carrying a small, brown, leather bag, given to me by the Abbess, containing a bible, some cotton underclothes, and my identity documents. I have very little money; Max and I agreed that, as we were travelling separately, our small reserve of cash would be safer with him. At the station, as expected, we find the entrance barred by soldiers in uniform. With cold fear crushing my chest so hard that I find it difficult to breathe, we approach the men and join a short line of would-be travellers.

When it is our turn, the young officer glares at us, wordlessly holding out his hand for our papers. Mother Mary Magdalene hands hers over first; he snatches them and, after a cursory glance, hands them back with a twist of his head that instructs her to proceed. He is not interested in older women, they are looking for young girl with a tall man.

I step forward next. "Remove the veil," he demands. I obey. His eyes search my face as he takes my small wad of papers; I hold his gaze for a moment, but then turn my eyes down, unwilling to intimidate him or attract attention. After studying each item, he thrusts the documents back at me with the same twist of his head; I step past him and join the Reverend Mother, replacing my veil, trying to control my breathing.

When Alice has been treated to the same scrutiny, he suddenly speaks to the three of us, loudly, for all around to hear.

"There is no room for religion under the new order," he pronounces in a deep voice filled with contempt. "The people have no need of your god."

With a sneer, he turns away, dismissively, and returns to his task of searching for the renegades.

Feeling slightly elated that we have passed through our first checkpoint, we enter the station. Alice and I go to the clerk and buy our tickets to Makaryevo. Mother Mary Magdalene is just there to see us off, she will not be travelling with us.

Chapter 46 ~ Another Train

When the train stops at Makaryevo, we look anxiously out of the window for the girls who are to join us; at least they are easy to spot in the crowd. We have been fortunate to find a group of seats to ourselves in the centre of the carriage, so I stay aboard to keep them while Alice leaps from the train to lead the three nuns to me.

As my four companions arrive, the train gives a lurch and begins to move. With nervous giggles, they stagger to the seats and flop down, then Alice introduces us. Sister Juliana and Sister Monica are about the same age and size as me, and it is obvious that a good deal of thought has been given to organising the group so that I do not stand out. Sister Agatha is a little older and taller, and has been chosen to act as the leader of our little party.

With echoes of my outward journey to Tobolsk, a year earlier, the miles pass beneath us with tedious monotony, and the first day passes slowly. Every hour or two, I walk the length of the carriage with one or other of the girls, either just for the exercise, or for one of us to visit the toilet compartment; we have agreed to do nothing alone, it is our first rule of self-preservation. Other travellers watch us as we pass, and we smile and offer a simple blessing.

There is a young woman, travelling alone but obviously at a late stage of pregnancy. She asks us to pray for her, as her husband has been killed in an accident and she is on her way to be with her family for the birth. Several other passengers gather around us as Sister Agatha chants a prayer, and they respond with us in the appropriate places. We finish with a song which, fortunately, I recognise from Alexandra's services and am able to join in. It is moving to see the happiness on the face of the young mother-to-be. I am beginning to realise that there is more to religion than just the rituals with which I grew up, a personal meaning that touches people deep inside.

~ ~ ~

The morning of day two, and as the train pulls into Danilov station, in the Yaroslavl Oblast, I notice that there are many soldiers, in groups of three or four, at intervals along the platform. The train stops, and I see the men near our carriage push aside the people attempting to board and climb the steps, brandishing their guns. It seems that we are about to be searched, and they are surely looking for me. The doors at each end of our carriage are thrown open, and soldiers burst in. There are gasps from the passengers.

With rising tension we hear them moving from one row of seats to the next, converging on the centre of the coach, aggressively demanding to see each passenger's documents. Suddenly one is looming over us, glaring down at us.

"Papers!" he spits, holding his hand out towards Sister Monica, who is nearest the aisle.

While she hastily fishes out her documents from her

purse, the rest of us prepare to hand ours over. He makes a sign to indicate that we must remove our veils, and nervously we undo them on one side and let them drop. One by one, he examines our little pieces of card and paper, scrutinising each of us in turn.

When he reaches me, I am so scared I can hardly breathe. It seems to me that he spends longer over my documents than any of the others, and his eyes probe mine; I manage to hold his gaze, though every part of me wants to turn away. Then he is thrusting my papers wordlessly back at me and turning away to face Sister Agatha.

Within five minutes he is done with us, and I hear him shouting at the people in the next seats, behind me. A few moments later, he and his colleagues are clumping down the aisle past us and disappearing through the door at the front. They are done.

Outside, a whistle is blown and the train begins to move again.

I realise that I am crying, and can hear one or two other women in the carriage weeping. The fear was so intense, the men's presence so intimidating, that I feel as though we have been physically beaten. I see that Sister Monica is similarly affected, and is shaking and sobbing, so I sit beside her and put my arm around her shoulder. She turns and rests her head against me, and we hold onto each other until, slowly, we both relax.

I turn to the rest of our little group. "I am so sorry," I say, quietly. "You should not have to suffer this for me."

I wonder if, when they volunteered to help, they

were aware at the time how dangerous it really was.

"On the contrary," Sister Agatha replies, quietly, "it is our duty and our privilege."

"But why?" I ask, puzzled.

"Because you are our future," she answers, simply.

"Me? How can I have anything to do with it?"

Sister Agatha fixes me with a look that frightens me. "Because only you can restore Russia to her former glory," she whispers.

I stare at her, stunned, wondering if I am reading too much into her words. Surely, she could not possibly know my secret?

"Sister Agatha, you have lost me. I am just a fugitive, fleeing for my life because I was unlucky enough to witness a murder."

She studies me intently for several moments, then nods her head, slowly.

"Perhaps I have said too much," she finally answers, quietly. "I am sorry, Sister Ephraimia."

By tacit mutual agreement, we say no more on the subject, and sit quietly looking out of the windows at the passing scenery. The sun climbs the broad, blue sky like a mountaineer, traversing from one small, white cloud to the next, until it passes overhead and begins to shine down into our eyes as we look ahead. As it starts its lazy descent towards the misty western horizon we cross the Volga, and I know that Moscow is close. I do not want to look out of the window as violent images flash unwanted through my mind from the last time I was here, of shootings and looting and the quiet dignity of people queueing for food. But at last I raise my head and see the city again, beautiful in the afternoon sun. It appears to be more peaceful, this time; I hope that it is not an illusion.

~ ~ ~

We emerge from the echoing, marble concourse of the palatial station building onto the streets of Moscow, blinking in the bright sunlight, and I look around for the nuns who are to meet us. I am searching for similar habits to those we are wearing, but Alice grabs my hand and drags me through the milling crowd towards two sisters who are dressed, not in black robes, but creamy white.

They introduce themselves to us as Sister Margaret and Sister Charitina, two ladies of middle years, both tall and slim, and each with that now familiar, far-away look in their eyes that indicates that their sights are set beyond earthly matters.

As we begin to walk slowly away from the railway station, Sister Margaret hooks her arm in mine and gives me a smile. "It is wonderful to meet you, Sister Ephraimia; stories about you are spreading throughout Russia."

She clearly thinks that I will be pleased, but the thought only worries me more. Too many people know of me, and seem think that I have something to give them.

We are led a short distance through wide streets, from the station to a square, with neat, walled gardens laid out in the centre. On one side of the square sits a beautiful white church set in green lawns, and it is to this building that we proceed. A large pair of oak doors form its front entrance, set in a carved stone arch beneath an icon of the face of Christ. High above, a bell tower at each corner is topped with a gleaming copper dome surmounted by a golden cross. They seem to shine against the blue sky.

We turn aside, however, taking a winding path through pretty gardens along the side of the building to a smaller and more modest entrance at the rear. This admits us to an annex, a simple, wooden-floored corridor with several plain doors off to the right and left and a flight of stairs at the far end. While Sister Charitina takes the others into what appears to be a chapel, Sister Margaret leads me up the stairs. There, on a small landing, she stops and knocks softly with her knuckles on a door. What follows transforms my day into unreality, for the voice that calls us to enter is eerily familiar, and my breath catches in my chest. No, it cannot be.

Chapter 47 ~ Elizabeth

I hesitate, confused. That sound, like a recording from the past, echoes in my head like the clamour of cathedral bells, like standing inside one of those bells as it swings, as the clapper hurtles past my head and smashes against the wall, setting up a reverberation that numbs the senses.

"Go on," says Margaret, "open the door."

Moving as though in a trance, I push the door and step into the large, bright room beyond, then stop; I cannot move. It is as though an arm has reached out and brought me to a halt, so that Margaret, following close behind, walks into my back. For crossing the room to greet me is Alexandra, Empress of Russia, alive as I never expected ever to see her again. I feel my legs becoming weak, see the room begin to sway before me. It is not possible! She is dead! I was there when it happened!

Sister Margaret quickly takes my hand and leads me to a chair, where I sit heavily, staring at the Empress, who is now seated in another chair, close to me.

"Hello Natalie," she says, "I am Elizabeth Feodorovna, Abbess of this convent, and elder sister of the Empress Alexandra."

I take a deep breath. Too much is happening, and my head is spinning. So this is not Alexandra? She has not risen from the dead, or miraculously survived the assassination? I feel such a mixture of emotions that I can hardly think; tears fill my eyes, and my hands begin shaking. The likeness is amazing, it is not surprising that I had thought it was her. She has the same eyes, mouth and hair-colour as Alexandra, and of course, her voice has the same accent. But closer, and with the benefit of new knowledge, there are subtle differences: Elizabeth is taller than her sister, stands straighter, her hair is cut shorter, her face is, somehow, older.

"I thought you were Alexandra," I stammer. "You are so like her."

She smiles at me. "Oh, I see. I wondered why it was such a shock to you. Well, take your time, just gather your thoughts. You have been through so much, and this has been another surprise."

As my mind assembles the latest information, I realise that Elizabeth is, herself, dealing with shock and grief. Her sister has been murdered only a few days ago, along with her whole family. I look into her eyes. "I am so sorry about Alexandra," I say.

She smiles, wanly. "Thank you. We were expecting it, but it is still distressing."

We lapse into silence, each in our own thoughts, and it is Sister Margaret, still standing nearby, who finally breaks it.

"You have much to talk about," she says, softly, "I will leave you for now. When you are ready, Sister Ephraimia ... Natalie ... I will show you where you will sleep."

I smile and nod to her. "Thank you, Sister."

~ ~ ~

After Margaret has left, I ask Elizabeth about the first thing on my mind, Max ~ his whereabouts, his well-being, thoughts that drum inside my head constantly, like a marching band going round and round in my skull.

"Ah yes, your man," she agrees, nodding. "The last information I have is that he is still with the circus, which has set up at Perm for an extra, last, stop before Moscow. It should be here in four days ... that will be next Monday." I feel like crying out with despair. An extra stop! I so desperately want to be with Max again, but things beyond our control are keeping us apart. Anger flares up in me at the way our lives are not our own. I cannot recall a time when I have ever been mistress of my own destiny.

Elizabeth studies my face. "Are you feeling any better?"

I cannot answer truthfully, for one emotion has flared up over the previous. I am no longer shaking from the mistaken belief that Elizabeth is Alexandra, but feel like raging against the world at the injustice of my situation. Will I never break free? Can Max and I hope for a simple future together?

I take a deep breath, and hold it, then let it out slowly; anger will not help me, I must be calm. After a moment, I manage a smile."Yes, thank you."

"You will be safe here, we will help you. I would like you spend the rest of today with Sister Margaret, finding your way around, getting used to our routines. But before you go, do you mind if I ask you some questions about Alexandra's last days?"

"No, certainly, I will tell you anything I can."

She smiles, that sad smile again. "Thank you."

She raises her head and looks across the room towards the window, though I suspect that she isn't really looking at it, just focussing her thoughts.

"How did it happen, the assassination?" she says, as though from afar.

The question throws my mind back to that night, a week ago. Has a week passed already?

Again, as I have so many times since, I relive the sequence of events in my mind, from the confusion when we were woken, via our obedient, silent procession down the stairs and through the house, to the violence of my rescue and the terror of our escape. I shiver.

"We were taken down to a basement in the early hours," I say, softly, looking at my hands, vaguely aware that my fingers are interlaced, so tightly squeezed together that the blood has ceased to flow through them. "The guards separated the family from the rest of us. Max managed to smuggle me out, but we heard the gunshots as we ran. He said that they were mercenaries from Hungary or somewhere, that did the deed."

As I finish speaking, I look up to see her nodding, thoughtfully. "Avadeyev is in charge?"

It is my turn to nod.

"He hates us all, you know? He deserted from the army in 1915, the coward, refused to serve the Tsar. Then, when Lenin started to rise to power last year,

Avadeyev reappeared as Yurovsky's right-hand-man in the Urals. They will carve up this land between them, if we let them, mark my words."

Suddenly, decisively, she stands.

"You go and relax, Natalie. We will talk some more tomorrow."

She leads me to the door, and down the stairs, where we find Margaret in the little chapel.

There, she leaves me, with a hug and a kiss on each cheek.

~ ~ ~

In a routine similar to that at the little convent in Nizhny Novgorod, and not very different from the one with which I grew up at Alexander Palace, six o'clock the next morning sees me back in the chapel, standing beside Margaret and Alice, listening while someone prays on my behalf to a god I still do not know. I feel ... disloyal ... for being so negative about something that clearly means so much to the people who have been good to me, but a part of me still baulks at their unquestioning acceptance of everything handed down to them, like scraps from the upper table.

Yet, somehow, the atmosphere is different from Alexandra's morning services. Everyone present obviously really believes what they are saying and hearing, or at least wants to believe it.

With my head lowered respectfully, I peep left and right at the ~ mostly young ~ women around me. Their lips move in silent prayer. There is something in their expressions, a kind of fervency, as though they are being transported to some wonderful place, and I find myself envying them. Is this what I am missing? They accept their hardships, while I rail against mine; their lives have a purpose, whereas mine seems to be carried in the wind. Perhaps I shouldn't resist. I try to open my mind, to push aside my cynicism and listen to the words of the chant that has just begun ... "Praise the Lord in the heavens, Praise Him on high, Hallelujah, Hallelujah ..."

As the words flow past me, meaningless, I start to form my own prayer in my mind. "God? Who are you? Are you real? What do you want me to do?"

I become aware that silence has descended, a lull in the voices. Then, when the Reverend Mother begins to speak again, I am surprised to hear my name.

"Heavenly father, who watches over all, bless our daughter Natalie Tereshchenko. Protect her in your service and show her the way."

The small congregation chimes "Amen."

I raise my eyes from the floor and look around. All faces are turned towards me.

Puzzled, I turn from one to another. They are smiling. Their faces have that same ecstasy that I noticed earlier, when they were praying, as though I am their God. Confused and embarrassed, I look back down to the floor, studying the patterns in the worn wooden blocks at my feet, until the chanting begins again.

Chapter 48 ~ Sophiya

The day is quiet. I spend some time reading, lying on my bed, though my mind wanders frequently, and I find myself thinking about Max. He is only three days away, now. I feel a quickening of my heartbeats as I contemplate his imminent return, and as I visualise the moment he will hold me again, my mind leaps back to our last passionate embrace. I close my eyes, and there is his face, close to mine. I hear his voice, singing softly, and feel his hands touching my skin. Immediately, I am aroused, and have to quickly open my eyes again before it overcomes me.

Blinking away the tears, I try to concentrate on my book, a treatise on the travels of Saint Paul ~ not ideal reading material for me, but all I could find.

There is a tap on the door, and Margaret enters. "Come with me," she says, mysteriously, crooking a finger. "Someone is here to see you."

I put down the book and accompany her to the door of a small room, which she opens and waits for me to enter. Puzzled, I step through, then let out a squeal of joy.

"Sacha!" I cry, rushing forward to embrace her. It is wonderful to see my friend again.

"How did you know I am here?" I ask, holding her hands and smiling.

"Oh, the White Underground is seething with news of your escape," she smiles, gazing into my eyes. "I am so happy to see you."

I cringe at the mention of my fame, but manage to speak.

"This is a lovely surprise," I reply. "How is your mother?"

She shrugs her shoulders. "Same as usual, over-reacting to everything. But she is well enough; strong as a bear, really. She has been busy on your behalf."

"My behalf? Doing what?"

"She has contacted your mother," she says, matter-of-factly.

I stand, wide-eyed, speechless. The last time ~ the only time ~ I met Sacha's mother, she had said that she would try to arrange for me to meet my own mother.

"She is on her way here to see you, now," Sacha continues, laughing at my amazement.

"My mother?" I stammer. "Coming here?"

She nods. "As soon as she knew you were safe, she wanted to meet you."

We cross the room to some chairs near the window.

"I don't know how safe I am, to be honest," I say, shaking my head as I sit. "The Reds are scouring the country for Max and me. I am just waiting for him to arrive in Moscow, then we can try to get out of the country. I won't feel safe until we reach England."

"Well, you have a few days to relax here before you have to start travelling again."

I grin. "Yes, as a nun. Could you imagine anything more bizarre, knowing how I feel about religion?"

She shakes her head. "It suits you, though," she says, appraising my habit.

"I feel like a fraud," I declare. "But enough about me, what has been happening to you, while I've been away?"

Her eyes become vacant as she recalls the events of the past year. "Father arranged for some troops to escort mother and I south, to a safe house he had arranged. We didn't see him, he was making his way to join some White units preparing to strike back against Lenin. He was with a regiment that tried to storm the Communist headquarters in Petrograd, last November. They were all killed."

"Oh no!" I exclaimed. "I am sorry, Sacha my love. I didn't know."

She shook her head slowly. "I had been expecting it. The outcome was almost predictable, the way he had been living his life, the risks he was taking. Of course, mother was distraught when the news reached us, went completely to pieces."

"I can understand that. How are you coping?"

"Oh I'm fine now. Obviously, I was very upset at the time, but it wasn't a complete surprise, so I had already been preparing myself. Mother and I now have new identities, and have rented an apartment here in Moscow."

~ ~ ~

There is a soft knock on the door, and Sister Margaret peeps in.

"Your other visitor has arrived," she says. "Shall I show her in here?"

My heart gives a sudden lurch, and I have to take a

deep breath before answering. Eventually I feel ready, and nod my head. "Yes please, Sister. Thank you."

With an anxious glance at Sacha, I stand to greet the woman I have never really met, but often thought about: my mother. What do I feel for her? Some sympathy ~ I can understand how it must have been for her when my father died. She was alone, unable to support me, and aware that Alexandra could give me a far better life than she was able to provide. But I also have a sense of alienation. For all that my growing years were frustrating, without real love from the Tsar or the Empress, they were still the only family I have known ~ this woman, my mother, is a stranger.

The person who bustles into the room is shorter than I am expecting ~ I can see from whom I have inherited my small stature. She is plump, with long grey hair tied at her neck, then falling like a horse's tail down her back. Her face is like that of a snowman, round and white, with little pieces of coal for the eyes, a stone for the nose, and a pinched, red-painted mouth. Despite the warm weather, she is wearing a large, Arctic-fox fur coat, but with summer shoes.

When she sees me, she throws open her arms and, with a kind of whimper, clings tightly to me. Rather than stand, mute and unresponsive, I put my arms around her, but I am feeling nothing.

After a short while, she steps back and studies me; she has to look upwards to examine my face.

"Oh my baby," she says in a whining voice, "you are so grown."

"Hello, mother," I answer, feeling embarrassed at

my lack of emotion. I turn towards the window and the chairs, where Sacha has also risen. "You know Sacha, I assume?"

"Yes," she replies. "Hello again Sacha. Your mother says she is looking forward to your return."

Sacha smiles, ironically. "I have been away only a few hours, and will be home this afternoon; already she is pining. Can I take your coat, Sofiya?"

She steps forward and helps my mother to remove her coat, which Sacha hangs on a hook behind the door. Sofiya ~ another little piece of information. Why do I still not feel the surge of love I had expected to overwhelm me?

We all sit, arranging our chairs into a triangle so that we can face each other. I feel that I should speak, try to make a connection.

"Thank you for coming to see me, mother," I say, politely.

"I am released from my promise to Alexandra," she replies, passionately. "That witch forbade me from seeing you. She also refused to accept you into the royal family, even though you are as entitled as any of her own daughters."

Somehow, she has touched the core of my childhood misery. I shrug my shoulders. "I resented it, until recently. Now I am happy to be a commoner."

"But you are not a commoner!" she exclaims. "You have a right to inherit the crown; you are a Romanov, the only surviving Romanov."

"Why should I want to do that?" I splutter. "Look at what has happened to Alexandra and Nicholas, and the children. It would be like accepting ~ no, inviting ~ a sentence of death. My life is in enough danger now, because of what I know and what I saw, without adding another reason for the Bolsheviks to hate me."

She leans towards me. "Don't you see?" she hisses. "You can only be safe if you take the initiative. Instead of running from them, you must turn and face them, confront them. The people only support the revolution because it offers them a way to break free from the bad rule of successive Tsars. But they loved Catherine The Great, and now they yearn for a return to her kind of rule."

"It's too late, Mother. The communists are in power now; they control everything. Even if I wanted to be Catherine The Great, which I don't, it would be impossible to organise an uprising against them."

She is shaking her head. "There is no need for that. Across the width of Russia, people are pining for the monarchy. When they learn that you are ready to repair their broken country, they will rise up and demand to have you as their sovereign."

Sacha has remained silent, her eyes following the conversation from Sofia to me and back again. When she speaks, it is softly.

"Natalie, you have seen the crude power of Lenin's armies, their lack of compassion, their brutality. That is the reality of the revolution. But there is another movement, hidden for now, that fears for the future of Russia under these beasts, and is willing to rise up under a queen they trust. A queen who will bring unity."

My mother is nodding, vigorously, and quickly resumes, cutting off Sacha.

"You don't have to carry a flag at the head of an army to lead a counter-revolution. The mechanisms are being set in place as we speak. You only have to consent, and they will begin the process of informing the people and negotiating with Lenin."

Chapter 49 ~ A Storm

Their passionate onslaught is making my head spin. Suddenly, I stand and excuse myself, leaving the room without giving an explanation. As I close the door I note their surprised expressions ~ let them wonder. I am close to tears. I feel, not for the first time, that my life is not my own, that I am being manoeuvred, controlled.

Unsure where to go, I head for the chapel, seeking peace, but find it occupied by several nuns, kneeling in silent prayer. Quietly, I turn and leave, then stand, at a loss. I need to think, to take in what Sacha and Sofiya (I find it easier to use her name than to think of her as my mother) have told me. I wish my Max was here, with his practical mind; he would know what to do.

Opposite where I am standing is a door that I know gives access to the main church, the one that is used for public services ~ I open it and slip through into a small, square ante-room. It contains a flight of stairs leading up to one of the bell towers, and there are some ropes of assorted thickness hanging from the ceiling, for the ringing of the bells. Another door, which accesses the body of the church, occupies the wall to my left. I open it and peep through into the half-darkness of the church.

My soft footsteps echo faintly from the high ceiling and hard walls as I step through, like a rustling of autumn leaves in the wind or the fluttering of birds in the rafters. I stop, self-consciously, looking around at the colourful, ornate icons on the walls, towering above me on all sides. A painted screen to my left, adorned with images of Christ and the saints, and scenes from the bible, stands as a barrier, excluding the common worshippers in the nave from the sacred altar it conceals.

It reminds me of all the royal palaces I have seen. Gaudy, ostentatious, flamboyant even, with its gold and bright colours, its self-aggrandising size and its exclusivity. There are no seats, it is considered irreverent to sit in the house of God, so I stand and look around, my eyes drawn upwards to the domed ceiling, trying to see beyond the trappings to heaven beyond. I suppose Myriam must be there, somewhere.

"What is it like in heaven?" I whisper, hearing only my own voice returning in sibilants and clicks from the far walls, mocking me.

"I don't suppose anyone feels like sharing a bit of insight," I add, ironically, then wait, not expecting a reply.

There is a faint, distant rumble of thunder, hardly audible through the thick walls.

"Am I to take that as an answer?" I mutter, bitterly.

~ ~ ~

Suddenly angry, I pull open the door through which I have just entered, and flounce back into the ante-room, panting. The truth is, I am frightened ~ afraid for my life, anxious about what is happening and scared of making the wrong decision. But what is the right decision? Can there even be a right or wrong one?

I feel myself being pulled, back and forth, by conflicting ideologies. From the time I became old enough to understand the world outside Alexander Palace, I have been critical of the way the royals behaved, and I have often longed to be in a position to do things differently. I know I could have been a better ruler ~ more sympathetic, more open to the ideas of others. So why, now that I may have a chance to prove it, am I so hesitant? Is it that I doubt myself?

Well of course I do! How can I be sure that I will always be fair and just? And what right do I have to make choices on someone else's behalf? I could be just like Nicholas and Alexandra, arrogantly passing laws and judgements based on my narrow view of the world, destroying lives without even knowing.

And what of the alternative, the "People's Government" currently taking over? My heart says that it is the right way, that everyone should have a stake in the wealth they help to create, and a say in how things are done, but I have seen it in action, and it is as cold and cruel as any monarch.

Another faint shaking of the walls accompanies the next rumble of thunder, closer this time. I decide to climb the stairs and watch the storm from the top of the tower. For a few minutes, it is good to have nothing more to think about than the placing of my feet on the spiralling stone steps in the almost-total darkness, one after the other. Slowly the light from above becomes brighter, and the sound of rain reaches me. Another rumble, loud and close, tells me that the storm has arrived. It feels, somehow, prophetic.

I emerge onto a little platform, where a row of bells in ascending order of size, hangs at head height from a wooden beam. I duck under them and stand at the balcony, feeling the rain-spray on my face and the cool wind through my hair. Moscow glistens in grey, watery beauty all around me. Occasional shafts of sunlight slip past the clouds for a few seconds, pinpointing random places ~ a factory, a church tower, a park. Off to my right, a rainbow gleams bright and pure. I jump as an arc of light leaps from sky to earth nearby, its crack of thunder arriving at the same moment. I can smell the ozone on the air. And though I am shaking from the shock, I laugh and thrust my head out into the rain, revelling in its cold freshness.

The power of nature is still greater than anything man can devise, and it has the effect of clearing my head. While I am absorbed in its beauty, I am freed from the agonising need to decide, and by the time it has passed, I am more relaxed. As the storm moves away, the bangs and blinding flashes slowly fading into distant rumbles and faint flickers, I feel a new purpose.

I turn and confidently pick my way down the stone steps to the ringing room, and then out into the corridor. For a minute, I stare at the door to the room where Sacha and Sofiya await my return, then, decisively, I open it and enter.

~ ~ ~

They have not moved. Or, at least, they are sitting as they were when I left. Sacha stands to welcome me back; Sofiya just glares at me.

"I needed some quiet time to think," I say, hating myself for being so weak as to feel that I have to explain myself. If I am to be Tsarina, I must learn to be stronger, behave more imperiously.

"What have you decided?" Sofiya snaps as I sit in the empty chair opposite her.

It seems to me that she has already adopted the manner of Mother of The Queen. Yes, she is looking forward to her new role. I look at her, holding her eyes until she has to lower her gaze into her lap. *That's more like it*, I think, but I don't answer just yet. Instead, I turn to Sacha.

"What, do you think I should do?"

She is taken a little by surprise, and has to think before answering. I am glad. If she had answered at once, I would have suspected collusion with Sofiya.

"You would be good for the country," she begins, carefully, looking across at Sofiya. "Many of us watched Nicholas and Alexandra with dismay. It was often as though they made decisions on the flip of a coin, so frequently did they take the wrong path. I mean, take the abdication ~ it handed control right into the hands of the Bolsheviks, and put the lives of everyone in the extended royal family in danger."

"What should they have done?" I ask.

"Negotiated," she says, emphatically. "Look at England. They still retain their monarchy, but with the illusion of a democracy behind it. Nicholas only needed to work with the Duma, give it more of a role, while he slipped into the background as a comical, harmless anachronism."

I find the thought amusing, and not exactly impossible.

"Would the Bolsheviks have been satisfied with that, though?"

"That's the whole point," she grins. "Their strength came from the people's anger at the Tsar. If the citizens had felt that the system was working for them, they would not have risen up, and the Bolsheviks would have had no army."

"So, is that what I am to be, a figurehead?"

Sofiya could not remain quiet for long.

"Natalie," she chips in, "that is how it would appear to be. But, in fact, all decisions would be yours, handed down through whichever government happens to hold office at the time."

I stare at her in amazement. She really seems to believe that what she envisages is a reasonable situation, and from what Sacha has just said, she agrees with Sofiya.

~ ~ ~

I cannot stay seated. I must stand again, and I head restlessly to the window, turning my back on the two women. I gaze out on the little patch of green garden, dotted with summer flowers, as I try to suppress my angry reactions. Ever since I learnt that Alexandra took me in, I have dreamed of meeting my mother, have expected to feel an immediate bond. Instead, I find that she is ruthless and ambitious, hoping to carve a better future for herself through me.

I take several deep breaths. I must not let my antagonism for Sofiya distract me from the very real decision I must make.

The storm has moved away eastwards, and the afternoon sun sits on the rooftops, slicing into the room like a spotlight. I consciously stand in its beam ~ today I have become very aware of how others see me, and how I wish to be seen.

Slightly calmer, I turn to face them, the glare from the window behind me creating an aura.

"What preparations have been made so far?" I ask them, suggesting that I could be amenable, but noting a new, sharper edge to my voice.

Sofiya smiles, as a hyena might smile, sensing that her dream of power is a step nearer.

"The White underground is throbbing with news of your escape," she says. "When I tell them that you are willing to lead them, they will begin a process of propaganda, telling all the people that there can be a new monarchy, better, fairer, willing to work with their chosen government, including the Bolsheviks, if that is who they want."

I shiver, hoping they will not notice. "And what is being done to get me to safety?" I ask.

"You are safe here," she says, quickly.

I take a step towards them, leaning forwards slightly so that my face is close to Sofiya's.

"No I am not," I spit, cutting her off. "I cannot be safe as long as Avadeyev and his gorillas are able to get to me. Whether I agree to your plan or not, I must not stay in Russia. Perhaps I can return, when the preparations are made, but first you have to get me out of the country."

She shrinks back a little, surprised at my outburst, and I stand up straight again, deliberately towering over her seated figure; I have learnt so much over the last twenty-four hours, I am no longer the malleable child she abandoned.

After a few moments' thought, she answers, subdued. "I will speak to someone. We will find a way to smuggle you out."

"To England," I stipulate sharply.

She sighs. "Very well, England it shall be."

"And Max," I add, quickly. "I will not co-operate with you unless Max is safe too."

"Yes, Max will go with you," she says.

But I can read the uncertainty in her eyes.

Chapter 50 ~ Dawn

And now it is nearly dawn. The convent is asleep, but my mind will not let me rest. I have lain awake all night.

The turmoil persists, pulling me apart, until I have finally slipped from my bed, quietly dressed, and returned to the bell tower. Climbing the stairs was difficult in total darkness, but I made it, clinging hand-over-hand to the iron rail, and carefully feeling each step with my bare toes. Now I stand again beside the set of small bells, looking out over the city again.

I have been here for an hour, savouring the cool, summer-perfumed morning breeze.

Yesterday's thunder-storm has washed the air clean and left the grass twinkling with moisture.

Now, the first rays of the morning sun, itself still hidden, light up the clouds near the horizon to the east with fluorescent streaks of crimson and orange, and bathe the rooftops in a warm reflected glow. Always nature finds ways to soothe me.

Sofiya and Sacha departed late yesterday afternoon, promising to make arrangements for Max and me to slip out of the country. In turn, I have agreed that they may begin to spread the news of my survival, although I am sure that will just make my situation even more dangerous. I need my Max, need his strong arms to hold me close.

Still the question spins in my head ~ can I unite

Russia? Because, if I accept the role of Tsarina, it will not be to continue as Nicholas and Alexandra did, blind to the suffering of the poor, driving the country deeper into poverty while they lived in luxury. Perhaps, working with the Communists, I could bring an end to class distinctions, make a new future in which everyone is equal? At least I am safe from the delusion that an almighty god has chosen me to rule.

A movement on the ground nearby makes me look down, and I see the grey shape of a man in uniform run, crouching, across the garden to hide behind a tree, facing the church entrance. The first edge of the sun peeps over the horizon, and a glint in the long shadows shows me where another soldier is already in position at the corner of a building, his rifle held vertical, close to his chest. Once I have begun looking for them, I see more, peering from behind bushes, lurking at corners, taking up positions all around the square, thirty or more of them.

With my heart pounding in my chest, I step backwards into the darkness behind the bells.

Armed soldiers surrounding the monastery? They can only be after one person ~ me. I cannot stay here, but what plans are in place for escape? Are there tunnels, I wonder?

Elizabeth will be able to tell me. I begin to make my tentative way down the dark stairs again, thoughts hammering at my attention. My enemies are at the door, if I cannot slip away unseen, then I am doomed.

~ ~ ~

The stairs from the belfry follow the walls in an anti-clockwise spiral. I descend slowly in total blindness, placing each bare foot carefully and holding onto the iron handrail. It is a welcome diversion, taking my mind from larger problems to the immediate one of reaching the bottom safely. Eventually I emerge into the ringing room, with its row of ropes hanging from the ceiling, but instead of hurrying, as I had first intended, to join the nuns and report the situation to Elizabeth, I stop and sit on the bottom step, deep in thought.

Why run? The question arrives, unsought, unwanted, in my head.

Why? Because if I do not run, I am dead ~ that is certain.

I remember Sofia's words "Instead of running from them, you must turn and face them, confront them."

Oh yes, they would welcome me with open arms:

"*Hello, I am your queen, take me to Lenin so we can have a nice chat.*"

"*Yes, of course, My Lady. Please be so good as to follow us.*"

And why would they want me? They have all the power; they are in control. If Russia has a future, it is in their hands. There will never be another Tsar, because the eyes of the poor have seen the falseness, the inequity, of a system in which all authority rests with the wealthiest ~ and they have at last rejected it.

Those soldiers, outside, they know I am here, and they have come for me. Perhaps they were following my mother when she came from Petrograd. What will they do next? I cannot imagine that they will storm the convent ~ or would they?

I smile grimly at the irony: it is a continuation of my life in service, but turned on its head.

First as a servant to a monarchy I rejected, now thrust into that very monarchy as its sole survivor, and threatened by forces dedicated to its destruction.

Everybody wants me for something, but what do I want? Nobody has ever asked me, and I have never really felt the right to allow myself that luxury. Now I can at least ask myself the question.

And I have an answer. It is already in my head, waiting to be heard. I know what I want to do, but is it the right thing?

"Myriam," I whisper, "you once told me to ask in the quietness of my mind, and you would answer. Should I act for myself, or for Russia?"

I close my eyes and try to clear my mind of all thoughts, to allow her to speak to me.

A vision swims behind my eyelids, Myriam as she had appeared to me when first she came.

"A day will come when you will hold the balance of history in your hands," she says again. *"I will not tell you what to do, the decision is yours, and you are free to choose the one that is right for you ~ but you must choose."*

"How can I choose? It is impossible! You can see in my mind what I believe is right, I need you to tell me if I am right or wrong."

"I am waiting for you, Natalie. I will hold your hand."

I understand what I must do. I stand and cross the room diagonally to the door leading into the church. In that expanse, with its whispering echoes, I pause briefly to glance at the brightly painted screen, then head purposefully to the opposite end of the nave.

~ ~ ~

The high, carved doors in the far wall provide the route by which the congregation passes from the narthex, a vestibule between the outside world and the sanctity of the house of God, into the nave. They are heavy; I notice that my hand is trembling as I push at one until it gives enough for me to squeeze through, then close it behind me.

My mind is made up, and what I must do next is not for Sister Ephraimia.

I remove my scarf, and carefully fold it, placing it on a little table, then the same for my outer robe. The room is not cold, but I shiver as I take off my inner robe and put it, also neatly folded, with my other garments. Am I putting off the moment by the folding of my clothes? Perhaps. It matters not.

The outer doors, though substantial, swing easily open with a single push. Naked and white, I step over the threshold into the half-light of dawn. There is a gentle breeze that raises tiny bumps on my skin. The sky is lifting, now dark blue, with splashes of salmon pink and deep red where clouds drift easily past. Behind me, I faintly hear the nuns begin to sing the first hymn of the day in the little chapel.

With an audible clunk, three spotlights leap into life

before me, one from each side and another straight ahead, pinpointing me like an actress upon the stage. I take two more steps, and stop beside Myriam, who is waiting for me, as she promised. She takes my hand and smiles, then shimmers from sight, and I stand alone in the spotlights.

There is the rattle of fifty rifles being cocked. I touch the silver necklace around my neck, which has been with me since my eighteenth birthday, when it was given to me by Alexandra, then I extend my arms so that my hands are at waist height, palms forwards, like a supplication.

The bridge is crossed, the action taken, I am committed now. There can be no turning back.

Whatever faults the communist system has, it is still the choice of the people. I have no right to take upon myself the authority to decide for them ~ the royal blood in my veins must not be passed on. Russia has chosen its future, and that is as it should be.

I am sorry, Max, my darling ~ I love you ~ goodbye.

I hear a shouted command, and see the puff of smoke from the first gunshot.

Also by Elizabeth Audrey Mills

~~~

The Other Side
Part two of the Natalie Tereshchenko story

As sole survivor of the royal family, Natalie could have been heir to the throne, but as a witness to their murder, she is a mortal enemy to the new regime, so she seeks obscurity. But instead, somehow, she finds herself working among the new communist leaders at the Kremlin, befriended by the those close to the top, who know nothing of her royal past.

With Max delayed somewhere along the way, Natalie, pursued by unknown assassins, begins to back-track her journey, seeking the man she loves and to whom she owes her life.

A Song For Joey

When your father has deserted you, and your mother died giving birth to you, when you are homeless, drugged and beaten, and someone is out to kill you, you may find that the best person to have beside you is the ghost of the boy you loved like a brother.

Meet Belinda Paolo and Rita, parents of Belinda, a girl with a wonderful talent. When Belinda is made homeless, Joey helps her to survive on the streets.

As Belinda pursues her quest to become a successful pop singer, she learns that love has many forms, but her past catches up with her, and a man she thought she had escaped threatens revenge in a terrible and brutal way.